20TH CENTURY
UN-LIMITED

Acclaim for Felice Picano

"Felice Picano is a premier voice in gay letters."—Malcolm Boyd, *Contemporary Authors*

Felice Picano is "…a leading light in the gay literary world… his glints of flashing wit and subtle hints of dark decadence transcend clichés."—Richard Violette, *Library Journal*

"Felice Picano is one hell of a writer!"—Stephen King

"Picano's destiny has been to lead the way for a generation of gay writers."—Robert L. Pela, *The Advocate*

"These stories [*The New York Years: Stories by Felice Picano*] are as well written and immediate as any contemporary gay fiction."—Regina Marler

"With *True Stories*, Felice Picano enhances his status as one of the great literary figures in recent gay history and does so with wit, verve and as much panache as we've come to expect."
—Jerry Wheeler, *Out in Print*

20TH CENTURY UN-LIMITED

by

Felice Picano

A Division of Bold Strokes Books

2013

ISBN 13: 978-1-60282-921-3

This Trade Paperback Original Is Published By
Bold Strokes Books, Inc.
P.O. Box 249
Valley Falls, NY 12185

First Edition: April 2013

Credits
Editor: Stacia Seaman
Production Design: Stacia Seaman
Cover Design by Sheri (graphicartist2020@hotmail.com)

Acknowledgments

Thanks to Steve Soucy, the earliest reader of *Wonder City of The West*, and to Ian Ayres, earliest reader of *Ingoldsby*, for their comments and help in making these fictional works become more fully alive.

for Len Barot

CONTENTS

WONDER CITY OF THE WEST

I believe the future is the past again, entered through another gate.
—Sir Arthur Wing Pinero

1

"The benefits of walking, especially up a hill like that one," Dr. Deanna Cheung had said, "are inestimable."

Little did she know.

Deanna was my blood pressure specialist at a clinic for such, attached to a hospital, and she insisted that I walk as much as possible, and that walking regularly would be even better than the lisinopril and amlodipine she'd prescribed and that I was taking for my moderate blood pressure issue.

"Our distant ancestors walked five to six hours a day," Deanna pointed out. "And they ate predominantly fruits, nuts, and vegetables."

I'm pretty good with produce, eat a lot. But I forebore from mentioning that our distant ancestors were three-feet-four tall, weighed sixty pounds at most, and lived until the age of about seventeen.

But the hill *was* there. I lived two-thirds of the way up a steep hill in the West Hollywood Hills, and it went all the hell the way up, a corkscrew road, with, once you got to the top, absolutely dizzying views.

Dizzying: that was the exact and actual word used by a visiting friend from the East whom I drove up to the top to show the view. As we were circling down, he closed his eyes tightly and said, "Tell me when we're out of the clouds."

I found it not so much dizzying, as expansive. Being so high above West Hollywood that I could take in all of that town, some of Beverly Hills, lots of Hollywood, all the way down across the basin to the Baldwin Hills and on clear days the airport and ocean even... It broadened my view of the world during a period when it seemed walls had begun closing in: Career walls. Financial walls. Personal walls. Stuff that happens when you reach retirement age and don't (or can't) retire as comfortably as you'd like to. So I walked up the hill three times a week—up to the top and back to my house: half hour or so. Great cardio exercise.

How can I better explain this hill?

What I told people was that it was ten minutes up the hill and three minutes down in a car.

By now you've got the idea of how steeply I was walking.

Which is how I came upon the friendly Bedlington terrier—Ralf.

Which is how I met the Bedlington terrier's master—I call him Mr. Morgan.

Which is how I ended up back in—but wait, I'm getting ahead of myself here.

Let's start with Ralf.

Rowf? Ralph? I never saw it spelled out.

Ralf was your ordinary gray-haired and unattractive wire-haired Bedlington. I've known three people in my life who have liked this breed and constantly kept them around. Margaret Darrieluex, our "house mother" and drug dispenser during the mid to late 60s in the West Village commune I hung out with. A neighbor of Boy Ondine, star of Andy Warhol's *Chelsea Girls* and costar (at least he told me it was his bobbing head) of *Blow Job*. And then Mr. Morgan.

Ralf would bark in a friendly fashion and wag his tail whenever I appeared, and then jump a funny little jump five inches into the air whenever I passed along the gated narrow strip of front yard before Morgan's house while trudging toward the top, which he was pretty close to. Then Ralf would bark and jump again and follow me again, back a few minutes later, when I went down the hill.

Which is why I finally saw Morgan, standing there through an open door, via a closed and locked wrought-iron fence. Morgan nodded. I nodded back.

Until after maybe the twentieth nod and half wave, when Morgan called me over to his front door gate, still all locked up, behind which he remained, and he said hello and he introduced himself and Ralf, and asked what I was doing.

"Oh! So you want to stay young?" he asked.

"Too late for that. I would like to stay healthy into my old age."

"How old are you? Maybe fifty-five?"

"Add ten years."

"No! Well, you are already healthy if you can get up this hill at that age. Guess my age."

"About the same. A little younger?" I said, generously. He looked older; wait, that's not right, he looked *odder*, not older.

"I'm actually over a hundred. A hundred and sixteen, to be exact."

"What's your secret? Armenian yogurt?" I'd heard people in some Armenian mountain town who ate a certain yogurt all lived long.

"I have a little time machine," he said with a straight face.

"Yeah, and…?" I was waiting for the yogurt—or the other shoe to drop.

"Yeah, and I've come back in time. I was born in 1995. In the year 2061, I used my time machine to come back a century. To 1961."

"That still doesn't explain how you are a hundred and sixteen."

"Well, I lost some years I had aged when I came back. I was sixty-six when I left there. But when I arrived in 1961, I looked about eleven years old. I had lost a lot of my acquired age. Add up the two spans I've lived and they total a hundred and sixteen."

This was the most interesting conversation I'd had in months.

"Did you bring anything from the future?"

To back up that statement, I meant but didn't say.

"I did. Want to see it?"

Ralf was barking his welcome too, so I stepped inside the now unlocked gate and into the house.

It was oddly furnished, although what I saw was the one floor. Very bare bones. Handsome, you could say, with maybe six pieces of furniture in each large area.

He sat me down at a Danish modern sofa and table and went away. When he came back he was holding out something that looked like a little transparent screen, something that you would put over the front of a BlackBerry.

He held it up to the light where it was iridescent. Then he put it on the table.

When I touched it, it spoke, and as it spoke it sort of went away and instead I saw a two-foot-high, pale, holographic video presentation of the U.S. Mint in Denver, and then the 3-D head of a young woman appeared in one corner and she said very clearly, "Mr. Fath Paul Morganna. You have seventeen hundred and ninety-nine thousand dollars on deposit at this location." It then said, "This is an official message. May thirty-first, 2061."

"Terrif! And that little video is what, exactly?" I asked.

"That's my last financial statement," he added calmly.

"I see inflation continues into the future," I said. "Or you are really well off?"

"Inflation continues. A dollar then is equal to about a dime now," he admitted.

He'd brought me a glass of juice that looked like pomegranate or grape.

"No banks in 2061?"

"No banks. Everyone keeps their money in the U.S. Mint," he said.

I was looking out the window at one of those amazing—dizzying—views. He meanwhile was looking at me curiously.

"So!" he said. "You keep walking up that hill and you'll live to how old?"

"Well, I've got longevity genes. My great-aunt is a hundred and six. Her brother died at ninety-nine and a half. My grandpa on the other side made it to a hundred and one. What do you think? Barring accident, maybe a hundred, hundred and five?"

"You won't like 2050," he said.

"I won't?"

"You'll hate it. You're too spoiled."

"War? Pestilence?"

"Only the usual amount of those."

"Bad climate?" I tried.

"Very bad climate. This area will be mostly unlivable."

"Because of jungle conditions? Wild coyotes and mountain lions and giant lizards?" I asked, thinking of global warming already evident.

"No. Because of icy roads. Ice and snow even this low, how high is this hill? Six hundred feet above sea level? It'll be impassable more than half the year. No one ever comes up this high anymore in 2050."

"Half a year of ice in the Hollywood Hills!? *That's* the result of global warming?" I asked.

"You've noticed our winters have gotten cooler? And our summers warmer? That trend will continue unabated. This used to be a temperate zone. A Mediterranean zone. Not anymore. And soon the cold will outdo the hot. Meanwhile, the rest of the country will heat up pretty well. Heat up. Melt down and drown lots of places. Become tropical and desert. But California gets a lot colder in the winter.

The entire West Coast freezes up like Alaska is now. San Francisco becomes unlivable most of the year. Far too cold. Blizzard conditions three months of the year. Only the flatter parts of the Bay Area are at all doable. Ever been to northern Chile? That's what it comes to resemble most closely."

"The Andes and the Atacama Desert?" I asked.

"You've got it."

"And Manhattan?" I asked.

"Ever been to Venice?"

"Italy?"

"Venice, Italy, is an underwater museum. Venice here—is ice skating heaven."

"Manhattan is underwater in 2050?" I asked.

"Manhattan, Philly, D.C., Boston, the entire East Coast up to the foothills of the Appalachians."

"While Portland, Oregon, is frozen tundra?" I asked.

"Huge packs of feral wolves up there. Caribou. Elk. Polar bear make a big comeback. Whales fill the Ess Eff Bay! My first dad used motorized sled-omnibuses to go up there with his buddies and hunt big winter game."

"Your 'first dad' because you had a second one when you came back in time to 1961?"

"Had to. I looked ten or eleven. I was adopted. But…you catch on fast. Some people can never get their minds around it."

"So tell me how awful it is in sunny Southern California in 2050 again?"

"Food supply is way down here, of course. Farms are gone. Ranches gone too. The Central Valley drowns and becomes glacial ice and taiga. The Rockies freeze over pretty well all year round. Huge glaciers the size of L.A. All those mountain cities and towns up there have to be abandoned. Boise. Salt Lake City. Even railroads can't get through by 2061. Cargo planes come into Burbank airport with fruit and produce grown in eastern Colorado and Wyoming. LAX is drowned, of course. But food isn't cheap. From Santa Fe over to what's left of the state of Georgia it's all desert. North of that, the Carolina plateau begins another green belt, mostly fed by the much-expanded Great Lakes and their inlets. Ashland is an island. Chicago, Cleveland, all drowned."

My cell phone rang and it was a reminder that I had to get home and shower and get ready to go out to dinner with an old pal who was in town for a few days.

"Thanks for the juice." I petted Ralf. "Gotta go."

"I hated it back then," Morgan said. Then corrected himself, "Forward then. The population of the country was under fifty million and dropping annually. So as soon as this thing worked, I sent myself back in time."

"You invented it?"

"I helped invent it. I've got to tell you, it was the best decision I ever made—coming here. I've loved living this second time, in this time. People here and now complain a lot. They've got nothing to complain about it. It's the peak of Western Civilization."

God help us, I thought.

"But won't you live till 2050 and then have to see it again?" I asked.

"Not me. I don't have any longevity in my ancestry. I've got short telomeres on my genes. I've got maybe another five, ten years. Tops. And like I said, I'm actually a hundred and sixteen."

"So you did! O-kay! Nice meeting you. I'll wave when I come by."

"Do more than wave. Ring my bell."

As I was stepping out and still petting Ralf, I figured he was a lonely old guy. So I said, "Sure. I'll ring your bell."

"Do so. I've got a very interesting proposition for you!"

"Bye, Ralf."

Refreshed, and pleased by the oddness of it all, I walked the third of the way down the hill in good spirits, enjoying the dizzying (wait! expansive!) views around houses perched on the roadside, until I was at my place again.

2

"I don't get it. Why exchange houses? Yours is much better than mine," I said. "Twice as expensive for sure, if not more."

We were in Morgan's main room again, Ralf on the floor where I could pet him.

"This house gets half knocked down and the other half gets

covered in a mudslide a few years from now. While your house is on the other side of the hill and escapes the mudslide altogether," Morgan explained.

"Then why give me this at all?"

"Well, if the time machine works for you, you will eventually arrive back here at 2010 and you'll be what? About ninety years old? And you'll find that you own a big house. You just might need a house! And if you don't, sell it! Live on the cash!"

"Okay, that makes sense. Tell me again how far can I go back?"

"The fuel cell we used the first time I traveled back was more than halfway used up by my trip and I couldn't fill it. So I'm figuring you have no more than eighty years. More like seventy-six or seventy-seven years."

"Back to the 1930s?" I asked.

"Right. That's why the year on the money you use will be important. There was a big new design and even a new paper-cloth mixture involved in the re-minting of U.S. money in 1935. 1935 bills were common for years, but now they're hard to find."

"And then the next design was when?"

"Not till 1960," Morgan said. "So, it's important. I managed to get in contact with a couple of numismatists and they've agreed to release some '35 bills."

"Bills, because metal won't travel back in time?" I asked.

"Only natural materials, except some plastic types did make it back with me, as you saw. So maybe plastic will travel too."

"Tell me again about the money."

"Well, it's a good idea to have cash in case something happens, so you're not a bum, right? I've managed to gather seven hundred and ninety-eight dollars of 1935 bills for you," Morgan said. "Mostly fives, tens, and twenties. They cost me more than double that."

"And that'll last me what? A couple of months. Great!"

"No. No, it'll last more than half a year, even if you never supplement it. Remember, all prices are *much* cheaper back then. You can rent a one-bedroom flat for about nine dollars a month. You can eat out for a dollar a day. A car'll cost you maybe five hundred dollars. A house maybe two or three thousand, even in a good neighborhood. What I've collected for you would be about equal to fifteen thousand dollars today. So, I'd suggest you lay low, open a bank account, be thrifty, and look for work. It was still the Depression in '35. There was lots of unemployment, although the movie industry was thriving and using many different kinds of workers then. You should arrive there aged somewhere in your early twenties. In that time period, with all the poverty and displacement going on in this country, you'll be able to live on your own without too many questions being asked. Unlike myself. When I got back to 1961 as a kid, I arrived into a tightly ordered society. I had to hide money, equipment, everything, for almost a decade."

"You really expect this thing to work, don't you?"

"I don't see why not. I repaired every part of it that was in any way frayed or not completely perfect. Had to wait until the invention of microchips to get it right. Then had to wait again for platinum anodization to get some stuff really miniscule. Remember, *you* won't be able to fix it until the mid 80s or 90s. I'll leave the mechanism in this house with your name on it, in case you want to use it again."

"But you don't advise it."

Morgan said nothing.

"My cell phone?" I asked.

"You can take it, but there'll be no towers. No satellites. It won't work."

"What about music?" I showed him my tiny MP3 player.

"That could go with you. What's the storage?"

"Up sixteen gigabytes with storage chips I can slide in."

He pried open the back. "I've got a battery half the size of a dime to go in here to keep it charged. It's made from exotic minerals. It will last eighteen, twenty years."

"By all means put it in!"

"First let me extend the storage to about twenty-four gigabytes. That's about a thousand hours of music. Download all that, and then I'll seal the USB port connection and use the battery. It's made of something that decays really slowly. Also, I'm noticing that this player's tuner is FM only. You'll need an AM bandwidth for the 1930s. FM only goes commercial in the late 1950s. I can fool around with it. Take a few tiny ear buds with you too, black ones. The only headphones they have are bulky things for crystal radio sets, and the plugs won't fit. Remember that is for *private listening only*. If anyone asks, they're earplugs. Oh, by the way, it'll probably be quieter most of the time."

"How quieter?"

"Well, cars are louder but there's a lot fewer. Ditto for trucks and busses too, which are smaller and fewer. Streetcars are noisy but they're limited too. And there are no commercial jets, which provide a lot of noise we no longer even consider in cities. So I believe it will be great deal quieter."

"Okay. To recap," I began, "I shouldn't carry metal, and I should wrap well any plastic like the MP3 player within clothing. I can carry a small duffel bag, made of canvas or cloth. Put what I need to wear inside that. What? A couple of changes of clothing. The cash. What else can I bring?"

"Clothing is crucial. I had to hunt vintage shops all over for my clothing once I knew I was headed back to the 1960s. I suggest wearing your windbreaker, because we don't know what time of year you'll arrive. It could be cold and raining, and if you need to you can fold it to the size of your hand and easily stash it. You'll need a cap of the era. A newsboy cap, maybe. Beaked. Not a baseball hat. Only baseball players wore those. Make sure it's got no logos. Cloth printing of that kind was pretty primitive back then. A short-sleeved and a long-sleeved cotton shirt with buttons down the front—and regular collars. No Izods or Ralph Lauren or Polo shirts. Maybe a white undershirt. Unprinted! Cut out all labels on your clothing, unless they're American made. A pair of light or dark chinos. Maybe work pants. And sturdy, all-leather shoes. Two or three neckties. No running gear. No denims: only farmers wore them then. When you arrive, buy yourself a good sports jacket. Take simple white briefs, or better yet, cotton shorts. Cotton socks above your ankles. This way, aside from the windbreaker, you won't stand out. Cut its label out too. The tighter the jacket, the better because you'll be younger and smaller."

"You've done a lot of research," I said.

"At one point I thought I'd go back again."

"But not now? Why not?"

Morgan shrugged. "You get tired."

"Tired of being alive—after 116 years?"

"The Hindu Vedas give a life span as 114 to 120. So maybe that's enough for me. Now! Don't forget medicine. Do you take any?" Morgan asked.

"Nothing besides my blood pressure pills."

"You probably won't need those. You'll be much younger. But

take a ninety-day script if you want to play it safe. I'd include some antibacterial ointment, and non-steroidal pain pills. They've got aspirin back then. But you'd better bring antibiotics—I've got a hundred Keflex I've stashed. Remember that people died of simple infections back then. All they have is sulfa drugs to combat them, and you might be allergic. Coming back here, I got minor infections from germs that I guess didn't exist in my time and had to see a doctor. Good thing I was a kid; kids get everything that's out there. That old Timex, wind-up wristwatch you've got on now is fine. Nothing digital and nothing with quartz or a battery, right?"

"Are you going to show me what it looks like? Your time machine?"

"It looks like a double mattress on the floor with electrodes all over your body attached to the mechanism, which is small. However, it uses a lot of electricity in one punching volt. So the neighborhood will have a blackout when it works."

"I still don't understand why you chose me."

"I didn't. Ralf did."

Almost asleep, Ralf looked up and barked twice.

"Why did Ralf choose me?"

"Ask Ralf. Listen. How many people will you need to sit down to explain that you're going away for a very long time, possibly forever?"

I thought so long that he interrupted me.

"You told me your partner died and you moved out here from the other coast. Since your partner died and you moved up here, you have no *real* connections down there, do you? No people who'll really miss you?"

"Not really. No."

"That's what Ralf thought…We'll work something out to make it look like you died here in an accident…I'll give you three weeks to get everything you need ready."

3

The last thing I remember Morgan saying was "Close your eyes tight. There's going to be a big flash."

He'd told me that ten minutes earlier and I'd said, "So that was you, making the big flash? I always thought it was some photographer who lived up this hill!"

No, it had been him, Morgan confirmed, trying to see if it the machine was up to speed before he used it on me.

I was on my back, fully dressed, with the duffel bag held tight in both of my hands, with all the electrodes on me: face, hands, torso, legs, feet, lying on the double mattress he mentioned before, the wires going into a bureau with a few dials and lights.

I remember thinking, "So this is how I die? Electrocuted by the maniac at the top of the hill who says he's from 2061. Well, it's *different*!"

There was a big flash even with my eyes closed, so I closed them tighter. Then I felt my body drop, like it sometimes does when you're in bed about to nod off and suddenly your body relaxes totally and you feel like you're falling and you try to catch yourself but you're not going anywhere, not really.

But this time I did drop, maybe four or five inches, and I grabbed both sides of the mattress and I felt—grass!

We'd been in his garage, I'd been on a mattress laid upon a concrete floor.

I reached out gingerly a little farther on each side. More grass, tufts of hard, wild grass.

I slowly opened my eyes. I wasn't in a garage. I was lying on grass and it was nighttime. I sat up and looked around and I zipped up my jacket including the extensible collar. It was chilly, and wet. Not raining but foggy or...

I tried to see where I was in the dark, in the light rain. It had been three in the afternoon when I lay down in that garage. Now it was definitely night.

The fog parted a bit and I could make out dim light far away and way down below.

Step by step, I told myself. Step by step.

I stood up. Looked around. Reached into the pocket and pulled out my phone and turned it on to operate like a little plastic flashlight. I moved it around.

I was on a hilltop. Well, not at the top. But twenty or so yards below it. All around me was grass. I tried peering down on all sides.

Just hillside. But below, wasn't that glow from old-time streetlights down there? I was almost sure that's what it was. But the lights looked impossibly far away. No houses. No nothing. Just hilltop.

I had been facing what had been the garage door: that meant a street had been put through here later. I closed my eyes and walked as I would do if I were walking out Morgan's garage and onto the narrow street. I stopped.

I looked around myself and it was still hill, but maybe a bit less hummocky here. I closed my eyes again and turned right, as I would do going down the hill from Morgan's house on my walks up the hill, and then after about twenty-five steps, I stopped, and closed my eyes again. I was assuming that the developers had taken the most natural route going up the hill when putting in the road. I knew this route by heart, having trudged up it so often. Next would be a left-hand turn down. Sure enough, the flashlight's tiny light on and off confirmed my footing, then after another fifty feet there would be a wide right turn, and here the fog parted again and I could see how very high up I actually was. Without a road and houses on either side, I was very high on a hill above what would later be West Hollywood.

The careful trek took me more than a half hour, with occasional stops to check my memory of the path with my eyes closed, and then to readjust and open them and move on. There was more chance for mistakes as the hill widened. At one point I was sure I was passing by the site where I had lived for years. It should have been the spot, and the terrain I could make out looked like it, although it was just trees and bushes. None of the tall eucalyptus that would grow later on, and of course there was no scooped-out section for the parking area.

Ten minutes later, the first sign of a house arrived suddenly. There was a paved road and a streetlight, and I knew exactly where I was: where North Crescent Heights Blvd. had joined Hillside Road right here in my time. Four or five houses were being built on what was now a cul-de-sac—barely a quarter of the way up the hill, but no street signs were up yet. It wouldn't remain a cul-de-sac for long. That house on the corner would become the green and white, half-timbered place that I'd driven past every day, and where Aldous and Laura Huxley had lived until the writer died of cancer, while taking a massive dose of LSD-25, in 1963. Another few sites down the road on each side, very widely spaced, and I knew now that this really *was* my road back in 2010: this was North Crescent Heights Blvd.

I was strolling quickly down that paved road and onto where it met Hollywood Blvd. where that famous road ascends and twists into the western hills only to peter out after curving around a few bends, a half mile later.

Proof, if any was needed, was here: Frank Lloyd Wright's Storer House, dully lit behind his carefully designed, tinted stained glass. So I now knew two things: 1) I had gone back in time because what else would explain my hill without houses and roads but an earlier time? and 2) I had gone back in time to sometime after 1924, because that's when this house was completed, when it had been the highest house on the hill.

Another residence far away on the same side, big and old, then the hill I drove down daily that curved down to cross Laurel Canyon Blvd. before it headed north to the Valley. I walked that familiar down-slope, and it was far less foggy down here although sheets of mist would blow across my view every now and then. It was cool and chilly—what season was it?—I was glad for the windbreaker.

What I saw looked familiar: the streetlights of Hollywood Blvd. level down there and moving directly eastward eventually into a lighted-up area of town. Palm trees eighteen feet tall, not sixty, as I knew them. Well, a dully lighted-up area of town, really, whether because lights were dimmer or it was later or who knew. I didn't care, I was suddenly ecstatic!

Fucking Morgan, I thought. That crazy motherfucker from the future Morgan had sent me back in time! He'd done it!

Even though Morgan had said it was "period-anomalous," I'd hooked a strap to my duffel bag and had it slung across my back and shoulder. I was able to lope down the road and onto the first level road, only two lanes wide, of course, and then across it and onto Hollywood Blvd.

All the two-story apartment complexes I knew were gone—or rather not yet existent. Instead, there were scattered little shanty-like cottages spaced apart. Not the "upscale neighborhood" I knew.

No one on the street, but then there, there was my first car.

It was a Studebaker pickup truck and it was black and it was old. Really old, but it looked brand new. The license plate—only one, and on the front bumper, next to the curved radiator grille—had three digits and a letter! How cool was that? I looked around and took out my phone again. No bars. No shit! I thought. But the camera worked. I shot the car. Front, back, and sides. And thought I heard a house door slam and someone coming, so I hightailed it around the corner, down Hayworth to Selma Avenue. Again, a few little houses here, and then I saw the streetlights of Sunset Blvd. slanting down the hill ahead, and that's where I headed.

I stood on the northwest corner maybe ten minutes—just looking around.

Only one building, a four-story apartment building on the opposite, south, side of the street, along with two little storefronts attached, was recognizable from 2010. But looking down Fairfax Avenue, the two—not five—laned road curved down just as it was supposed to.

What time was it? I had no clue. My watch read 4:06. My phone's clock was out, of course, flashing and useless.

Then a car went by. A big old sedan, maybe from the 20s, speeding along Sunset, headed east.

Another, newer, car came down Fairfax and turned on Sunset, and began going east too, but then pulled to the side of the road in front of the apartment building. The guy driving looked out his window. Then he waved at me.

I gestured at myself—"Me?"

He nodded—"Yes."

So I crossed Sunset. It was the first wide double-lane street I'd seen so far here, with a single two-color street light dangling high, hung in the middle of the road by a cross wire. All of Sunset as far as I could see in either direction was lined every fifty feet or so with tall, wooden street poles. I went over to the driver side window.

This was a tan coupe with a darker tan or brown roof, very nice-looking, with swoopy side fenders, and it was shiny, possibly new.

"You were gesturing at me?" I asked.

The guy inside was wearing a felt brimmed hat and black overcoat with the narrow cloth collar up. His profile reminded me of the old-time actor Edmund O'Brien, but when he was younger; sharp and yet soft in places too.

"You lost?" he asked. Surprisingly high voice. "You look lost."

"Kind of," I admitted.

"You jump ship?" he asked.

Because of the duffel bag and the jacket.

"No. Nothing like that."

"I thought I saw you coming out of the canyon. You lose your ride there? He go down Crescent?"

He had looked toward and thus he must mean down Fairfax Avenue. Note to self: it's called Crescent. I lied, "Yes."

"Well, I'm headed this way," he said, pointing east. "If you're looking for a berth for the night, downtown's your best bet."

"Downtown where?"

"Geez. You really are lost. Downtown Hollywood. Unless you need to go to downtown Los Angeles?"

"No. Hollywood's fine."

He gestured and lit a cigarette. "Get in!"

Once I was inside the car, it was odd. The cloth on the seats was thick and nappy and the Bakelite on the dashboard was amazingly smooth and gleaming.

"It's a Chevy Six." He shrugged. "New."

"It's neat."

He laughed, offered me a cigarette, and I declined. I noticed he didn't start up the car yet.

"So what's your story?" he asked.

"You mean because I'm walking alone on Sunset at what time is it, even? I think this watch stopped!"

"It's just after one a.m. But…you were on a boat, right? I've picked up enough hitchhiking Merchant Marines and sailors to recognize an ocean brat when I see one."

I thought fast. "Right again. I signed off some bucket up in Santa Barbara, and I hitched down the rest of the way. Took all day," I added, I hoped, for verisimilitude.

"So, now what?" he asked. And I thought, is this guy gay or is he just bored or interested or what? I couldn't tell. I couldn't read his signals at all, and that stopped me. Really stopped me. What if that would be what tripped me up here in this time? Not knowing the intuitive gestures and language of the era?

"I mean a kid your age and looks, nine out of ten come down here and try out The Pictures. Was that your idea?"

And now I resisted, I mean seriously resisted, getting up in the seat and looking at myself in his dashboard mirror, to see what I looked like.

"I don't know. The way you say it, it sounds like probably I shouldn't do that."

"I didn't say anything of the sort. It's just, well, I've seen some good kids go bad fast once they hit this place, you know? Especially when they get hitched up to pictures."

"Relax. I've got no illusions," I said. "But I did hear there were a lot of, what do you call 'em, craft jobs, around all the studios. You know: Electricity? Carpentry? I've done some of that."

"On board?" he asked. "Well, that's more sensible."

He threw his cigarette butt out the window and I resisted the urge to tell him it was a thousand-dollar fine.

"So where to?" he asked. "The Hollywood Y is closed until seven a.m. tomorrow morning. I'm guessing you're not terrifically loaded, and you didn't plan on staying in the Roosevelt or the Knickerbocker hotel."

I turned to look at him and smiled. I liked him. But he was totally serious looking back and I now noticed he somehow had large soft eyes. Light eyes, maybe gray or green. But soft because of the heavy eyelashes top and bottom, and those were the only soft features in what was an otherwise masculine face. Thin mustache too. A 30s mustache, I remembered, from old black-and-white movies I'd seen.

"You got that right," I said.

He sighed. "Well, you should go to the Y tomorrow. But you won't. And I don't blame you. They lock the doors at nine. Tell you what…I know a place not too far away that some kids told me about. It's cheap and they've got someone at the desk all night who'll let you in."

He pulled out a silver flask and offered it to me, but I nodded no, so he took a few sips and then looked at me. As if to ask, really, no hooch?

I remembered: this was Prohibition. He was just being friendly. So I nodded no again.

"You hungry?" he asked. "I've got half a baloney sandwich."

He reached behind us and took that off the shelf that was there in place of any backseat, and he handed it to me. It was wrapped in waxed paper, of all things, inside a brown paper bag, and it consisted of two slices of white bread, baloney, and maybe a smear of yellow mustard. Nothing else. I wolfed it down.

"What I oughtta do is turn around and drive you up the other end of the canyon and send you back home."

"I told you I don't come from there. Anyway, I've got no family."

"Oh, geez." He took another sip from the flask and this time I could smell it and guess it was rye, and he lit another cigarette. "Then I oughtta bring you over to Father Flint at Immaculate Heart. Let him put you up and send you home on a bus."

"You're a nice fellow," I said through my eating. "But one: I'm not Catholic, and two: I've got no home to be sent home to." I remembered that this was the Depression, and so I added, "I've been on my own a coupla years already." What I wanted to say was: hey, cool off, not only that but I'm an old guy of sixty-five.

"Okay! You win!" he said, taking another few puffs. He reached behind me and opened one of the fake leather cases I'd seen back there and he took out a fountain pen and a little pad. "I'll drop you off at the Alsop House. But I want you to have my address." He wrote on it and tore it out. I read, *Lawrence Allegre. Free-lance Jewelry Jobber.* There was a business address on Wilshire Blvd. and a phone number that began Aldine 6, with four more numbers.

I folded it up neatly and put it into my shirt pocket.

"Anything at all goes wrong, you ring me. Okay? By the way, my name is Larry."

The name I'd prepped with Morgan before had gone clear out of my head. I did notice his Saint Christopher medal, and I thought and then said, "Christopher."

We awkwardly shook hands.

"That's unusual. Sounds British and all that. Okay, Christopher." He took my hand in his large, meaty paw of a hand and released it reluctantly. "You trust me, right?"

"What, are you kidding? Why would I trust you, Larry? I just met you!" Then I added, "But I will phone you if I'm in trouble."

"Okay. I can see you're no pushover. That's good!"

He threw another butt out the window—the fine was up to two thousand bucks—and he turned on the ignition, engaged the clutch, released the brake, and we took off.

We only stopped twice before we hit Cahuenga Blvd. and he veered left. We went up a block and he stopped and parked in front of a five-story building that dominated one side of the street. Maybe five cars total were parked on the entire block, all of them old.

"Let me go in with you," Larry said.

Fine with me. I wondered if he got some kind of kickback for bringing in strays.

He had to knock on the glass pane until someone looked up from a desk a few feet away where he'd been snoozing. Old guy, very thin, lots of messy hair. Wearing pants too big for him, held up with suspenders over a long-sleeved shirt I wouldn't want to get too close to.

"Yeah!" he mumbled as he opened the door an inch.

"Evening, Pops! Got a young sailor wants to check in."

Pops looked at me and turned around to go back to the desk. Larry caught the door before it slammed shut, and I followed him in.

Behind the desk was a curtain that I guess led to another room, possibly a daytime office. We were in a small, stepped-down lobby. Two chairs with Braque-like tubular metal of some indeterminate alloy on its arms and legs and a green, plasticky-looking leather seat and back. Between the two stood a table—high metal ashtray with what looked like a much-stained yellow plastic tray and cigar or cigarette marks on it. Completely out of place was the third piece, a faux–Queen Anne side table, completing the lobby furnishing. It was covered with a soiled doily and held two magazines. I longed to pick one up to check the date.

Pops slid over a register. "Half-month rate is three dollars."

"I'm not sure how long I'm staying."

"He'll stay the two weeks," Larry said for me. And when I looked at him for explanation, he said, "It'll take you that long to settle into that job."

"Oh, right!" I said, playing along.

"Always glad to have residents with jobs," Pops said. This close up, he had an amazingly big nose with a growth on it and a sterling case of strabismus. His thin, steel-rimmed glasses were tiny: they barely covered his eye sockets. "But if you don't start up right away, you can go with the other fellows in the morning, up to Paramount or the Warners. They got omnibuses that pick up folk they'll need as extras every morning but Sunday. Stops on the corner of Hollywood and Cahuenga. Okay, sailor boy, three bucks, up front. Fill in here."

He pointed to an empty line below one signed *Joe Schmoh. Paducah.* Clever, I thought. Why not "King Kong, Skull Island"?

I wrote *Christopher Hall* and had two surprises as I did so. First, my handwriting was good: my hand was steady and neat, the letters utterly readable. No one had been able to read my handwriting in twenty years; not even me. Second, the last name had just come to me. The same way that the name Christopher had. I'd not chosen it, it had chosen me. Next to it, as a home address, I wrote *Santa Barbara.*

"Nice moniker," Pops said. "If they use you in the pictures you won't have to change it none."

As I fiddled in my wallet for singles, he said, "You'll get a bath towel and hand towel and a bar of soap. Those and the sheets get changed once a week. More than that is a dime a change. Anything extra you need like a toothbrush or comb, you can get tomorrow at the Five and Dime up the street."

I looked at the top for a date, but all it said was April.

I looked next to my name—"What does this slash mean?"

"You share the room. Only four shares left. No full rooms at-tall!"

"No problem," Larry said, "Chris here is used to bunking in a hammock on board a ship."

Pops couldn't have cared less. But he did say, "You're sharin' with the cleanest one I got."

He handed me a set of keys on a leather thong that could go around my wrist or ankle. There were two normal-sized keys and a smaller one.

I held them out. And Pops pointed to them: "Building door key. Room door key. Lock box for your valerables."

"What kind of lockbox?" I asked.

He rummaged behind the curtain and pulled one out matching the key number. It was gunmetal, about the size of an old-time cigar box.

"You're all set," he said, handing it to me. "I don't want to hear about anything going missing. You got me?"

Pops almost fell asleep before I was finished saying good-bye to Larry and thanking him.

"Can I buy you a cheap dinner sometime?" I asked.

"Sure you can. When you get yourself a job."

"No. Really. I got paid on board."

Larry pointed to a dark space at the end of the little lobby, opposite the stairway door. "There's a pay phone. All it takes is a nickel."

"I'll call."

"Sure you will. Just get on that bus Pops mentioned when it comes by tomorrow morning and go look for the electric and woodworking shops once you get to the movie studio."

I saluted. "Yes sir! Captain, sir!"

"Wise guy!" But he smiled and his eyes looked like they would melt.

On the third floor, I knocked on the door, then thinking my roommate might be asleep, I quietly used the key to let myself in. It was dark except for the light from two windows facing me. One was open an inch or two and a fresh cold breeze was coming in. The fog had picked up again and everything was visible outside only through a scrim of haze: some lighted-up hotel and "eats" signs, a few dull yellow streetlights. I used my hand to search for a wall switch, found it, and wondered if the light would wake my roommate.

I flicked it on fast and saw: no one else in the room. It was an old brass standing lamp with a flared, circular top bowl and three incandescent bulbs laid around it in a ring. Only two worked. I saw that the room was about ten by six, and had a sort of open-work closet on the left side of the door, where hangers held a few items. There was also a tall dresser. Two spindly-looking chairs. But where was the other bed?

I dropped my bag and went downstairs again and had to awaken Pops.

"Pops! There's only one bed in the room!"

"So? I told you I was giving you the cleanest feller, didn't I?" Pops said, in an aggrieved tone of voice. Then he added, "Oh, I forgot to tell you. The lavs and the shower rooms are all public, and with stalls. You gotta water pitcher and little sink in your room, but no terlet. And I'd suggest knocking before you go charging right into either of those places."

"Because…?" I asked.

"Because I don't go up there much except to clean up, but any place with almost a hundred young fellows in it, there's goin' be some, whadayacall it," he gestured with his hand, "jerking around? Funny stuff? You know what I mean?"

"Yeah, I do, Pops. I was on a ship. Remember?"

"I forgot. You could probably teach *them* how to do it!"

I laughed. "You're a riot, Pops! Listen, my roommate wasn't there."

"He'll be in soon. There was some goin'-away party up the street. Nice guy. From up north around Portland or some place like that. You might have been on a ship, but you're still just a kid, you understand. And a friend of Larry's too. So I'll look out for you."

"Thanks, Pops. You're swell."

"Ah, heck. I was young once. 'Bout a hundred years ago. I'll tell him you're up there snoozing so he don't wake you up."

I looked at the magazines on the lobby table. One was *Popular Mechanics* and it read March 1935. The other was *Saturday Evening Post* and it read March 24, 1935. I was in 1935! I'd come back more than seventy-five years!

"Go on, take one," Pops said. "But make sure to return it in the morning."

So I took the *Popular Mechanics*. Smart to brush up on what actually existed and what actually worked in this to-me-still-unknown time.

After I locked my valuables (MP3 player, money, phone) away and put the lockbox under the bed, I went out of the room and into the single big lavatory at the end of the floor. It sported six booths with doors on one side and an open brass single urinal trough on the other wall, like what I'd seen animals feed out of on big ranches. At the end was a clear space with two windows on each side, and in the middle were three small separate sinks with old brass taps and a single torso-high mirror above all three. I was planning to wash up and brush my teeth.

And that was my third big surprise.

I looked maybe seventeen, eighteen years old. Slender. Thin, really. With curly black hair, long on the front and sides, that needed cutting, and nothing even close to a shadow of a beard. My skin was clear and perfect. My oh-so-familiar-after-sixty-five-years eyes were fresh and dewy and large and dark brown, and elaborately lashed. I had not seen this particular "me" in many years, not since I'd come across a photo a few decades before.

I smiled a little lopsided smile that I remember cultivating at that age and then I winked slowly at myself.

And why not? I was totally fucking adorable!

4

"So, Hank, what gives? We don't have enough competition for work and dames, but you gotta bring us some city slicker who looks about twelve and is sure to take 'em with both hands and leave us holding the bag?"

That was Sid. Sidney Devlin. A redheaded, tightly built little bantam shorter than me but about my weight with blue eyes a little too matte to be called attractive, and a bump in his nose, but otherwise as sweet-looking a Son of Erin as I'd ever come across.

"This is Chris." Hank Streit introduced me to the others. We'd just arrived at the Anderson Diner, their usual hangout, around the corner from the Alsop House. "He just got outta the Merchant Marine. Looking for work as—what did you say? An electrician?"

We settled at a table in the window. The place was filled at seven a.m. The two other diners at the table also shook hands with me.

"Jonah Wolff," the dark-haired one said with a distinct Midwest accent. He had dark eyes and thick brown curly hair, what I'd call "Hollywood hair." Some *Mitteleuropean* in his genetic makeup. Maybe even a little Jewish mixture. Hooded eyes. Kind of sexy with a little scar on the side of his mouth like a comma. Not at all my type.

He asked, "You comin' with us up to Warners today?"

"I thought I would."

"Ducky." The thickly muscled, bigger guy water-pumped my hand in greeting. Like Hank, he was some German-American combo, with thick, wheat-colored hair and dark blue eyes, and good-looking, standard features, though not as good-looking All-American college boy as my roommate, Hank—Henry Anthony Streit, Jr. as his ID read—who was from Belmont in Washington state. He was scrumptious, or at least I thought so. Almost golden hair. I mean like a gold metal; bright blue eyes; even, symmetrical features, with a little bit of a flat, cat nose, i.e., just enough individuality to make it "interesting." As opposed to Ducky's stouter, straighter nose and bigger lips, all of which features would thicken early. I recalled that in 2010, the only actors who looked as butchly "All-American" as these two guys were usually Canucks, Aussies, and an occasional Kiwi. The four of them were all about twenty-two years old. Maybe Jonah was a year older. It was hard to tell. Given my own true, advanced age, it had been several decades since I'd been around this many young men, and I was enjoying their youth and freshness at the same time that I remained cautious. The one thing in my favor as a newcomer was that I looked much younger, and so I was less of a threat.

Hank had come in after I dropped off to sleep, although I awakened at one point and knew he was in bed too. In the morning I got up and went to take a shower. When I got back to the room, Hank was trying to wake up, still tangled in the sheets, with a guinea tee on, and loose white boxers that couldn't hide a boner, his golden hair all which ways, his eyes barely open. I'd fallen for him in the spot.

"Geez, but you got soft hands!" Ducky commented to my shake. "What did you do on board that ship?"

"Radio communication," I lied.

"What a soft spot, eh? No wonder."

"What's Ducky short for?" I had to ask.

"Short for Dutchman. I'm Deutscher. Daniel L. Deutscher. County Wide All-Varsity, Edgemont High, Altoona, P.A."

"So now you're playing football professionally?" I asked.

"Nah! Long story."

"Ducky's going to play for the Hollywood Bulldogs," Hank said.

"I haven't even tried out."

"You will. And you'll get on the team," Hank insisted: a good friend.

We'd been served coffee in small, thick, white porcelain mugs when we'd first arrived. As the waiter had passed, the other three had ordered, but not Hank. I was looking at the menu above the metal stove hood that listed coffee and a refill for a nickel, with a ham and eggs, toast and fries platter—for the royal amount of twenty cents!

"Aren't you ordering?" I nudged Hank.

"Nah, I'll wait."

"My treat. One time only," I added. As the waiter came by, I called out, "*Garçon!* Two of those ham and eggs plates. Easy-over for me! Hank? What's your desire?" When he stared at me without answering, I said to the waiter, "Eyeballs for him."

The waiter took off, and Sid asked, *"Garçon?"*

"It's French," I said.

"Geez, Louise. A nine-year-old off a boat and he already speaks French. And what's with the 'eyeballs' business?"

"It means two eggs fried straight up. That's waiter lingo."

"And you know that because what? You were a waiter in your youth, many years ago?" Sid asked.

"Something like that!" I admitted. The other guys were extremely amused that I had Sid flummoxed.

Ducky stopped chewing toast long enough to say, "Baby-Boy here's probably got a wifey and few kids stuffed in some little bungalow somewhere."

"Lotsa competition, Sid," Jonah said between bites of his eggs. "You're not the Golden Boy anymore. Junior here's got you beat." He turned to me. "Ever been in the moving pictures?"

"Not yet," I said.

That set them all laughing again, except Sid, who said, "Not yet? So what? You're going to do that this month? And next month learn to fly a plane?"

It was all I could do to restrain myself from telling him I'd already had a few lessons in a single-engine two-seater, back in 2005.

I left it at "Well, you know. I get around."

That set the others laughing again.

When Hank went into the john, Ducky said to me in a low tone of voice that only the other two could hear: "That was a swell thing you did, kid. Hank's broke and he wouldn't've taken a handout from any of us. They'll give us all a sandwich or maybe some stew for lunch at the studio. But until then…"

"I was just being prudent, Ducky. Who knows but Hank might turn around and *eat me* during the night."

They all guffawed this time.

When we paid, I was about to leave a tip on the sixty-cents-with-no-sales-tax-tab that the two meals had cost me, but I saw that no one else had left change on a table or on the counter. Remember, Christopher Hall: this is the Depression!

Even so, I was last out the door and I dropped a quarter into the waiter's apron, saying, "Found this on the floor. You musta dropped it."

He looked at me with dead eyes. "I can die happy," he said in a tight voice. "'Cause now I seen everything!"

There was a line waiting for the omnibus: mostly young guys; a few older men, and two or three older women.

The bus was a clackety old thing from the 20s, I couldn't tell what make, possibly General Motors from the worn-out badge on the hood, and with wooden slat seats and rope handholds, and we five were jammed in the back. I was in heaven. With these four I felt young again for the first time since I'd come back. It slowly chugged, climbing the narrow Cahuenga Canyon road—there was no Hollywood Freeway 170 yet in 1935, of course—at times I thought we might have to get out and push. But once we made it over the crest of the hill and a small vee of the San Fernando Valley was in sight, all the younger men gathered at the back of the bus gave a big cheer and applauded.

The driver was a big, fattish, good-looking African-American guy of about forty, who the guys called Jungle Jim, Sid told me, because he took "bits" in every movie set in any jungle anywhere at any studio in town. J.J. waved his hat back at us.

The Warner Bros. extras lot was where the 2010 WB easternmost parking lots of the studio were located. We took a dirt road off Barham Road to get in. The studio seemed to consist of wooden, some quite tall, Quonset huts, where the actual indoor filming took place. Behind those were these little wooden shacks that I recalled would still be there three-quarters of a century later, used as producer's offices.

We were let out into a big yard filled with people. As we entered, we were sorted into age groups, which kept the five of us together. My new pals knew their way around and also knew some other extras, I guess from coming here regularly. They found a spot with some shade and a bench with a couple of guys sitting around in folding chairs, and a doubled-over piece of cardboard between their knees being used as a table. They were already playing cards.

There must have been about five hundred people there altogether, mostly standing around or hunched down, waiting. Meanwhile, men in three-piece suits and fedoras wielding megaphones would come and go out of what must have been a casting office, going around every once in a while, and calling out numbers, film titles, even names. If you'd been an extra in a film the day before and had been called back, Hank told me, you went over to that doorway, and they checked your name and then siphoned you from there onto a queue, and would then walk over to a costume set-up or to a stage inside one of the Quonset hut–like structures. That is, if you didn't need to change.

But everyone had to check in first. And, of course, as a new extra I had to check in and give name, residence, and even a phone number. All of which, Hank, playing my protector, supplied. The rotund middle-aged man whose eyebrows were in sore need of a clipping knew the Alsop House, of course, and its phone number and street address.

"Any acting experience?" he drawled at me, in a bored tone of voice, around the stogie he was chewing on, and I could see his pencil poised over the "no" box.

"Well…a little," I said.

He checked off "yes" and looked up at me. "Roles?"

"You wouldn't know it, I don't think. It was a new play in my hometown."

"That being?"

"New York City."

The stogie moved around a bit before he said, "Don't tell me it was Broadway?"

"Off Broadway."

It had been my own play, in fact. When I had to cover for the lead, when everyone was out with the flu. But I didn't say that.

Pencil poised again: "Other roles?"

"*Romeo and Juliet*?" I said.

"Role?" he asked, his curiosity even more piqued!

I screwed up my eyes, afraid to say it: "Juliet's father."

"What was it? A kindergarten production?" he asked and the stogie fell into his lap from where he quickly retrieved it.

"Just write it down, Mack," Hank Streit insisted behind me. When we moved on, in a lower voice, he added, "Sid's going to have a conniption when he hears this!"

"I told you I got around…Look, Hank, don't tell them. Please."

"Okay. But I'm sticking close, kid. Who knows what'll come up next."

An hour later I was admitted to the poker game when two guys playing were called away to extra on the set of *Charlie Chan in Paris*.

Of course the game was the kind we played as kids, but I still couldn't recall if four of a kind beat or was beaten by a straight, when the megaphone announced, "All you on *Fondly Yours*."

The other four got up and so did I, but as I approached the doorway where the group were being collected and sent out via the open doorway, my interviewer with the stogie from before came up to me, along with a woman in her fifties with close-cropped gray hair under a cloche hat and big glasses and a leather satchel slung over one bony shoulder.

Stogie guy pulled me out of the line and held on to me tight.

"Here he is."

She looked me over, head to toe.

Ducky and Jonah had gone through the door. Now Hank was being let through. Sid was looking back at me. Watching what was going on.

"I've got to go with my friends," I told her, pointing to the doorway.

"He'll do fine," she said to the stogie chewer. "You're coming with us!" she said, and grabbed my other arm.

"Sid!" I called out.

He had just gone through the doorway, and he turned and yelled, "Where are they taking you?"

"He's a juvenile," the woman spat back at him. "He's coming with me."

Sid's face opened up in a huge grin and he threw his cap in the air and caught it, then spun around and ran to tell the other guys with glee that I'd been busted.

All four of them were gone now.

"Stop pulling, young man!" she insisted.

"But what did I do? Why are you throwing me out?"

"Throwing you out? I'm not throwing you out! I'm taking you to MGM in Culver City. We're short two juveniles in a film being cast today."

"You're kidding."

"Do I look like I'm kidding?" she asked, and her eyes resembled hard little pebbles.

The stogie chewer said, "He didn't even want to tell me he'd acted before, with his friends around. I had to pry it out of him," he lied.

"Boys!" she expostulated, as if we were a breed known for every possible excess. "Here!" she mumbled and I saw her hand him a green bill. He looked around, I guess to see if anyone was observing, and then quickly put it into his pants pocket. Evidently he was her point man, on the lookout for unsuspecting juveniles.

They marched me out through the fence we'd first come in through, where a big black limousine was parked. A uniformed and capped chauffeur opened the third door and the woman all but pushed me into the back. There was a pretty young lady at the far end of the big backseat who smiled at me. So I got in. The doors snapped locked. The chauffeur got in one door and the woman in the cloche got in the other, up in front, separated from us by a glass partition with closed, pleated blue curtains.

"I see they nabbed you too!" I said, still a little breathless.

"I hope so!" she said in a lovely voice. "It's only an audition, but I understand they're suddenly short because a couple dropped out and they're beginning initial shooting tomorrow. You're very nice-looking," she added, "so I'm sure they'll take you."

"Well, you're very pretty, so they'll probably take you," I replied.

Good God, I thought. I'm in the middle of some inane Andy Hardy script. "What film is it, anyway?" I had the sense to ask.

"I don't know the title. But the trades said it would star Billy Bartlett. From the *Mickey McGuire* movies. I just love those!"

I had no idea what she was talking about.

"Don't you?" she prodded.

"I'm not really that familiar…" I began.

She jumped right in, animated and enthused: "Well, Mickey Rooney plays this kid named Mickey McGuire, and he's just gotten a gang of pals together and…"

As she went on, I thought, wait, I've met Mickey Rooney. But he was about ninety at the time and actually that meeting hasn't even happened yet, so he'll never recognize me if he's there in the studio. So—no problema!

She was just finishing saying, "I've been waiting for so long for a part like this. My agent says it could make me."

"Waiting for how long?" I asked.

"Over three years. Since I was sixteen."

"You look sixteen now."

"Thank the Lord," she said. "I've done bits. But this is the real deal."

"It's not like…singing and dancing? Is it?"

"If they take us both, we'll be a new couple," she said. "We'll work on lines together and I'll show you the dance steps. They're usually pretty simple. Don't worry about singing. Unless you're a star, they can dub in the voice on the soundtrack," she added knowledgably. Then, "Maybe you should say you're agented by Frances Wannamaker too, when they ask. Otherwise you could end up with a bad contract. She's my agent."

"Okay. But you'll have to back me up."

Eventually we pulled into the famous gate at MGM when it still was that, and not Sony Inc., and she got excited again.

We were far more ceremoniously treated by the woman—Pamela Cullen, she now revealed her name—once the chauffeur had opened the door and let us out onto the studio street.

We headed into the building, side by side, through what looked like a big lobby and I could see my companion's excitement growing, so I took her hand, which had begun shaking, and I mimed taking deep breaths. She looked at me with a "thank you" look and regained her composure with a few deep breaths as we entered a big casting office through open double doors. I thought, no way this is happening.

Three people got up to meet us, and Pamela went to the back of the room, her job done for the moment.

The taller and balder of the two men, with a good-sized mustache, greeted us, taking both of our hands and having us come over to the other side of his desk, which opened to a little garden area. It had two medium-sized winged chairs that he had us sit in while he gazed at us. I thought he smelled of lilac and wondered if that was an aftershave lotion of the era.

"Sue-Ann Schiller," my companion introduced herself.

"Christopher Hall," I said.

"I'm Dominick La Cosse, casting director. You're both very attractive. Do you know the Mickey McGuire movies?"

I let Sue-Anne gush about them for a while and I smiled at what I hoped were appropriate points.

"Well, this movie is somewhat different," La Cosse began. "It's older kids. Boys *and* girls. And…you've acted onstage, correct, young Mr. Hall? Even so, there probably won't be many lines."

"I learn lines easy," I said casually. "We both do. Sue-Ann and I will coach each other."

"Well!" La Cosse said. "We've got two little professionals here!" And all the adults laughed politely. "How unexpected!" He turned around and said, "Thank you, Pamela. You've come through at this difficult moment for us very nicely. Very nicely indeed! This will be noticed upstairs."

She simpered thanks and left the room.

"And of course you're not represented…?" La Cosse began.

"But we are!" Sue-Ann said. "Frances Wannamaker!" we added in one voice, then looked at each other and smiled.

"Okay. Of course we know Mrs. Wannamaker. You kids look great together, you know. Schiller and Hall, huh? I've got no problem with your names either. Melv? What do you think?" He looked at someone behind us and concluded, "Yes, the names are fine. So we'll send over contracts for you to Frances, by messenger. But first we'll have to meet Mr. Seiter,.He's the director. Have you ever been on a film stage before?"

We both pretended we hadn't. La Cosse took us gingerly by the hand as though we were breakable and his underlings silently followed us out into the studio street and then up into the first of two motorized open autos waiting to take us to the soundstage.

A half hour later, we were learning dance steps from the choreographer, and Sue-Anne had been right. They weren't that difficult.

Frances Wannamaker herself came to pick us up after the first rehearsal and the preparatory "lighting shoot" that afternoon, at five.

She'd driven her sky-blue Terraplane station wagon with real, two-toned, painted wooden siding, and matte-black running boards and roof, a car that I looked over carefully. I'd only seen photos of this Hudson model before.

Frances wore her long blond hair in back in a style I knew to be called a French log. She'd been attractive not too long ago, but she also looked like she'd been around the block a few times. No wedding ring but a tan line where one had been recently.

"Are you hungry? I assume the studio fed you lunch at the commissary. Right?" she asked.

During the lunch break we'd eaten in the studio's lunchroom, along with the other seven young dancer couples but not with the star: excellent club sandwiches with a side of coleslaw, and lemonade.

The front seat was big enough, so first Sue-Anne, then I got in, while Frances spoke to someone she knew.

Sure enough, right there on the car's steering column was the Bendix "Electric Hand" I'd read about as a vintage car enthusiast. This was an early precursor of the automatic transmission that Hudson had introduced the year before on this model only, and had four preset buttons. I looked on the floor, and there was a clutch pedal, but I knew this Terraplane also had an automatic clutch.

When Frances got in, I pointed to the "Electric Hand" and asked how it worked.

"I start up the ignition." She illustrated, and then she tapped the clutch once and hit the Electric Hand button #1, for first gear. "That disables the clutch and I don't have to keep pumping it every time after I brake."

"So you just hit second and then third buttons when you want more speed?"

"That's right."

"What happens if the Hand here fails? It's some kind of electrical and levered pump, right?"

"I don't recall all the details," she admitted. "But that sounds right. If the Hand doesn't engage, I have these buttons here!" She showed me where they were, under the dashboard radio. "These work as gears. You sound like you drive."

"I have for a few years now. But I never drove one of these."

In those three weeks between Mr. Morgan's offer and my jump back in time, I'd gone out of my way to learn how to use a manual transmission, a talent I'd long forgotten. "I'd like to try it out some time."

"For years? You're some kid, Christopher."

"I'm not a kid. I'm an adult, Mrs. Wannamaker. Eighteen," I told her.

"Chris has already been in the Merchant Marines," Sue-Anne offered.

"Is that right? Well, then, Mr. Hall, I'm very glad to hear it. It'll make life a lot easier for me. Dealing with child actors can be dreadfully exhausting!" She laughed. "That said, like Sue-Anne here, you look years younger than your age. That fellow I was speaking to? Thom Rafferty? He said they like you two already. He's big in future development at the studio, and he told me that the Lion is banking on teen movies as the next big thing for the next five years! So, Mr. Hall and Miss Schiller, if you behave yourselves, and don't hit the hooch and white powder too hard, I can probably get you both all the work you want."

"Don't worry, Mrs. Wannamaker," Sue-Anne assured her. Then in a dreamy voice added, "Oh, Chris! Think of it! We're in the movies!"

"Terrific!" I replied. "Where do I sign?"

Frances looked at me suddenly. Oops. Had I been a little too ironic?

"At my office, naturally. That's where the contracts are."

5

"That's wonderful news, Hank," I was saying. We were leaning up against the side wall of the Anderson Diner blocking most of the Dugan Auto Body Shop mural-advertisement, waiting for the other guys to show up. "So all of you got bit parts?" I.e., more than extras, they would do or say something on film, and be paid more.

"Just Sid and me. It's good. But nothing like your news."

"When do they pay you? End of the week?"

"Sure. A buck a day. Why?"

"How about I front you a loan until then?" I asked.

"What if it's only one day's work?" Hank argued.

The sixty-five-year-old me wanted to say, don't worry. I'll take it out in trade. The eighteen-year-old me said aloud, "I'm making twenty dollars a week, Hank. I *think* I can afford it. And don't say no, because you'll make me angry and you don't ever want to see me angry," I added.

"I don't?" Hank asked with an indulgent smile. In this light he reminded me of the young Don Murray, with that square jaw and that really kissable thin-lipped mouth.

"No, you don't. I'm a terror."

"Yeah! But you're a *juvenile* terror," he said, and laughed. "Wait'll Sid hears what happened. He'll blow a gasket."

I handed him the five dollars, my older self tempted to say, "Same time, next week?" loud enough for two passersby to hear. But I restrained myself.

Ducky and Jonah showed up first, and as it was beginning to rain, we all went in and found a table. The waiter was the same one from the day before and he gave us what Jonah Wolff called a "fish-eye": he probably thought I was going to ask for my quarter back.

Hank told them my news and Ducky clapped me on the shoulder. Jonah said in his flat voice, "I know your type."

"You do?" I asked. I still hadn't figured out his type.

"You slip in dog-doo and it turns out to be chocolate pudding."

"Funny. Well, Jonah and Ducky, I sacrificed to the Goddess this morning and She promised me you'd get parts too."

Hank was amused and Ducky had no idea what I was talking about.

"Not me," Jonah said. "Other people's luck doesn't rub off on me."

I was about to suggest he not be so defeatist when Sid showed up, using a piece of cardboard he'd found somewhere as an umbrella, that he left at the door.

He shook himself like a dog next to the table and then ordered breakfast standing up. When he sat down next to me he said, "Ducky was sure we were goin' have ta bust you outta Juvie Hall!"

I put my hands out as though I were being cuffed.

"They got me, Sid. Took me in a seventeen-foot-long Lincoln." I rubbed it in. "Automatically locked doors. No getting away. One other backseat passenger. The lovely and talented Sue-Anne Schiller. Obviously an alias, as she was clearly a career criminal, like myself. We were forced to sing, dance, act, and then they made us sign our lives away in some bogus contract. We were marched over to a soundstage and stuck there all afternoon. Sure, they fed us on club sandwiches fatter than my hand with green goddess dressing, but who knew when we'd ever make good our escape or see freedom again? Not to mention your mugs?"

Hank and Jonah and after a while even Ducky did all they could to not burst out laughing. But I could see that every word was another blow to Sid's ego.

"Geez!" Sid said. "What an imagination this kid has. He's another Edna Ferber!"

The others exploded at this: food and drink went all over the table.

"Tell you what, Sid," Hank said, once he could hold down food again and not giggle. "You shave really close tomorrow and Chris'll bring you by his director's office when he goes."

Jonah added, "Try to look sweet, Sid, and you just might pass for a particularly perverted teenager."

"What a bunch a bananas," Sid said, not losing his cool. He turned to a man with a newspaper at the next table. "And these are my friends!"

"Congratulations on your part, Sid," I said.

"It's nothing. They really wanted Lover Boy there." Meaning Hank. "I'm just along for the ride." Not a stupid young man.

"For contrast?" I asked.

"Something like that."

"They picking you up in a limo today too?" Ducky asked. Naïveté was his long suit and it looked good on him.

"No. My, ahem, talent agent is getting me. At ten!"

"Will that Sue-Anne be there?" Ducky asked.

"I guess. She's staying not far from here. You want to meet her, Ducky?"

"Ducky likes girls but they make him…nervous," Jonah said.

"Are you kidding?" I said. "If I looked like you, Ducks, I'd be dating three girls at any given time."

"Not on my bank account, you wouldn't."

"She's probably staying at Miss Irene's Hotel for Young Women," Jonah said.

"Words uttered by someone who must know every brick in that building's façade," I said.

Jonah blushed. "Well, I have known a girl or two who stayed there."

And I realized what it was about him I'd not been able to put my finger on before: he was a cocksman. A quiet and unassuming one, a non-bragging one, but definitely a cocksman. I'd bet he made out like a bandit with those out-of-town girls.

A friend of theirs, a guy named Russ with lots of almost white-blond hair, came by the table and joked with us. He had a larger "bit" part in *Charlie Chan in Paris* and knew a couple of the guys in the crew. He mentioned that they were looking for French speakers.

"Junior here speaks Froggie," Jonah announced. And before I realized he meant me, he added, "But he's got an agent."

"That's okay. It's a legit role." Russ wrote down my name and said he knew Wannamaker Talent. "You're kinda young. But who knows?"

When he'd left, Jonah said, "He'll get a five-buck tip if they sign you."

"Fine with me."

Sid muttered, "You do high-wire too? I hear Ringling Brothers is looking for an aerialist."

"Except it's for an aerialist without a net, right?" I asked, and Sid smiled—complicit. So that was it: Sid and I were going to have a friendly-rivals relationship.

The rain had stopped and the street was misting over when we left the diner. I joined the others headed up to the Warner's omnibus stop. At the last minute, Jonah begged off saying he felt a headache coming on, joking about "this damn California climate, sunny every day of the week!"

The bus came not a minute after that, and three minutes later I was back at the Alsop House with a newspaper someone had abandoned in the lobby.

I mentioned Jonah to Pops, who was awake and listening to *The Trials of Helen Kent* on the lobby's console radio, which was about the size of a 1960 Fiat 500 I'd owned in my youth. But once the commercial came on, Pops turned down the volume knob and said, "He didn't come back. Only you."

Leaving me to wonder exactly where Jonah had gone for his "headache."

I sat and read in the lobby, waiting for him to come in. The front-page articles were mostly local: Teenage girl didn't come home. When the Griffith Park Observatory would—finally!—open, in late May. One little article was about drought conditions and high winds in Oklahoma.

There was a photo of a huge and ominously black cloud hovering over a tiny shack of a house with a barefoot girl looking up at it. The caption: *She's praying for rain.* I was aware that this would soon become the Dust Bowl tragedy, and by next year, that little girl would be one of a million trying to survive on the borders of Kern County in the Central Valley, not that far from where I sat.

Sue-Anne was already in the front seat of Frances Wannamaker's Hudson. So I climbed in back. The ceiling of the Terraplane was high and curved in back. I thought that Magic Johnson could be comfortable back here.

Frances half turned. "I got a phone call just before I left the office. What's this I hear? You speak French?"

"Bien sur, madamoiselle. Mais seulement un peur."

"That sounds genuine to me."

"Certainement, mon cherie! Mon chaufleur!"

Sue-Anne turned—her pert little mouth open in an astonished "o."

"From what Casting at Warners told me on the phone, it's about five lines in one scene. They'll probably glue a mustache on your face and put you in a French cop uniform."

"Je sera—un flic?"

"It'll have to be early in the morning. Since you've got eleven o'clock shoots all the rest of the week. If I or someone else can't meet you, I'll send a taxi over for you. The pay is hundred bucks flat."

"Magnifique!" I said.

We were stopped at a streetlight. She turned again to face me:

"Two film jobs in one week your first week in town and you're cool as a cucumber! Enough to joke about it. In French, yet! You don't really care one way or the other, do you, Chris?"

That got Sue-Anne riled up. She defended me, telling Frances how hard I'd worked at the day before rehearsal. "Tell her, Chris!"

What she hadn't understood was that for the past few days I was reveling, absolutely reveling, in the health, strength, and especially in the easy dexterity of my *new eighteen-year-old body.*

"I think it's all wonderful for me and for us both, Mrs. Wannamaker. I'm willing to do whatever it is to keep me working and to provide you with your ten percent."

One shapely, mostly penciled in, eyebrow lifted and Frances

muttered, "Oh, brother! And I thought I had to deal with bad acting at auditions."

The car took off again.

In the backseat I found a copy of *Screenplay* magazine: on the cover was an idealized illustration of the head of Greta Garbo. To one side, the cover copy read, *Marriage predicted for Garbo!*

I let out a guffaw.

"What?" Sue-Anne asked and I handed her the magazine. She squealed: "Oooh. I'll just bet she's going to marry John Gilbert."

"I'll just bet she's going to marry Mercedes Acosta," I said.

"Who's he?" Sue-Anne asked.

"I heard that," Frances said, trying to act shocked.

A minute later, she let out a big laugh that she tried to stifle.

6

"Cut! That was terrific, kids!" our director said. "Take ten!" And we went to one side of the soundstage where food, and more importantly juice, had been set up. Most of the girls raced to sit on the folding chairs there; they'd been dancing in low heels. Most of the boys wolfed down whatever looked edible. We'd been shooting the scene—an utterly forgettable song-and-dance number along with the "lead couple," Bill Bartlett and a young woman whose name I didn't catch—for what seemed to be hours: i.e., since we'd gotten there at eleven that morning. Lots of chatter, and catching up, and complaints among us.

But I noticed the "star" himself in what looked like animated conversation with the director, and a few minutes later, the set producer joined them and it became even more animated. Finally all of them headed in a direction that I knew was where some of the "kids" went to smoke: outside.

When they returned ten minutes later or so, they seemed to have agreed upon something. All of them but Billy and the executive producer, who evidently had also joined them, seemed annoyed, biting their lips, looking aside, etc. From which I gathered that the star had thrown a hissy fit and his wish had been granted.

The script boy came over and tapped me and then Sue-Ann and took us over to the group with our star.

"Nice work, kids," our director said. "Tell me, would you two be comfortable moving up in the line and going right behind and to one side of Billy and Milly?"

That was her name: Milly!

"Sure," I said.

"Isn't that where Henry and Jane are now?" Sue-Ann asked: the sixty-four-thousand-dollar question.

"And that's exactly the problem." Billy came up and joined us, acting all chummy all of a sudden. "Thom and I saw yesterday's rushes and those kids looked totally out of whack!"

He meant Thom Rafferty, Frances Wannamaker's connection at the studio and the executive producer on the picture: i.e., he answered directly to M.G. or M.

"We thought maybe you kids could try it. We all like your look and your dancing," Seiter, the director, said. He sounded long-suffering.

"But aren't they professionals?" Sue-Ann argued. "We just got here!"

"Don't underestimate yourselves," Billy said. "You kids are terrific."

Sue-Anne was about to protest again when I grabbed her hand hard. She shut up and looked at me.

"We'll try it out," I said. Then I added to Billy, "Thanks for giving us the spot!"

He clapped me on the shoulder and off everyone went.

The second director then had the less pleasant job of telling Henry and Jane that they were relegated to the back line. I could see Henry doing a slow burn. Jane turned around to hide her tears.

But we still weren't ready to shoot. Billy, the director, and the set director went into another huddle, so I grabbed Sue-Anne and marched her back to the ousted couple. Sue-Anne went over to Jane and tried to console her.

Henry, a good-looking, auburn-haired kid of about eighteen, was evidently still livid.

"You two can't dance as well as we can!" he said.

"No we can't, Henry, and we both know it too. But that seems to be exactly the point!"

That stopped him. His face froze up for a second. "What do you mean?"

"I mean you and Jane are so good that you're showing up those two clod-hoppers! With us next to them, *they'll* look like the pros."

The look of sudden enlightenment on poor Henry's face at the iniquity of the world was almost too much to bear. I touched his arm. "I'm sorry, Henry. But don't worry. You'll get another chance to shine."

Now his face darkened with the realization. I could see Sue-Anne telling Jane the same thing, only she cried even more.

"It's because he's blowing off that exec," Henry said, his mouth a hard curved line.

"Blowing off" was a American 30s slang term, meaning not "ignoring," as I was used to hearing the term in 2010, but instead "blowing," period.

"Who is? Bartlett?" I asked.

"Sure. I saw the two of them in the Derby on Wilshire a couple of nights ago, next to each other, thigh to thigh. He's blowing off that Rafferty for sure. I had the chance to do it myself, a few months ago, you know." I just bet he did, handsome as he was. "Rafferty invited me out to a nightclub and all. And stupid me, I turned Rafferty down. Said I didn't do stuff like that. Not even for a movie."

"Well, maybe. But it's Bartlett's movie, Henry. He's got the name."

"Betcha he blew off that Rooney guy to get in *Mickey McGuire* too."

So I let Henry blow off—some steam. When he was a little calmer I suggested we go help Sue-Anne with Jane. We'd just accomplished that when we were all called to our soundstage floor marks.

"I'm really sorry, Henry," I repeated. "You know I am."

"I know. I know. Thanks. It's my own fault," he said, ruefully, and he and Jane took what before had been our places.

"Are you nervous?" I asked Sue-Anne.

"No, I'm mad."

"Then dance, girl! Dance like mad!" I whispered.

She made a cute smile at that.

We did okay. At least we didn't mess up. And the scene took only four more tries before a beleaguered Seiter yelled "cut!" And then the set producer yelled, "That's it for the day. Tomorrow at eleven a.m.! You've got the scene number and page. Costumes at ten a.m."

We joined Jane and Henry as they were leaving and we repeated our apologies.

"I forgot to tell you," Sue-Anne said to me. "Frances can't come today for us. And anyway, we can't have her come get us every day. There's a studio bus that'll get us over to a streetcar line."

Fine with me. I wanted to process what had happened that day.

In fact, we were about to step onto the studio bus when a car horn got our attention. It was Henry and Jane in a canary yellow open-top '33 or '34 Cadillac convertible with coffee-au-lait fenders. Very nice! They called us over. He was at the wheel, she in the front passenger seat.

"Where to?" Jane asked.

"Downtown Hollywood?" I asked.

"We're going straight up Crescent," Henry said. Meaning Fairfax Avenue. "Then turning left." I.e., probably to Beverly Hills.

"We can take a Red Car from Crescent and Santa Monica," Sue-Anne said. She obviously knew the streetcar lines. She joined Henry in front, while I joined Jane in the backseat.

"Nice car!" I said. "Is this yours?" I asked Henry.

"I wish! No, it's Jane's. Her eighteenth birthday gift from her uncle."

"Is it a straight eight?" I had to ask.

"Vee-eight," Jane said. "He's driving because I'm still upset."

"Bummer!" I said, then remembering the lingo, added, "You kids got a really bum deal today."

"Tell me!"

"It's your car, huh?" I said. And once Henry took off, I added, "Is there any way I can butt in on this friendship that you and Henry have going?"

"You're pretty fresh, aren't you?" Jane asked, delighted.

"Watch out for Chris, Jane," Sue-Anne said from in front. "And remember: he's been a sailor and gone halfway around the world."

I wanted to correct that and tell them all that I'd gone completely "around the world," more than once.

Up close, Jane was good-looking, with more solid and mature features than Sue-Anne and what used to be called "chestnut brown" hair and with big, pretty, green eyes.

"Jane's uncle is E. B. Gilmore!" Henry said.

I'd heard that name.

"Watch where you're driving, buster!" she said. Then to me, "I heard you were a Merchant Marine. You don't look old enough."

"I lied."

"I guessed you for the lying type too." Jane continued to flirt.

"Well, anyway, I'm just flirting," I said, the obvious. "You know, because you're pretty and we're thrown back here together."

"Well, don't stop now!" Jane said, and covered her mouth as she laughed.

We'd driven east on Venice Blvd., which was only two lanes, and just as I was wondering if I'd recognize anything from my time, the odor of baking bread came my way. "Helms Bakery?" I asked.

"We're stopping there," Jane said.

We did stop and the girls went in through big, double front doors to the shop to get bread and rolls. I gave Sue-Anne money to get some sweet rolls and doughnuts. After today's workout I could eat a horse. But I watched as Jane pushed Sue-Anne's hand proffering the cash away, with a look that said, "What, are you kidding me?"

"So, you two are an item?" I asked Henry, once I was alone with him in the car.

"No. I'm nuts about Jane, but she's still shopping around. She's looking for excitement. Then she'll allow her folks to marry her off to some other millionaire."

"Yet she dances as hard as any girl there."

"Jane's a trouper." He mused a little. "I'm not a gold digger. Although, you know, that would make everything a lot easier if I were. But how can I convince her folks?"

"I understand. My advice is stick around her as long as you can. Maybe once all her excitement is done, she'll see you still hanging around and figure…?"

"Nah. That only happens in the movies," wise Henry said.

"So her family is rich?"

"The Gilmores? They own a big chunk of L.A., from Wilshire all the way up to Melrose and over to La Brea. You'll see. We go right by it."

The females went into the backseat together and I contented myself with feeding Henry and myself doughnuts as he turned up Crescent (i.e., Fairfax Avenue, not renamed until the 1950s). After about five minutes, he said, "See, over there!" He pointed left at San Vicente Boulevard. "That's the Carthay Circle Theatre. We're going to a premiere there Sunday. You should come with us. Right, Jane?" he yelled.

She leaned forward between us. "I've already invited Sue-Anne. Come with us, Chris! It's Garbo in her new picture: *Anna Karenina.* Had to pull a few strings for those premiere tickets," she added.

At Wilshire, we passed the construction of the Mays department store, in all its *Moderne* glory. In 2010, it would be long shuttered, and then part of LACMA. The rest of the street here was all shopping. It was, after all, "The Miracle Mile," and it even sort of looked like Fifth Avenue—although a Fifth Avenue with palm trees!

Just beyond it was—not the housing development called Park La Brea I'd lived in for a few years—but instead oilfields! Pumping oil wells as far as the eye could see, from Crescent (Fairfax) on east.

"And now, *North* Gilmore Island!" Henry announced.

On the northeast corner of Third Street was the farmers' market, without the wooden clock tower or any permanent buildings at all. But some were being erected, and would soon be followed by DuParr's restaurant and another building that I knew from its location would become the first Gilmore Bank.

Beyond that, as we headed north, was not CBS Television City. In 1935, television was still in experimental labs—the plaything of Philo T. Farnsworth. Instead, on that future site was a big stadium! On the outside it read *Gilmore Stadium—Home of the Bulldogs!*

"The Bulldogs are what?" I asked.

"They're my uncle's football team," Jane answered.

"You couldn't, by any chance, get me in there too?" I asked Jane.

"Cheapskate! Tickets for tomorrow's afternoon game are only ten cents."

"I'll buy the tickets! What I really want is to meet someone in charge of the team. You know, for a tryout."

"No offense, old man," Henry said with a fake British accent, "but while you may pass at a distance for a Latin Lover, you're too small and skinny for that team!"

"Wise guy! It's for a pal of mine."

"After the game, go down in back to the dressing rooms," Jane said, "and ask for Willy Jantz. Tell him that you and your pal are close friends of mine and that I sent you."

"You are wonderful," I said. "And beautiful, and talented, and…"

But something had caught my eye beyond the stadium.

"Wait, Henry!" I pointed beyond the stadium. "What is that?"

"That," Jane said, "is Uncle E.B.'s newest project. The Pan-Pacific Building."

Located where Pan-Pacific Park would be in 2010.

"Can we see it?" I asked.

"It's not open yet," Henry said.

"He's right, Chris. It doesn't open for a few months."

"Can we drive by it?"

"Chauffeur!" Jane called out. ""Right, please!"

Henry hung a turn, and just past the stadium's rough, dirt-field parking lot was landscaped park surrounding what might have been Norman Bel Geddes's best building design, burned down and gone by the 1970s. Brand new, it looked like a barely grounded ocean liner, with its four turrets and its curving lines and three-tone paint job: the epitome of Streamline design. I felt I'd died and gone to Art Deco heaven.

"I've got to get inside," I said.

"Not till May twenty-fourth," Henry said.

"I can get you in a week early. It's opening with a model home exhibit," Jane said. "How about we all go?" she asked Sue-Ann.

"Maybe we'll see our little housey there!" Henry said, with fake sweetness. "Right, little wifey dear?"

"Drive on! Drive on!" Jane commanded.

A lot of the shops on Beverly were recognizably the same buildings I knew. Of course the Mexicano excesses of El Coyote Café weren't there yet. It was still located more quietly, around the corner, at La Brea down on First Street.

Henry turned right onto La Brea and drove north, headed up to the hills, and passing only one building that I knew from my time, the Showcase movie theater.

Sue-Ann reached forward and tapped Henry's shoulder. "We'll get off here."

"Oh good," he said. "We go the other way. Truth is I don't think I'm a good enough driver for downtown traffic."

He meant downtown Hollywood Boulevard traffic, where we'd

pulled to the side of the road for us to get out. I could see maybe four cars and a bus; I almost laughed, it was so empty.

A streetcar took us over to Cahuenga and I walked Sue-Anne up to her building, which in fact was Miss Irene's Hotel.

"Well," I concluded. "All's well that ends well."

She looked at me closely. "How did you get to be so smart? And don't tell me in the Merchant Marines."

"Why? What do you mean?"

"I mean, Jane and Henry could have ended up hating us, but instead I think we'll all be friends. You did that!"

"So did you!"

"I followed my instinct, which is to be nice to people who've just gotten hurt."

"Well, fellows have instincts too!"

"Yes. Usually bad ones," Sue-Ann said. "Not...Another...Word! And Jane's right. You are wonderful!"

She then bussed me on the cheek and ran inside the foyer, not even looking back before the door slammed on her.

Oh. No! I thought. I had two girls who thought I was wonderful. When all I wanted was a boy who thought so too!

7

My roommate, Hank Streit, used his little pocket knife to carve pieces of wood he picked up anywhere and everywhere into little sculptures: a car, a biplane, a little house. So he was reluctant to give up his blade even for a minute, until I promised him he could watch me use it and he'd have it back "in a jiffy."

I cleaned it with a towel and then I used it to scrape flakes off the bar of soap until I had a handful. I collected those in an envelope, and by this time I had Hank's deepest attention.

I picked up my two soiled undershorts and one undershirt and I went out and into the bathroom with the three sinks, gesturing for Hank to follow. I filled one sink with hot water, and put in the shaved soap and the clothing and thrashed them about until it got all soapy and foamy, and then I stood there letting them soak a while.

"Nice knife," I said. It was a Bowie with a bone handle. Not cheap.

"High school graduation gift. From my folks. It was supposed to get me to join my dad and my brothers at the mill."

"The lumber mill?"

"Cor-rect. Instead, I hit the road for a few months, took all kinds of temporary labor jobs. Did anything *but* join the mill."

"And ended up here?"

"Girl up in Fresno said I looked like some fellow in The Pictures. So I figured why not?...It could still work out."

"Watch!" I gave the clothing one more thrashing, drained the sink, and then began to rinse the clothes in cold water. When I was done, I squeezed them, rinsed and squeezed again, and marched us back to our room, where I hung them on the curtain rod to dry.

"Not perfect!" I said. "But I can wear them for a day or more before they have to go to the Chinese laundry."

"Mine smell kind of ripe too," Hank said.

"So I've noticed." That had been one reason for the demonstration.

Before he could say anything, I said, "Get out the knife, and I'll walk you through it, step by step."

As we were waiting again for his clothes to soak well, I asked, "No one special waiting for you up in Washington state?"

"No one," said in a hard voice.

"Sounds like there might be someone you're avoiding."

He shrugged.

I remembered he was the youngest of four boys. "An older brother?"

He shrugged.

"Or was it more than one?"

"End of discussion," Hank said.

"Sorry I brought it up. Okay. Now drain the soapy water and run that cold water to rinse all the soap and dirt out."

"You learn this in the Merchant Marine?"

"I told you, I got around. Squeeze it good. Then rinse again."

"I see Sid looking at you funny," Hank surprised me by saying.

"Yeah, well, Sid's not my biggest fan!"

"When fellows look like that at other fellows, if they aren't fairies, it means something. And it's not just Sid, either."

That was news. "Why? What does it mean, Hank?"

"It means they envy you. It means they want to be you. It means you have what Sid calls moxie. It means you can be a movie star."

"What if I don't want to be a movie star, Hank?"

"Why not?"

"Well, if it happens, I'll take it. But it's not what I really want. And I think it's the same for you."

He shrugged.

"Okay, rinse again and squeeze them dry," I said, and as he was doing that, I added, "By the way, I got us tickets and all of us guys are going to a football game tomorrow," I said. "The Bulldogs. One p.m. I know someone there. Also, I'm bringing Ducky down to the dressing room to meet someone after the game. It'll be a surprise."

"He's been trying to meet someone there for six months."

"Well, you heard what Jonah said, I'm the chocolate pudding kid."

"Yeah…?"

"Yeah! And I met someone who can help Ducky."

8

The Saturday game was "exhibition" only, and even so the stadium was three-quarters full. I knew L.A. in this time was already a football town, what with the Trojans and Bruins in competition. Our seats were surprisingly good, three rows up from the forty yard line, and we were able to see pretty much all that happened.

I knew the rules would be different, but I'd forgotten how different the uniforms would be. There scarcely were uniforms at all: certainly not much in the way of protection. The helmets were leather caps with ear cups. Some guys wore what looked like heavy sweaters, though the pants seemed doubled up, and the shoes were "regulation"—whatever that meant.

From what I could gather from conversation around us, a few UCLA as well as USC former players who'd been big shots on school teams were now on the Bulldogs, including a quarterback who stood out for his sheer nerve at making big amazingly dumb plays. It did make for a fun, exciting game, even if it was exhibition.

My friends enjoyed it, and I enjoyed them enjoying it. Jonah went so far as to call me a "humanitarian," while Sid admitted that it was a great way for the group to be together. I caught him looking at me a couple of times, as though I were Mephistopheles and he was waiting, just waiting, for me to demand his signature in blood.

I'd prepped Hank to grab those two away after and lead them to a local diner while I led Ducky—all unknown—to his destiny. To my surprise it came off without a hitch. Partly because Ducky hadn't been at a game in a year and he was so worked up about this one; what this player had done right, what that player had done wrong. It wasn't until I'd maneuvered him down the stairs and into the long, echoing corridors under the bleachers that he said, "What gives? What are we doing here?"

"The others are across the street, waiting to get into Dillman's. We'll join them in a few minutes. I need to see someone here."

He followed me over to the door of the "Club Office," which I blithely entered. Two older men at the desk looked up, cigarettes dangling off their lips.

"Willy Jantz?" I asked.

One pointed through a door. The other moved to stand in front of it.

"We're friends of Jane Gilmore Ellis," I said.

Magic: they opened the door and we went through, not into an office but into the dressing room, another echoing corridor with lockers and players and shower steam from nearby. Ducky looked around himself in amazement.

I located Jantz's office and opened the door to hear him yelling into a telephone receiver. I pulled Ducky into the office and we stood there while Jantz loudly fumed.

When he was done and had hung up, he asked, "Yeah! What?"

"We're friends of Jane Gilmore Ellis. Ducky here is your new defensive back."

"Says who?"

"He was county-wide varsity star in baseball, football, and all-around star athletic three years running at Edgemont High in Altoona, P.A." I repeated what Ducky had told me.

"So was my mother."

"When can he try out and show you his moves?"

"Who're you? His baby brother? You sound like a talent agent."

"I noticed the roster board outside said you were having tryouts on Monday afternoon. We'll pencil his name in. It's Deutscher. Daniel J. Deutscher. Thanks for your time, Coach Jantz. He'll be here promptly Monday afternoon at noon."

I grabbed Ducky, who had stood there not saying a word in his utter astonishment, and I pulled him out of the door. I found a pencil hanging up on the roster board and began writing his name in.

"He's got to sign it himself!" Jantz said, hanging half out of the office door. As Ducky went to sign it, Jantz gestured me closer.

"A friend of Janie's, huh?"

"Yeah, Janie and me are in the pictures together at MGM. She sent us. Her uncle'll probably ask about Ducky when you next see him," I lied.

"Okay. Okay. Calm down. He'll try out Monday!" Jantz looked at Ducky. "He's big, I'll say that. Well built too. Altoona, you said."

"P.A.," I added.

"Lots of good footballers there in that part of Pennsylvania," Jantz mused. "Must be something in the water."

"Your QB, Wendell? He looked good out there today. But nobody on that offensive line is protecting him. Next real game? He'll have his scrotum handed to him. Put Ducky on his butt and Wendell will be safe and he'll be able to go to town with his sneaky little moves."

"Okay! Okay," to me. "You're a good observer, kid. Write your phone number and address too!" Jantz yelled at Ducky, who jumped to do so. "You coming on Monday too?" Jantz asked me in a lowered voice.

"Wish I could, Coach. But we're shooting a picture all day."

"Well, thank the Lord for that. 'Cause you'd be one little son of a bitch to have to say no to. You don't seem to understand the meaning of the word," he added.

"Neither does Ducky when he gets going, Coach. Don't say no."

"Get out of here! The two of you!" he yelled. "Hey, Grimes! Get these two Palookas outta here."

His assistant hustled us out. At the dressing room door, I turned around to catch Jantz winking at me. "Go on. Get going! Both of you!"

Out on the street, Ducky turned to me with questions all over his young and baffled face. He looked about ten years old.

"So! That went well," I declared.

"Uh…? Do I come back Monday or what?"

"Of course you come back. And old Jantzy there'll take you onto the team. On waivers. Which means at a temporary job, I'm afraid, and at temporary pay."

"But…But he said…"

"He needs you, Ducky. Didn't you see? He needs you to make sure his spoiled little candy-ass quarterback doesn't get clobbered."

Dillman's diner was two blocks up and crowded with attendees of the game. As we arrived, our friends were in line outside and just being let in the door and shown to a table.

"Where did you two monsters go off to?" Sid asked once we were all seated.

When Ducky told them he had a tryout scheduled, they cheered.

The other tables yelled out, "Go! Bulldogs!" in response. Ah! I found myself thinking—boys!

Now, I thought, looking at my four happy, smiling, laughing, and for the most part really nice-looking faces: which one of you is my *next* victim?

9

Jonah Wolff was in the Alsop House lobby with me listening to the radio when Frances Wannamaker came by, driven by our executive producer himself in a big chrome-fendered Buick Special Ten, to pick me up. Sue-Ann was already in the car, but all of them got out to say hello and change the seating so that Frances's date, Thom Rafferty from MGM, of all people, and I would sit in the front seat and the women in the back.

We'd both donned outfits sent over earlier from the studio to wear at the premiere of MGM's newest film: *Anna Karenina*. That was Thom's doing. For me, a tuxedo with white tie. For Sue-Ann a flouncy pale blue dress and a discreet gold neck chain with a single garnet. Our agent looked divine in an emerald gown with high neck, short sleeves, and long matching gloves. A kind of semi-snood held her hair in place in back.

I introduced Jonah to all of them and he definitely had eyes for Sue-Ann, but I also noticed that he and Frances exchanged words, and upon her initiative. Hmm.

Once we were moving through light traffic, Rafferty said: "You kids are very clever to have wangled tickets to this premiere! It's our big spring movie and all the studio people will be there. Of course, there's an MGM dinner after at Forelli's that you're invited to—now that you're part of the MGM family."

The restaurant he mentioned was on Wilshire not far from the Ambassador Hotel.

"Terrific!" I said. I could hear Frances giving Sue-Anne the same news in the backseat.

San Vicente was closed off several blocks away from the theater and only cars going to the premiere were allowed through. We crawled forward. As we were one car away from getting out and handing the keys to a valet for parking, Rafferty moved over in front of me in the big front seat where streetlight was pouring in and said, "I think there's something at the edge of your eye."

He lifted a piquantly scented handkerchief to just below my left eye, and I looked at him while he pretended to get it off. Pale blue eyes. Not bad features. Clearly a shark in shark-infested waters. But back in this time period, I often felt so in-the-know that I was more like a giant squid, wasn't I?—and sharks better beware! So I stared back at him, not defiantly, but innocently, all the while sizing him up. He was what? Thirty-three? Half my real age. The bigger they are, the harder they fall, had always been my motto: I could handle this one easily enough, if I had to.

"Doesn't Chris have the biggest brown eyes you ever saw?" Sue-Anne said from the backseat and I could have kissed her.

"Yessss," he drawled, adding, "They'll film wonderfully."

"Especially in a close-up," Frances said. I could have kissed her too.

He looked me over so hungrily, I expected his tongue to dart out and lick me.

"Did you get it?" I asked, adding, "The cinder at the edge of my eye?"

"Yessss!" he drawled and sat back in his chair. Was that wood in his lap, or was he carrying a .38?

Someone had told Billy Bartlett that he was going to be the youngest MGM star present and he and Milly were dressed to the nines, if dressed a lot younger than their actual ages, unlike me and Sue-Ann. But he soon got over his unhappy surprise when we joined him and Milly inside the big entrance court in front of the theater where a red carpet had been laid out. Frances Wannamaker got Rafferty to describe all four of us as the MGM's quote Stars of Tomorrow unquote, and so we were all photographed together—a lot! By studio photogs and by the no doubt previously bought-off, fawning, press.

Before the film, there was a short and two cartoons and only one coming attraction! We took advantage of that to go and "freshen up."

I saw Henry in the big men's room lounge and told him, "Rafferty's in our row, if you want to switch seats with me and try your luck again."

Henry laughed. "You're wasted in this movie. You should be in vaudeville. You're a real card!"

As I came out of the stall, Henry wasn't there but I noticed a well-dressed African-American man of middle age in the same colors of uniform as the ushers and other theater staff I'd seen so far. He was sitting by the sink, next to a basket of white cloth napkins.

I went to wash my hands and he leapt up, turned on the faucets, and handed me a little oyster-shell shaped, milled bar of soap. But if that was surprising, I was even more amazed when, after I had rinsed off, he handed me the towel. "I'll take that, sir," he said when I was done and took it from me and deposited it into a can I'd not noticed before. Just as I noticed loose change in the basket, he held a little brush up to me. "May I, sir?" he asked, and began lightly brushing whatever might be on my jacket lapels and sleeves. The last time I'd seen this kind of thing was at a debutante ball in Manhattan when I was a teenager, and even then it had been an anachronism. But in a movie theater!

I realized with a start that this was his job, remaining here in the men's room all night and helping men clean their hands and jackets and step outside looking good. I felt myself begin to color, and to allay my shame at what I was feeling, I pulled out a dollar and put it into the basket, and turned to leave.

"Sir!" he called out, and I turned to see him holding out a handful of change.

He had such a dignified look on his face that I had to stammer, "What is the usual *good*…?" Good what? Tip? Tariff? Charge?

He handed me three quarters back and said, "Thank you for your *generosity*, sir," and went to open the door for me, and only then did I notice he was wearing sparkling white gloves.

Out in the lavishly velvet-walled corridor with its Persian carpets and gilded light sconces and spun silver décor, Henry was speaking to someone else that he soon stepped away from. He grabbed me by the shoulder and marched me toward the ladies' room to meet our dates.

"You look funny, Hall. Something happen in there?"

Something had happened in there. For I had suddenly realized that the bathroom attendant was *proud* of his job. It was a *clean* job, working at this *high-end* establishment, filled with white people in the film industry, and he went home *proud* of the money he earned and of where and *how* he earned it. He would probably be able to put his children through high school, maybe even vocational school. In this Depression era, it would be *a very good job*!

"No. Nothing! Nothing!" I insisted, for the moment devastated.

There were some things about this time I didn't think I would ever get used to, things that other people—nice, good, caring people like Henry—didn't even notice, never mind think odd.

After the film, I made sure that Henry and Jane joined us when we were paraded past Sam Goldwyn and Louis B. Mayer and their wives later on, at the restaurant. Milly and Sue-Anne and Henry were pretty closed-mouthed, but Jane said she had met Mayer before, at a Gilmore wedding, and they chatted. I smiled benignly at all and attempted to look wise beyond my years, without saying anything beyond hello.

Then my gaydar went on at "full red alert" when our group was approached by two genuine movie stars: Joan Crawford, looking young, thin, soigné, and approachable, with her beau of the night, the top film comedy star of the past several years, William Haines. Behind them was another good-looking man I guessed was Haines's boyfriend, accompanying Marion Davies, who was glittering with jewelry.

Crawford buzzed past the MGM bigwigs with a "Hiya, Sam! Hiya, Louis!"

But if Haines saw them at all, he acted as though he hadn't but instead slid right past them, with Crawford as his shield, ending up close to where we had moved.

"Her Nibs show up?" Crawford asked, about the star, Garbo. She looked as though they'd been drinking in the car.

"Not yet. But she's due any minute," Rafferty said. And we heard a hubbub at the front door. Alas, it was only Garbo's costar, Frederic March.

"I wouldn't lay odds on that particular horse arriving at the finish line any time soon," Crawford said breezily. "Friend a Billy's here says she's got serious cunt cramps." She laughed at her own joke and went on, "But then, my opinion is she always acts like she has serious cunt cramps anyway. No?"

Everyone enjoyed that. Crawford just then noticed me.

"Oops. Sorry, Lamb Chop!" To Haines, she quipped, "Let's get outta here before I corrupt more of America's youth!"

Just then two other actresses whose names I didn't know approached and stole her attention away.

I watched Haines and Rafferty exchange taut hellos and butched-up handshakes. Haines had been at MGM for years. Rafferty was probably there when the actor was fired for being too homosexual and for not playing the game by making a fake "lavender marriage."

"And who is this apparently still uncorrupted and quite sweet-looking American youth?" Haines asked.

"Young Mr. Christopher Hall here is your biggest fan," Rafferty suddenly lied, although why I had no idea, probably to keep the star's attention on me.

It worked: Haines would not let go of the hand he was shaking—mine.

"It's true," I lied on glibly. Then I added, more truthfully, "But I'm surprised to meet you and see that you are so, well, so well-built, close up!" I added in a lower voice, "The screen doesn't do you justice."

He looked at me then the way hungry rodents usually gaze upon a perfectly aged gorgonzola, but with twinkling rather than feral eyes, and said, "If you want to be in a lot of movies, Christopher, you really have to meet a lot of people in the movies. Of course I'm stuck in Poverty Pictures—true name, Raff, that's what we're calling our new studio, Jimmie and me. But you know what?" he added, to me. "I'm having a big party next Saturday night. Everyone who's anyone—under fifty—will be there. Why don't you come, Christopher? Thom will tell you where and when." Only then did Haines let go of my hand and move on.

I thought: Finally! Some famous fags to hang out with!

We didn't eat a thing until most of those "important folks" from MGM were long gone. Then we found a big plumped leather corner booth in Forelli's and piled in. Frances and Thom meanwhile had their own, more centrally located booth, where they seemed to be busily confabbing. "Business," Sue-Ann commented.

"How do you eat wearing all this white?" I asked Henry. I tried putting my cloth napkin in front of my shirt. "With a bib?"

"Disregard any stains on your shirt," Jane said. "Especially if the studio owns the tux."

That made it a lot easier. A few other people from the studio— mostly colorless business types I'd never noticed before—were dining nearby with people I guessed to be wives and girlfriends.

I began noticing other things: all the waiters were white men, even those who bused the tables. I'd begun noticing that kind of thing more and more over the past few days; how *white* a world it was that I had found myself in. So much so that African-Americans like the Warner's bus driver and that fellow in the men's lounge had stood out very clearly. I hadn't seen anyone Latino or anyone Asian at all! Would it all be like this: lily white? If so, wasn't this the period that all those Conservative Republicans in 2010 wanted our country to return to? I'm not sure why. I, for one, was already missing the other races and the "color" they brought. Good thing there were some Homos around.

10

By Wednesday it was established that Jane and Henry would drive Sue and me partly home to Santa Monica or Hollywood Blvd. and there we would get a trolley or bus or walk the half mile or so farther east through "Downtown Hollywood."

That evening we got off before her usual stop at Wilcox Avenue, as I wanted to step into the stationery shop we passed every day.

Sue-Anne was amenable to the few blocks' extra walk, and she actually wanted to get a "stationery mailing set" herself. This was a score of sheets of nicely lined, embossed paper, and an equal number of envelopes. One packet even had two-penny postage stamps. "I'm way behind on my correspondence," she admitted.

I meanwhile bought an 11x17 inch pad of fifty sheets of different unlined paper, most of it light with a few heavier vellum pieces in the back. Along with those, I bought three pencils with softer-than-number-two lead.

As we walked on, however, we passed a bookstore, and in the windows were several books, with a sign: "Just Arrived." The titles were *Life with Father* by Clarence Day, which would later become the hit movie; *God's Little Acre*, by Erskine Caldwell; *Taps At Reveille*, a collection of stories by F. Scott Fitzgerald; and—noted as "Back in Stock"—James Hilton's blockbuster best seller that year, *Lost Horizon*.

Now, before I'd left 2010, Mr. Morgan and I had discussed the niceties of wealth amassment in the past. He'd said, "I discovered that as long as you do it discreetly, and sort of naturally, it'll work out. If you go out on a limb and do something big because you remembered some horse that won and made a bundle, you'll probably lose it again."

I'd always collected good old books. What better way to shore up my future than getting first editions of twentieth-century classics. So I pulled Sue-Anne inside the book store, to which she replied: "Who would have thought? He can sing, dance, act, and he *reads* too!"

"Don't be sassy," I said. But she'd already begun to blush at her outburst.

She bought books she was "dying to read" by Edna Ferber and Helene Vardis. Helene *who*?

I walked out with seven, count them seven, first editions, with a plan to return the next time I got paid and buy another seven. I did not get the Caldwell, and the Hilton in the store I scorned as merely a second edition. But I did pick up the other three in the window, as well as Faulkner's *Pylon*, *Tortilla Flat* by the still unknown John Steinbeck, Hemingway's reportage in *The Green Hills of Africa*, and Thornton Wilder's *Heaven's My Destination*. They were each wrapped separately in brown paper, and then wrapped together in brown paper, and all of it was tied together with string that I could hold it by. Total cost: $8.60!

Before I was done that month, I'd gotten copies myself first editions of *Studs Lonigan*, T.E. Lawrence's *Seven Pillars of Wisdom*, Wolfe's *Of Time and the River*, *Lost Horizon*, and *Goodbye Mr. Chips*, as well as a first edition of Fitzgerald's *All the Sad Young Men* and a copy they managed to scare up in the stockroom of the first printing of *Tender Is the Night*. Also two of Faulkner's older titles, *Sanctuary* and *Light in August*. And to top that off, Burrough's *Tarzan and the Leopard Men* and Laura Ingalls Wilder's *Little House on the Prairie*, all brand new. But it was another new title, Sinclair Lewis's *It Can't Happen Here*, that would have a bigger impact on me when I finally read it. It was a fantasy about what was going on in Germany and how something like National Socialism might also happen in the U.S.

"The mystery deepens! Junior turns out to be a scholar!" my roommate declared, and I knew Hank would tell the others soon.

I'd swept my books into a cardboard carton, kept on the floor by the bed, and I moved the floor lamp away from the door so I could read in bed. But after a few days I found Hank reading the Tarzan book, as well as copies of *Black Mask*, *Amazing*—with stories by Del Rey and Campbell—and *Weird Tales* that I'd bought at the local magazine and newspaper shop. The latter sported Margaret Brundage's amazing illustrations. Those too would eventually become valuable collector's items.

I left the pad I'd bought open with a pencil whenever I wasn't there because my next victim had already shown himself to me clearly. Not only did Hank Streit carve things out of wood, he also drew things upon any piece of paper that came his way. Using a little stub of a lousy pencil, he'd drawn on napkins from diners that he'd stuff in his jacket pocket, on light-colored or white magazine and catalogue covers; upon anything and everything. What he drew was even better than what he carved: futuristic cars, trucks, busses, trains, houses, buildings, stadiums, skyscrapers, his own versions of the Hollywood Bowl; his own versions of the new Bullock's department store. He also drew façades and interiors. Some detailed a corner or a cornice or a flower box. He threw away most of what he drew—but I retrieved it and kept it.

By the end of the second week at MGM, I had a handful of those drawings and the pad I'd left around, which he had sketched in just as I'd hoped he would, filling all but one or two leaves. That morning, I carried the lot of it to work in a paper bag.

During lunch break I approached the second director, asking who I could show the drawings to.

"Bring it to Design. I'm going right past there now. I'll give you a lift."

At the rear of the big design building atelier was a long desk, and I laid out all of the pieces I had, and then two fellows working there came by, curious.

"Not bad. You do this?"

"My roommate."

"Who's he?"

"Where's he?"

"He also carves wood beautifully into little sculptures." I pulled out the "futuristic Ford coupe" he'd given me and showed it around. "And he's done carpentry. His family runs a lumber mill. Woodworking is in his blood." I knew most art direction models in the studio were wooden carvings.

"Where. Is. He?" a tall pale, gray haired man with thick-lensed glasses very pointedly asked.

"Not here. Not yet."

"Then get him here!" he ordered.

"Is tomorrow morning okay?"

"Faster the better. We're doing twenty percent more sets and models this year than last year. We're perpetually short of help."

"How do I get him into the studio?"

"The kid needs a hall pass?" one artist quipped.

"Shut up," the tall guy barked and went to his table and tore off a piece of MGM stationery. He wrote on top. *Appointment. Design. Ten a.m. for—* "What's his name?"

"Hank Streit. Eee, eye, tee."

"Give him this. It'll get him in."

The stationery's embossed staff read, *Owen Barclay—Sets/Art.*

When I showed that to Hank that night and told him what happened, he looked at me in astonishment.

"Geez, Chris. I'm not good enough for a job like that."

"Well, then you will hear that you are not good enough for a job like that *in person*! Because I made an appointment for you! You are coming with us tomorrow morning. Like it or not."

I dressed him the next day and Hank tried to weasel out of coming three different ways and then he argued with me all the way to Wilcox off Fountain, where we would pick up Sue-Ann. When she stepped out of the hotel he quieted down immediately.

I introduced them, and Sue-Anne, bless her, said, "Everyone loves your drawings, Mr. Streit! It'll be wonderful if we're all working together at MGM, won't it?"

She flounced on ahead, going to mail a letter.

Hank stared after her, unbelieving.

"Coming, Da Vinci?" I asked Hank as I caught up with her.

Hank was waiting for us outside the soundstage when we broke for lunch some hours later. We invited him to join us at the commissary.

Sue-Ann flirted with him. He said almost nothing. She pretended he was responding in depth and range. Soon enough I felt *de trop* and I left them alone. After she'd gone into the "ladies" to clean up, Hank said to me: "Jonah was right."

"I fall into chocolate pudding, huh?"

"Chocolate pudding is right. Moxie is right. Luck is right. *All* of it is right."

"What's that in your hand?" I asked.

I took and read. *Temporary, free-lance contractor's agreement.*

"Were you ever going to tell me that Barclay showed some sense and hired you?!"

"It's only temporary, and I'm not going to be able to do all that design," Hank argued.

"You'd better!" I threatened. "My reputation in this joint is on the line."

The assistant director was going past the studio's main office and I asked him to take Hank to Personnel to have his contract notarized and signed so his salary would be set up correctly. I was beginning to learn the studio ropes.

"We'll be leaving around three o'clock today," I told Hank. "Why not stick around a while and we'll all leave together? Including Sue-Ann."

Hank mumbled some reply for why he couldn't possibly join us, but I just walked away without listening. And he was there, at 3:21, when we exited. He even had a "temporary employee" decal on a card pinned to his lapel.

"Oh isn't that *wonderful*," Sue-Anne said when she saw the card. "Isn't it *wonderful*, Chris?"

Hank turned about ten shades of red from carnation pink to magenta in that many seconds. I knew I'd lost him as a potential boyfriend, stupid me. But then, I'd always suspected he'd been hiding the fact that he was a flaming hetero anyway.

11

The party house was one that Billy Haines was renting while Paul Feher added to his famous Stanley Ave. home murals. This was a big ranch set on a large corner property several streets away from what would soon be the extension and the guest cottages of the Beverly Hills Hotel. There were already a dozen cars parked around the property when we arrived; eventually there would be twenty-five or more.

The double front door was wide open when our director, William Seiter, and I entered together. I had told him I was invited and he had declared, "You are *not* going into their home alone." Fine with me.

The interior was wide open on both sides of the foyer with what looked like two living rooms, already filled with people. Music from a phonograph was playing on one side—was that Jolson singing?— and on the other side, people were at the piano singing and fooling around.

I knew that Haines would soon become a decorator full-time and that his boyfriend Jimmie Shields already was one, but this pared-down décor was hardly the grand, Graeco-Roman with spots of *Chinoiserie* style they'd become known for. Here was natural stone, colored wood, and light-colored upholstery: the SoCal Ranch style.

I also noticed that there were three men for every woman, and the latter tended to be in single among a group of men.

"Don't wander too far," Seiter warned. "*You* shouldn't even be here tonight."

"I was in the Merchant Marines," I lied, glibly. "Remember? I think I can handle myself."

"It's not *you* I'm worried about. It's your reputation… Hi, George. This is George Cukor, the highest paid movie director in Hollywood," Seiter added, chugging the long arm of a man with oddly shaped, curly black hair, wearing a tan sweater over brown slacks and smoking a cigarette in a long amber holder. Another known Homo I already knew. "He's hot as hell now, thanks to his hit movie made from—of all the books you *didn't* read in high school, *David Copperfield*!"

Seiter introduced me: "This brat is Christopher Hall, who is actually thirty years older than he looks."

I spied our host, Billy Haines, sitting on the counter bar between one living room and what must have been a serving pantry. He was wearing a strange short-brimmed hat with bright blue ribbon around it maybe two-thirds of its height, showing it off. Seiter went toward that group.

"Supposedly all the rage, in New York," Cukor said with a soigné accent. "A Pugaree hat. Who did you say was your lover, Mr. Hall?"

"Mahatma Gandhi."

"I see you aim high. But isn't Gandhi celibate?"

"Would *you* be celibate if you were my boyfriend?" I asked back.

"Point taken."

Thom Rafferty arrived where we stood, holding drinks.

I sniffed. "Could they afford the gin?"

"*They* easily could. *You*, however, cannot. George, I see you've met our newest addition?"

"Mr. Hall was describing various postures from the Kama Sutra to me," Cukor said in a bald-faced lie.

Rafferty looked perplexed. Like most people in '35, he'd never heard of the Indian book of amatory postures.

"I was pointing out to Mr. Cukor," I added, "that most of those erotic maneuvers require the attendance of a small water buffalo and a liter of clarified butter."

"Sounds like you're already friends!" Seiter said, rejoining us.

"We might be," Cukor said, extending a languid hand for me to shake. "But I think I'd have to get up a great deal earlier in the morning to stump this lad." He smiled a sort of downcast smile and looked at me suddenly, and then bent down and to one side of me. "Now, *that's* a good angle for this one, Willy. Look!"

Seiter joined him bending down and they had me move my head

to one side an inch and then had me turn my body an inch, going "Ah!" and "Even better!"

When he moved away Cukor said to me, "*Aufwiedersehn, schatzlein!* I'll see *you* in the movies!"

"*Au revoir!*" I replied.

"Hold still, Chris," Seiter said. "Look at him now, Thom."

"I do see."

"Gosh, I wish I had Cukor's eyes," Seiter said. "He can see 360 degrees and top and bottom too, all at the same time."

"I'll say. Can you use that angle later?" Rafferty asked.

"I thought in the letter scene!" Seiter mused.

"What letter scene?" I asked.

But no one answered me, and they went on talking, so I wandered off to the piano and then to the library, inspecting their bookshelves.

No one else I.Q.-tested me. I did meet a great many people and spoke with them and I would let Seiter and Rafferty talk about me—and Sue-Anne. If neither of them added her name, I invariably did. Leave 'em guessing.

Crawford arrived with two fellows, both of who looked big, straight, horny, and half-drunk. Robert Taylor arrived, looking more stunning than on the screen with a so-so pretty girl on his arm who was more interested in him than he was in her. He looked me over very carefully indeed, and I found myself more or less striking poses back for his greater edification: lots of poses; everything short of Madonna's *Vogue* video. But Taylor remained with his date and left with her after only fifteen minutes or so.

"What was *that* all about?" I asked Jimmie Shields, who had caught most of it.

"Difficult to say. He might have been sizing up the competition."

"Yeah, right! He's a foot taller!"

"Not quite. Cukey says you're a great wit, for one so young."

"I'm just good at the art of the riposte."

"An art not to be sneezed at, Christopher, is it? Great name! Now you're going to spoil everything and tell me it's real."

"As a matter of fa—"

"Oh!" Shields's attention flew to the front door. "And here. At last. Is—Archie!"

"Archie" was Cary Grant. Outside the still-ajar double doors I could see someone else hurrying up the entry pathway behind him, even taller, blond, with a perfectly gorgeous tanned face and smashing pale blue eyes.

Shields and "Arch" hugged and bussed each other.

"Where's the new meat?" Grant asked in his characteristically deep growly voice. "Oh, my! I didn't see *you* there!" he said to me in a much higher voice.

"Christopher Hall," Jimmie intro'ed me. "Real name. New at MGM. And as brand new as new meat ever gets around here."

Grant had fixed his amazingly large, dark eyes upon me, in some kind of pre-hypnotic gaze, when I moved aside a bit, enough to see my all-time idol while growing up, his buddy and no doubt his date tonight too, Randolph Scott, just lightly holding on to Grant's linen-jacketed shoulder while saying hello to other people.

"Hi!" Scott said, and I reached past Grant for his big hand with its little thicket of blond hair and I almost wouldn't let go.

"But...he's a child!" Grant made a big act of pushing me aside. "Don'tcha know, Jimmie, children always steal scenes from you."

"Not from Fields they don't," I said.

"He's got you there, Arch."

"Yes, yes," Grant explained carefully to us all, "but I'd have to grow at least three more inches to my nose." He drew his own out with two fingers, overillustrating his idea, overacting the entire bit, in fact, and I remembered he'd been a vaudeville star first: a clown.

"You've got a wonderful nose. Don't touch it," Jimmie said. "Right, Rand?"

"Right," Scott answered, distracted. "Where's the bar? We drove from the beach with the top down and I'm parched."

I joined them at the bar and Seiter arrived to re-introduce me.

"See," I said mostly to Scott, "I'm a grown-up. Anyway, I'd never dream of competing with you. *Either* of you," I said, I thought more to Scott.

Grant, however, answered. "We can't be too careful," enumerating: "Jackie Coogan. Jackie Cooper. And now that escapee from a crib, what's her name, Rand? Oh yes! Shirley Temple! They're all taking money out of our pockets with both hands."

A half hour later the party was in full swing. I'd ended up near the doors because all the cigar and cigarette smoke was so thick that it was choking me. No one smoked in L.A. in 2010 or if so only outside, on the streets. Then Haines closed those doors. He explained why: "The neighbors! The noise!" So I ended up stepping outside the back door, where I'd seen people going before.

The rear of the single-story house showed the shallow vee of the two wings on either side of the big back lawn, with its rectangular, white stone terrace and twisted metal, white wrought-iron lawn furniture, and big rectangular swimming pool. Beyond it, in the shadows of the trees over and behind, stood a pool house with hanging curtains of interpolated panels of patterned satin and pleated gauze material, all of them shivering in the light breeze.

It was one of those uncharacteristically warm spring L.A. nights in which the fog hung low to the ground, but above it the stars were all out, and because the place was so much less populated than seventy-five years later, I could see a great many stars and could even recognize constellations.

I popped into a chair and put my feet up onto a low, wrought-iron table and for a minute or two I stopped and just absorbed it all: the night, the laughter from inside, the music, the handsome movie stars, the cats going at it in some nearby alleyway. Barely a whoosh of auto traffic, and no decibel-drenched helicopters chugging by, two by two, headed to a car chase on the upper 405.

There was noise behind me and I turned to see a young bartender setting up an outdoors bar. He kept coming and going indoors with glasses and bottles. Evidently this wouldn't bother the neighbors.

Once when he was indoors and I was alone, I heard what I thought was a groan and then two voices from another direction.

I stood and followed the sounds: around the side of the pool.

There was a streetlight that periodically and only a little lighted the pool house's evidently open, deep interior, but with the breeze and the trees and the curtains all moving, I had to stand very still in the right place to see anything at all.

Then I did see a glint, then I saw the glint again, and then I realized that I was looking at a hand with a big ring on it. But the hand was curved around something dark. I started hearing groans again, a lot more regularly, and I edged forward more, and now I saw it was curved around the figure of a man wearing a lighter shirt and darker pants, and two hands were placed, gripped really, around those pants at hip level.

And then I recognized the ring as Thom Rafferty's fat silver high school ring, with a big shiny sapphire in the middle.

Very quickly now, the fellow standing gave the characteristic moan of someone trying to keep an orgasm from getting too loud, and his figure shook, visibly shook. Then the ring was gone, the hands were gone, and there was a laugh, a word spoken low, and the man standing turned and raced around the pool and into the house, almost crashing into the bartender, who was coming out with a bucket of ice.

I tried moving back, but Rafferty seemed utterly unfazed that I'd caught him, as it were, *in flagrante*. I'd vaguely recognized the other fellow from the party.

"And *there* you are," Thom said.

So I played it utterly blasé myself. "And *there* you are, too."

He moved us toward the bar.

"I thought you'd be here with Billy Bartlett?" I said. The bartender was forlornly gazing inside through the angled, cottage-crossed panes of the kitchen windows to where the party was happening. Thom tapped on the table and ordered for the two of us, directing him to "make the second one weaker."

While Haines's outdoor bartender was bent down looking for limes, I straightened out Rafferty's collar.

"Lipstick on your collar told a tale on you!"

"What did you say?"

"Or in this case, semen on your collar. An old song," I said, though it wouldn't be written for twenty years, then to be sung by Connie Francis. "We were talking about Billy Bart…"

Rafferty moved me away from the bar. When we reached the other side of the pool, we sat and he said in a hoarse whisper, "Billy is over!"

I was processing that statement when he added, "Billy made a large tactical error…"

"Don't stop now," I prodded.

"…when he had Henry and Jane moved to the back line."

"Why? Did her rich uncle kick up a fuss?"

"Oh, no. It's better than that," Rafferty said, enjoying himself and tasting his drink. "We've been looking at rushes for the past two nights."

"'You' meaning, 'you fellows in the suits'?"

"That's right."

"And?"

"And Bartlett looks bad. Six o' clock shadow even through the makeup. Looks thirty. Dances like a whale. Milly looks skinnier than Olive Oyl. She dances like a wounded elephant."

"Oh no! Don't tell me they're shutting down the movie and canning us all?"

"Not quite, sweet Christopher Hall. Because guess who *does* look good—well, *better* than good. Guess who *can* dance or at least *fake* dancing well enough? Guess who looks like a half-pint Ginger Rogers? And guess who else looks like a baby John Gilbert with legs? That's right, Sweet Sue-Anne, and Dapper Dan himself."

"Surely you jest!"

I was hoping he'd say "don't call me Shirley," but that movie was forty years to come. Instead he said, "The camera loves you two. It loves her. It *ah-dores you*! It's undeniable. So…We'll finish this film, and we'll juice up your two parts with a new scene or two or three and we'll cut Billy and Milly's parts back a scene or two or four. Thus getting audiences ready for—ta dum!—Schiller and Hall in the next: who knows what the next teen stupidity to come out of our Scripts department will be titled?"

This explained "the letter scene" Seiter and Rafferty had mentioned, for which Cukor had just given my director the lighting cues. Evidently one of the new scenes I or Sue-Anne and I would be shooting.

I wanted to say, but wait a minute, this shouldn't be happening! Because in 2010, Sue-Ann Schiller and Christopher Hall are *not* a name. *Not* a team. They are not *anybody* in movie history.

Instead I said, "Does Billy Bartlett know any of this yet?"

"No-oo! Seiter will film all their scenes, and then film all your new scenes without Billy's knowledge, and then Seiter and I and the editor will make the new film in the cutting room."

Shark in sharkskin all right!

"So, Billy will know when?" I asked. "At the premiere?"

"*If* he's invited," Rafferty said, and I thought, ice water in the veins.

But it did explain something: why Thom Rafferty, who clearly was attracted to me, didn't make anything like a move on me. Someone—not Frances, but someone at the studio—had said "lay off this one, Raff." And Thom knew where his bread was buttered.

I clinked my glass against his and said, "Well! This has been *most* informative, Mr. Rafferty. I'm awfully glad I came tonight."

"You're taking this bit of subterfuge rather well, Christopher. What are you going to do," he asked, "now that you know?"

"Me? Not a thing," I made big innocent eyes at him. "I'm just a Tool of Fate."

"Well, and maybe a Tool of Marketing?"

"A Tool of Fate *and* a Tool of Marketing," I added. "The one problem I will have to deal with at some point will be with Saint Susan-Anne of Miss Irene's Hotel for Women, who will fall over herself weeping and *geschrei-ing* alongside the victims of this particularly backhanded, if rather spectacular if I do say so myself, purge!"

"She'll care? She's the genuine item?" he asked.

"She is completely so. She is a doll. While I…well, let's just say I've been around."

"Don't tell me your stint in the Merchant Marines prepared you for this sort of thing?" Rafferty said.

"Thom, I don't think being in Caligula Caesar's palace court would have prepared me for this sort of Byzantine plotting."

He laughed. "You'll do all right, kid. Because you don't take any of it that seriously."

"Just show me the money, honey!" I said and cracked up.

As we entered the house through a back door and darkened little mudroom, he moved in quickly and bussed my cheek.

"First and last time," he said. "So I can say I was the first one. Because, Christopher Hall, you're going to be a star!"

12

Two days later I had left Jonah in the lobby of the Alsop reading a copy of *Popular Mechanics* when we all returned from Anderson's Diner, but he was already gone when I got back down there not five minutes later. Sid and Ducky, Jonah's roommate, had no idea where he'd gone.

"Where does he go all day?" I asked.

"Beats me!" Ducky said.

"Don't look at me!" Sid replied, aggrieved.

Pops chose that moment to inform us that room number 225 was moving out and there would be a full room empty at the end of the week. Did any of us want it?

"You two have been waiting longer than me," I pointed out.

"Not this month, Pops," Sid said, holding out empty trouser pockets. Ducky said the same.

"Hank is working now. Do you think he'd mind if I moved out?"

"Ask him," Sid suggested.

"Pops, can you hold that room a day for me?" I asked.

"Sure, kid."

"By next month I'll be able to afford my own too," Ducky said. "*If* the Bulldogs keep me in training."

We both assured Ducky that they'd keep him in training.

"Hey, Pops! No paper today?" Sid asked.

"None was delivered."

"Cheez. This joint is goin' downhill every day," Sid declared.

"I'll get one. I want to see something anyway," I said.

"Who cares? I got no horse at Santa Anita Park," Sid said and rang for the elevator.

I stepped out anyway and around two corners to the little place I'd found on Selma, right off Vine, that sold newspapers and magazines.

A few nights before, at the Haines-Shields party, I'd overheard Randolph Scott saying that he liked having breakfast at the Derby there, if he was in Hollywood. Good-looking and healthy as my Alsop House pals were, none of them had turned me on as totally or as instantly as Scott in person had. I'd nosed around a little at the party and gotten these facts about him: he came from a wealthy Virginia family; he'd been a football star in college; he'd recently married a woman named Marion Dupont, yes, those Duponts! A woman who lived most of the time in New York and the rest of the time on the Riviera, while Scott shared a beach house in Malibu with Archie Leach, i.e., Cary Grant.

In other words, all of it was "suggestive" that Scott was gay, or if not gay then bi. So I was going to see if he was breakfasting in the Vine Street Brown Derby, which he'd mentioned he liked, while I was collecting an *L.A. Times* and a few magazines, and if Scott *happened* to be there, I'd drop in too.

He wasn't, and I'd gotten a paper and was wondering whether to go back to the flat or into the Derby to sit at the counter and wait around, when I spotted Jonah up on Hollywood Blvd. getting onto a streetcar headed south on Vine, i.e., toward me.

Sue-Anne and I had a late "call" for shooting that day, some time after lunch, so I held the newspaper up in front of my face and hopped on the back of the streetcar at Selma when it stopped and I stood in such a way that I hoped Jonah would not see me.

After fifteen minutes, the streetcar turned off Vine onto Wilshire to go east, and Jonah stayed on. For one minute he and I were the only passengers and I hid. Then it loaded up with passengers and I was hidden from him again.

I wondered how far this trolley went and at one stop popped off to look at the sign on the back of it: *Franklin to Hoover.*

Fifteen minutes later Jonah dropped off just as it went into a final stop and turnaround at Hoover and I dropped off behind him.

There was a row of shops along Wilshire, with Westlake Park on the other side, so I kept behind him a bit. Maybe Jonah had a job he wasn't telling us about? He always had money. Not a lot, but enough for most of our simple and inexpensive activities, though he seldom got film work like the others. Where did he earn the money?

He walked alongside the park and then up the next block. I lost him temporarily when he turned a corner and I had to hurry to catch up. A couple of bigger buildings here amid the two-story shop fronts and restaurants and I almost walked into the huge lobby of an office building, thinking he'd gone inside there, when I spotted Jonah hurrying across the street and then on the other side. He walked up another two blocks and turned into what looked like the boarded-up doorway of an old wood-sided, three-story house with third-floor dormers and with no glass windows, only paper and boards across the window frames.

I walked past it, and then seeing no one coming out, I moved the piece of barely attached wooden door hanging off one hinge that he'd moved and I went in too. The powerful smell of dried urine and a few pieces of rags and several newspaper nests with clear imprints of people who had slept in them showed me that it was a nighttime hangout for the homeless.

It was an old building from the first boom hereabouts in 1900—or even earlier. Maybe even an old farmhouse, surrounded by city later on. All the doors to rooms down on the ground floor were locked and padlocked and the locks looked rusted over, and thus not opened in a while.

A long wooden stairway going up one interior side of the house rose two times with two well-defined landings, and that smelled bad too, so I held my nose as I went up. I'd tightly rolled the newspaper as a potential weapon, but I encountered no one.

Empty rooms with maybe one small piece of built-in shelving or bookcases on the second floor. I thought I heard the shuffling of feet above.

I was more cautious ascending there, but like the second floor, at first all I encountered was a hallway with closets and even an old sink room, and then I heard shouting ahead, and I sidled along the wall.

A man's voice shouting, and then a woman's pleading, and then— wasn't that Jonah's voice saying, "Well, I'm *here now*. So let's get started!"

The man said something and then there was the noise of things being moved about and suddenly an area in front of me where the corridor opened up was very brightly lighted from the left.

Slowly I crept forward toward that light. So slowly that I'd only gotten halfway when I saw Jonah stepping into my line of sight and I flattened myself against the wall, even turning my head with its light-reflecting eyes away. When I slowly turned my head again, with a hand visoring my eyes, I saw the following:

Jonah stripping off his clothing, one piece at a time, and placing each piece upon a different rung of a tall, old-fashioned, wooden clothes tree nearby. He didn't stop when he'd gotten to his singlet, which he slipped over his head easily, and then he dropped his rather gray-looking shorts and he began to play with his penis while staring straight ahead. His shoes and socks were still on, however, which added a rather Rene Magritte touch to it all—what? No hat?

I thought for a moment he was going to turn and stare directly at me, and what, I mean, but *what* would I think to say in that moment? "Hello, sailor"? But instead, he said, "Ready" in a loud voice, and Jonah was rock hard and bouncing as he moved forward out of my view.

For a few moments I heard the other male voice saying stuff I couldn't make out, and then the woman's voice either complaining or explaining. I thought: Is this what I think it is? If so, *this* I *have* to see!

I slid forward and then back into the corner of the big room, but still hidden from view from the others, and edged along it until I could see Jonah from behind, and he was clearly butt-naked, standing and having intercourse with the woman bent over in front of him on the edge of the bed. The lights were bright, but the photographer-director was hidden from me, and so I could move quite forward until I could make out not him, but instead the "set." This was of a portion of a bedroom, with a sink cabinet topped by a tall, gold-framed, wasp-waisted mirror, and bureau with tasseled drawer handles and a very ornate iron-work bed with several mattresses propped with pillows.

There were no periodically popping flashes, so it was a film, not snapshots. Jonah looked good from three angles and he had a good profile and his manhood looked the right size, or at least a good size as he took the woman. Then the director barked out something, and Jonah pulled back out of her, and I slid back along the wall. But then evidently she changed her position, and this time, Jonah leaned way forward over her in the missionary position and thus completely out of my view except for those black socks and dark shoes.

I thought I heard a door below us make a noise or thought I heard feet on the stairs, so I decided on discretion and backed away and slid back along the corridor walls.

Just as someone came up the last stairway and into the third-floor corridor, I brushed past him with the newspaper up, blocking half my face, and he said something I couldn't make out and I said, "No. I'm just leaving." I sped down the stairs and out onto the street and down the street and into the doorway of the Bradbury Building, from which at last I did peek out.

But no one had followed me or looked outside for me and I thought, "Well, Jonah, sweetie, honey pie. I know your secret. It may be only be '35, but you, my buddy, is a porn star!"

At the studio that afternoon, I got my second surprise of the day. As I sauntered in, Seiter came up to me and said I had to go to the studio doctor.

"I'm fine."

"I know, Christopher. But we need a full health exam for the insurance people. All"—he whispered—"*featured players* need to have the exam. Sue-Anne will go later today, once the nurse comes in." So he was confirming what Thom Rafferty had said to me earlier. Sue-Anne and I had been bumped up in the credits.

One of the fellows on the set took me there in his open jalopy: it was at the northern edge of the studio lot—a little cottage-like extension of the larger building, with a plaque outside.

"I half expected Lew Ayres to welcome me," I said to the thirty-year-old tanned, casually dressed physician, who was relaxing in an armchair reading a movie magazine.

He didn't catch my reference to the actor who'd made famous Young Dr. Kildare the famed movie doctor, and I wondered if I had the year right for it. Probably not.

"Give me a minute and I'll do a quick change," he suggested.

"Never mind. I'll take you as you are."

He put on a lightweight white jacket and we went into the bright little examining room, which looked totally official. Diplomas from medical schools decorated one wall. Harold S. Weissman. Once we were there, he asked me to sit on a stool in front of a rose-vine-covered cottage window, picked up a stethoscope, and asked me to take off my shirt.

In between putting that cold little metal cup upon me all over, front and back, and asking me to breathe deeply, Weissman touched my collarbones, the back of my neck, my upper arms, and then at one point, he had me stand up, and he pulled my trousers and shorts down an inch or two and touched my hip bones. He took my blood pressure twice and counted my pulse. With a little flashlight device, he checked my eyes, the inside of my ears, the interior of my mouth, my scalp, and then he palpated my lymph glands around my jaw and under my armpits.

When he was done and went to his desk to begin writing, I joshed, "Will I live, Doc?"

"For a long time. You know, Christopher, your papers say that you are eighteen years old and I know you were in the Merchant Marines for two years. Did you show them a birth certificate when you joined up?"

"No."

"Do you even have a birth certificate?" he asked. He wasn't being unfriendly.

I thought, well here it is.

"I didn't show them one and no, I don't have one."

"How old are you?" he asked, "Really?"

Really? I'm sixty-five!

"I have no idea, Doc!"

"What do your folks say?"

"What folks? If I had parents, I never saw them. Or they're long dead. Or they left me for dead. All I know is that it was somewhere on the East Coast. I sort of found my way here," I added, "after a long, long while."

He took a deep breath. "You know, I hear about this from my colleagues all the time. From doctors at downtown hospitals. Hell! Even at West Side hospitals. But you're my first. I studied anatomy in med school, and you are slight for your age. Or perhaps maybe…you were underfed, growing up?"

I decided to play up that angle. "You can say that again, Doc!"

"You're what? A runaway? From some home? Some orphanage? Or what?"

Now, I'd read enough books of the period before coming and I'd screened several documentary films about the Great Depression years in America, and so I'd already cobbled together what I hoped was a maudlin yet pretty sturdy tale.

"You know, Doc, all that happened such a very long time ago, I no longer remember where I started out from. What I do know is that I've been on my own for a long time. I've lived by my wits. I got people to feed me, and to put me up, sometimes as long as a few months at time, and then…well, then I just moved on."

He looked at me with narrowed eyes and I realized in that moment that this doctor—this stranger—held enormous power over me. I don't know what he had found in even his simple physical exam. Was my blood pressure too high? Or what? In my sixty-five years of life I'd had measles, German measles, mumps, chickenpox, mononucleosis, hepatitis B, gonorrhea, syphilis, and amoebic dysentery, most of them by the time I was forty. And he must have seen the result of one or another. Which ones? I *did* suddenly understand that if he didn't give me a full certificate of good health as a featured actor, that MGM wouldn't be able to get insurance on me. And if they couldn't, neither could any other studio in town. And so my sweet new life as an actor would be over. Suddenly, this was a crucial moment in my new life. I decided to handle it the only way I knew how—straight on.

"Doc, this movie deal is going to be my big break," I said, making my eyes as big as I could and even managing to bring up some water around them. "This will be the first time in my life I have a real job. The first time in my life that I'll have any security. Or a speck of dignity. It'll be the first time that I have a family too. They treat me like I'm a kid in their family out there, you know! They don't know anything of what happened to me all these years. They don't know what I've been through. They don't know about all the cheats and the liars and the heavy-handed louses that I had to put up with to get a crappy meal, or the ones who did whatever they wanted with me. And I'll never tell them, Doc. I won't! But please don't make me go back to that kind of life! Please let me have this one break, Doc! Please don't tell them I'm in bad health, Doc! Please! I'm begging you! *I'm begging you! Doc!*"

I was in tears at this point and I had dropped to the floor onto my knees and I was clasping him about the lower torso, sobbing into his trousers and thinking holy cow, where did this come from?

After a while he lifted me up and he clasped me close, chest to chest. When we separated, his eyes were wet too.

"Don't worry, son," he said, his voice hoarse with emotion. "Don't worry. None of it is your fault. None of it! I won't *ever* say a thing to anyone."

"Really, Doc?"

"I swear it. I do. C'mon, now. Dry your face! There! Now get dressed. I'll be in the office outside waiting for you."

As I was turning to put my shirt on I heard him say, "This goddamned country! How responsible people could allow this to happen to all you young…Why am I telling you all this? You know it firsthand!" He stormed out of the room.

When I was dressed and put back together again, I looked in the mirror where I was straightening my tie and I said to my reflection, "Christopher Hall! He bought that act hook, line, and sinker. He totally bit! And you, my lad, seem to have a gift for acting!"

Where *had* that come from? Sixty-five years of being alive? Of having to act at times? Or was it sheer necessity of the moment? Who knew? But it was another asset: a definite asset.

Weissman gave me a soda pop, cherry, my favorite flavor, and I kept my eyes cast down as I sat there sipping and he wrote up my health report.

"I said you'd live a long time and you will, Christopher. But your life of wandering and of—well, of homelessness and poor diet and all the associated trauma and turmoil—has actually taken a toll on your body, I'm afraid." He sounded quite serious now. "I'm frankly surprised you're as grown-up and healthy as you are, given what you had to go through for so long. It's proof of your basically solid constitution. But the fact is, Christopher, I spotted a flutter around your heart, in one ventricle. It's nothing serious yet, nothing dangerous...not yet! It's just—I couldn't approve you for any real heavy 'action' on the set, you understand? I can't approve you for any crazy stunts or anything like that. Horse riding is fine. Some running is okay. But not for fighting or wrestling with guys larger than you on the set. Do you understand?"

"I don't plan to do any of that. But a flutter, Doc?" I continued my innocent act, but I was also curious. "Is that like a heart murmur? I've heard of a heart murmur."

"It's not that bad. I think you contracted some kind of disease, a bad flu or a streptococcus virus along the way or, I don't know, maybe even rheumatic fever. Who knows what? It went untreated and you managed to throw it off, but it did leave a mark on your heart. In general I think you'll be fine. Keep dancing, maybe do more swimming. All that's good for the heart. But the truth is, if you tried to enlist in the real Navy with their more stringent health requirements, or any of the other armed services, I'm afraid they would be forced to turn you away."

I wondered which of the diseases I'd had before could have caused that. Or maybe it was all of them and then just simple wear and tear. Dr. Weissman had said whichever disease it was that I'd had, it had left a scar. I had to admit that was kind of unsettling. If I thought I had a free ride here, I'd just gotten notice that limits were being set.

He signed my health certification papers, and as I was getting up to leave I shook his hand hard.

"You know, son, if you do well, maybe someday you'll feel strongly enough to tell your story. People ought to know what kids like you have had to go through. Maybe if they knew, they'd support Roosevelt's programs more."

"I'll seriously think about that, Doc. I will. But not yet. I'm just a kid in a teenager movie."

"Sure. Of course!" and I was halfway out the cottage door when he called me back, and I wondered until he slid a little box of condoms into my hand. "Given all of what you've been through, I'm guessing you already know what these are for."

"Thanks, Doc," I said, pocketing them.

"Any girl or woman you're with? You use one of these. You don't want to get 'caught,' now, do you, Christopher?"

I couldn't tell whether he meant caught with venereal disease or caught knocking up a girl. Nor did I ask him for particulars.

13

The next morning, when we were done breakfasting at the diner and the others went up to their rooms, I stopped Jonah Wolff. "Got a minute?"

He said he did and I slid most of those condoms into his open hand.

"What this for?" he asked suspiciously.

"I can afford these now."

"You plan on using them anytime soon?" he asked, giving away nothing.

"I don't know. But I'll bet you could use one soon."

This time he shoved me up against a wall. He'd been chewing on a wooden toothpick and he looked pretty mean.

"What's that supposed to mean?" And when I didn't answer, "You been snooping around in places where you shouldn't be?" he now asked, looking very dangerous. I didn't like the grip he had on my shirt collar either, and I was trying to get it off me.

"I won't tell anyone."

"Won't tell anyone what?" The toothpick fell away and his canines were exposed and now I was feeling his hand on my throat a lot more.

"I don't care where you go!" I managed to get both hands under his one and could breathe a little better. "Or what you do."

"And...?" He wasn't buying it.

"I just want to make sure you don't catch anything. That's all!"

"Why do you care what I catch?" he asked and gave me a further shove, but he let me go, and he left. Just in time, I noticed, since two other Alsop House guests came by us.

I managed to squeak out a greeting to them and followed them closely in case Jonah was lying in wait for me upstairs.

Later on that day he must have thought about it and had a change of heart. I was sitting in the Alsop lobby, reading a story by H.P. Lovecraft in an old copy of *Weird Tales* in a wooden carton being thrown out. I was waiting for Hank, who was making a phone call, when the stairway door opened and Jonah sauntered in. He didn't look any friendlier than he had been earlier.

"Ducky is meeting the rest of us up the street," I said. Meaning that Jonah was welcome to join us.

"I've been thinking, kid, about your unusual concern for my well-being."

He let that hang for a minute, and I wondered how much of a threat it was, while he took up another magazine on the table and pretended to look at it. "And I want you to know that I've come around to appreciate your sudden interest. But if you're really that concerned, you should also be willing to…how should I put this? Invest in my future?"

"Meaning…?" I responded cautiously. I wished Hank would finish his phone call and get over here.

"Well, perhaps you'd be interested in the reason why I've taken up a…certain line of work?" Jonah asked.

"I don't need to know. And I'm not down on you, Jonah. Believe me!"

"Okay, but see, let's say I really needed the money that…line of work provided," Jonah went on in a lower tone of voice. "And that other lines of work I've tried do not provide. Let's say that I've decided that if I'm ever going to amount to anything here in this city of Los Angeles, that what I really need is not so much a new occupation, as an automobile. So I'm doing that line of work to more quickly save up to buy one."

This was news.

"Okay. Let's say that," I agreed. "How much do you have saved up?"

In an even more confidential voice, he added, "Let's say I've already amassed a hundred fifty dollars..."

So porno paid well, even in 1935.

"A new Lafayette costs five ninety-five," I said. "That's the cheapest car on the market."

"I know that, kid. But a fellow I heard of from another fellow I know has a Willys-Knight that's few years old, and he'll sell it to me for three hundred bucks."

"What'll who sell for three hundred bucks?" Sid asked, coming upon us in the lobby.

Jonah quickly stuffed the condoms I'd once more held out to him into his jacket pocket. "Nothing."

"A previously owned Willy-Knight," I said. "What model?" I asked Jonah.

"A '31 sedan. Hard top. Six windows."

"That's not a bad price for the top of the line," Sid opined. "What's wrong with it?"

"Nothing," Jonah said.

"When you going to show it to us?"

"When I get another hundred fifty dollars," Jonah pointedly said, looking at me.

He was right, though— to really get around L.A. you did need a car.

"How about I go in halves on it with you, Jonah?" I asked, all innocence. "I've got the cash. We can work out a schedule of use."

"How do you know if this previously owned Knight," Sid said, "is going to even run after you get it back here? It could be a dud."

"We don't," I said, then thinking fast, I added, "But I'm guessing you would know!"

"Well, yes, I would," Sid admitted, with no false modesty.

"Because...?" I prodded.

"Well, because my father and my uncles own an auto repair shop in Flatbush and so I sorta grew up around internal combustion engines. I helped fix up an older Knight engine too. The originals came over from England, you know. Along with the Rolls-Royce and the Bentleys."

"Guess who's getting a ride home in a '31 Knight," I said to Sid.

"If it runs," Sid said.

"The streetcar fare going there and coming back too, if need be, is on me," I said.

The following day was a Friday, and after lunch none of the three of us were working, so instead we were standing inside the sparkling new Chevrolet dealership showroom that had opened on Vermont, two blocks north of Beverly.

"This sweet thing," referring to the Knight, "is my own ride, bought brand new," a fat young salesman declared. He was in a three-piece, light brown suit and sparkling white collar and cuffs. "Boss told me I had to turn it in and drive a Chevy. Said it was bad for business, me driving another marque."

"Sid here's going to take a look at it," Jonah said.

"You got the money?" Fatty asked.

"*We've* got the money," I said.

"Oh, it's one of *those* deals?" the salesman said.

"One of *what* deals?" Sid asked.

"Nothing, I didn't mean anything."

"You got a problem with my money?" I asked.

He saw it was three to one and he calmed down. "It's just, you know when fellows are in the pictures…"

"We're paying cash!" Jonah pointed out. "Cash!"

"How do you know any of us are in the pictures?" Sid asked.

"*He* sure is." The salesman pointed to me and walked us back outdoors and up Vermont another block where two workmen in gray overalls were just finishing putting up a movie poster for *Hey! Hay Fever!*

"That's you, isn't it, up there?" the salesman asked.

"Well, I'll be!" Sid mused.

"What'd I tell you?" Jonah asked him.

"Chocolate pudding?" Sid asked.

"More like chocolate soufflé with this kid!" Jonah corrected. "No wonder he's got cash. He's a featured player!"

Sure enough, there, bigger than life, and not much doctored except for colorization, were photos of me and Sue-Anne Schiller holding hands and smiling in our costumes. We were pictured quite large and in front, with a far more doctored and almost unrecognizably touched-up photos of Billy Bartlett and Milly dancing behind our heads. Musical notes were interspersed all around us and around the imperishable copy line: *They're just like your own friends! And they're coming soon to a Movie Theatre near you!*

"Can we look at the damned car?" I asked the salesman.

"Sure. Sure."

Sid acted like a pro. He folded back the multi-panel engine cover and stood high up on the front edge of the running board. He took out a hanky and wrapped it around his right hand and he touched this and he touched that and at last he hopped down and wiped both hands.

"Battery's old and all but fused to the connecting leads. But that's all right since you keep brand-new batteries right here in the garage and can replace that old one, right?"

"Where?" the salesman asked and looked at the engine.

"While you're in there," Sid said, "check out the spark plugs. One or two look pret-ty rus-ty to me. Those'll need to be changed too."

"Oh, yeah. Oh, yeah. Well, you know, it's just been sitting for a few months."

"And naturally we'll have to take it for a spin to see what else happens to fall off or seize up," Sid said, with a slick Brooklyn professionalism that gained my immediate admiration.

"Naturally. Naturally."

While they were doing all that, I asked to use the salesman's desk phone inside the Chevy showroom and called the studio, asking for Rafferty.

Without identifying myself, I began: "I just want you to know that the cat is outta the bag big-time on *Hey! Hay Fever!* I'm looking directly up at myself and my costar, both of us twelve feet high and sweet as can be, on Vermont Avenue in Mid-City Los Angeles, for every passerby to see."

Rafferty laughed. "B.B. knows already."

"Not from me, he doesn't."

"No. From the script boy. Who apparently could *not* be trusted and who I assure you will *not* be a script boy again anywhere in *this* town."

"Just as long as *you* know," I said. "I didn't want this to come as a horrible surprise at some meeting or other," I added.

He laughed again. "Thanks for the tip…I knew. By the way, where are you? Come in today. We've got lots of new lines for you to learn."

"Maybe Monday. But first I'm going to Frances Wannamaker's agency, to sign my fat new studio contract."

"It's there, waiting for you." He laughed again. Then, in a lower voice, he added, "Did you know that little prick was doing it with the script boy *and* some other nobody *and* who knows who else on the set?"

"If it were a *little* prick," I replied, "I doubt that you or any of them would all be interested. Anyway, I suspect I know who else," I said. "But I'm torn between telling you and blackmailing him myself."

"I believe you would!" Rafferty said, highly amused.

"I would. If it's worth the effort. Which…I doubt."

The others soon arrived back from their "test drive" without any apparent harm to auto or to any living creature, and so I got off the phone and we all went into the office, because it was, after all, despite the salesman's line of bull, an official sale through the dealership. I made certain that Jonah's name and my own were on the bill of sale. The salesman then even provided us with an official state registration of the vehicle and a license plate, and we were set.

As we all tooled into the car, I said to Sid, "So you can drive *and* fix cars. Any cars?" I asked.

"I ain't seen one I can't yet. But that doesn't mean there's not some Chinese model out there I never heard of."

"Why not come to the studio with me Monday? I'll introduce you to the vehicle shop manager. He's always bitching that he's short of experienced help. He holds up shooting. He may be able to give you part-time work. They pay the highest in town. And," I rubbed it in, "every once in a while they're looking for drivers on film sets too. That's hazard pay even if you're driving an old lady at four miles per hour."

"I think I may be free Monday," Sid allowed.

"Yeah, Sid," Jonah said, "check your busy schedule! You wouldn't want to miss your afternoon appointment with Jean Harlow!"

We arrived at the Alsop House and Pops and a few other residents came out and looked over the car. Pops said it was "a lot better than that Gosh-Darned Flivver I used to burn up." He then amazed us by saying there actually was a "garage across the street for paying residents." Who knew?

"Hey, kid," he added to me. "You got a phone call. That Wannamaker lady."

I phoned Frances from the lobby pay phone and she was breathless. "There's been a palace coup!" she said.

"Well, not quite. But I know all about it, and as we speak the posters are going up around town."

"Thom sent the new contracts here. You'll both have to come in."

I gestured to Jonah, and asked would he want to drive me and Sue-Anne over to Wannamaker's office on Robertson Blvd.

He was game. So we picked her up, and although Jonah was interested in her, he was a total gentleman, which kind of surprised me.

All was mayhem at Frances's office, the reason being that her pregnant assistant, Gloria, had left early due to what her boss called "morning, afternoon, and just general all-day sickness!" On top of that, the messenger service hadn't come by yet and the Wannamaker Agency had stacks for them to take around.

"We've got our own messenger service," I said and called Jonah indoors. I once again watched Frances size him up and like what she saw, and so I decided to shove them together.

I explained that Frances needed—what was it?—five or six places he would have to drive to that afternoon?

"Maybe…seven. I'll pay for your services, Jonah, is it?" Frances said. And knowing what I did of Jonah now, I thought, will she ever!

Sue-Anne and I got our ride, along with the signed contracts, down to MGM, and as we directed Jonah to the main office where he had to go to deliver the contracts we'd just signed, Jonah took me aside.

"Listen here, Little Mary Sunshine. If you're planning to fix me up in the studio here the way you're busy fixing up Sid and Ducky and Hank, you just forget about it!"

I made big eyes at him and said, "Why, Jonah Wolff, Junior, I have no idea *what* you are talking about, and I resent even what I *suspect* you may be hinting at.

"Come on, Sue-Anne," I said, grabbing her by the shoulder. "Enough of this riff-raff, girl! You and I have *lines* to *learn*."

14

"Who wrote these lines?" I asked Seiter, not at all rhetorically, the next day I was back at work shooting.

"Who knows? Someone in Scripts. Why?"

"Teenagers haven't talked like this to each other since Marie-Antoinette lost her head over a *brioche*. Tell him, Sue-Anne."

"Chris is kinda right, Mr. Seiter. This dialogue is... What's the word I'm looking for, Christopher?"

"The word *I'd* use is different than the one you're looking for, Sue-Anne, and it's also unprintable. The word you are looking for is 'unbelievable.' Let's see, perhaps also 'archaic.' 'Antique.' 'Irrelevant.' 'Risible.' Am I getting warm?"

"I suppose *you* could do better!" the director said, throwing the script down on the table and going over to the coffee urn in the room, always kept full and hot, and leaking with a cloth towel folded beneath it.

"With my eyes closed, one hand tied behind my back, and a full frontal lobotomy! Yes, I could do better."

"Okay, hot shot. We're shooting scene 74A tomorrow. You come in with better dialogue and we'll look at it."

He stormed out of the room with an audible "little know-it-all son of a—" cut off by the door slamming on us.

"I *can* write better than this...dog-doo." I softened the last for her. "And if I get stuck, you'll help me. Right, Sue-Anne?"

The next morning at nine a.m., Jonah dropped off Hank, Sid, and me at the studio. "I'll probably be by sometime later," he told Sid, "if you need a ride back." And when I looked up at him, Jonah said, "She said she had a big fight with that cockamamie messenger service. So I said I'd help her out."

"She" being my talent agent, Frances Wannamaker.

"Who knows, but I may be stuck being her errand boy until she finds another service," Jonah concluded. He didn't sound that upset by the fact that he was "stuck" with a real job.

Hank went straight to the design department. He had taken the news of me moving to my own room philosophically, but then he'd asked, "Can I come sleep with you every once in a while? I got used to you."

To which I had assented, thinking, this boy is too damn sweet for you, Chris Hall, you manipulative old bastard.

But I also noticed that being alone did him good last night, as he came in this morning with a pad full of ideas from being alone and up half the night.

I myself had stayed up until after one a.m., rewriting not only scene 74A, but 74B, 74C, and then 77A, B, and C too.

"This is Sidney Devlin, of Flatbush, Brooklyn," I introduced him to James Phyllis, our Vehicles Department head. "His mother breast-fed him on high-octane petrol with a motor oil chaser."

Sid meanwhile was looking around the enormous garage in wonder. Not only were there cars and trucks, decommissioned streetcars and city busses of varied makes, models, and vintages, but even the first three cars of a steam engine last used to supposedly crush to death Garbo for *Anna Karenina.*

"Will ya look at that one?" Sid said under his breath to me at a 1926 Stutz Black Hawk yellow-bodied roadster with ink-black fenders, chrome trim, and black leather seats. It looked like a giant dragonfly that had just landed for a second.

"Flatbush, huh," J.P. asked. "You a Dodgers or Giants fan?"

"I was a Dodgers fan. Now I'm a Black Hawk fan!"

"A beauty, huh? That was owned by Priscilla Lane. She said it went too fast. She couldn't slow it down. So we took it off her hands. Now take a look at this old Mercer Raceabout. Some bozo told me…"

I left them together in auto heaven and popped into the Scripts department.

A young male assistant at the front desk with a mop of fuzzy yellowish hair and big tortoiseshell glasses, altogether resembling a very young Marx Brother, was reading a newspaper. He looked up surprised and seeing pages under my arm, he quickly said:

"No one's in yet. I don't expect them till eleven."

"What about the typists?"

"The fellows do their own typing."

"Fine, I need a typewriter and an office for an hour. If you have any problem with that request, call Thom Rafferty."

It had been decades since I had used a typewriter, but their Royal manuals were kept oiled, cleaned, and in generally tip-top condition, with erasing ink nearby and nice soft paper and bright new ribbons in the carriages. Even better, the typewriter tabs were already set for the specific indents needed for an official screenplay page: for scene, then set-up; farther in for character name and out again for dialogue; so after a few minutes of reacquainting myself with all that and the noise it made, I was speeding along.

At eleven on the dot, one writer showed up and was told that someone was in the empty office typing away, so he peeked in.

His comment: "When did we begin a high school program?"

"I wish the script for *Hey! Hay Fever!* was that funny," I replied and kept typing, although by now my fingers were aching. Ten minutes later they were all collected around my office door when I exited, the new typed script pages in my hands.

"Gentlemen," I said, and tipped my smart, brand-new little fedora to them as I walked out.

"Who's that?" I heard one ask.

"That's your replacement, Garson."

"He's twelve years old."

"Remember what you looked like when you first arrived?"

"Don't remind me."

Seiter and Rafferty both liked the changes.

Sue-Anne said, "Oh, these are perfect, Chris! My lines are *just perfect!*"

Probably because I made Sue-Anne's character speak just like she did.

"What'll we do about the writing credit?" Seiter asked.

"Chris," Raff asked, "You got another name up your sleeve?"

"Blaine Anthony," I said, thinking quickly, recalling and then reversing the name of the Evelyn Waugh character I most wanted and probably had the least chance ever of getting to play onscreen.

"He's got a million of 'em," Rafferty said, with a sigh. "I'll send Frances another, temporary, contract for your writing."

By the time we'd finished shooting two weeks later—yes, five weeks shooting altogether!—everyone in the set had asked for line changes from me. Even Billy Bartlett, who, amazingly, had no hard feelings about what had happened.

"I always thought I looked like a prison ex-con on the silver screen," he explained to us one day, philosophically.

"But you're not giving up show business?" Sue-Anne asked.

"For a while. I'll go fishing, I think. Deep-sea fishing."

He would end up with his own yacht and a business on the ocean. Out of Port Hueneme, up the coast.

The wrap party for our dopey little movie ended up at the Brown Derby on Selma and Vine. To my great satisfaction, Marlene Dietrich was there also, along with a bunch of Germans including Sacha Viertel and Franz Werfel. At our end of the place, people were making toasts, and I was forced to stand on a chair and bow repeatedly for "saving the movie" via my script changes.

I could see Dietrich narrow her eyes as she looked me over then, and I thought, I would be only a tiny canapé in her vast, gorgeous, lipsticked mouth.

Then Randolph Scott showed up and she gestured him over. He stood by her side and I suppose she asked who I was. But instead of gesturing ignorance, I could see his lips saying my name. So I had made something of an impression on him at the Haines-Shields party. Good!

Later on, he was at the counter with two nice-looking young women when I walked by. "I'm free tomorrow," I said. "My film wrapped today. I hear *Roberta* wrapped too. So you must be free yourself...I was thinking I'd come by and take a dip in your piece of ocean. Say at noon?"

"Just you? All by yourself," he asked. "You know our place has a *terrible* reputation."

"Everyone calls it Bachelor Hall," one of the women said.

"I know," I said.

"How old are you anyway?" Scott asked.

"I'm of age."

He looked me over.

"Actually, I'm a whole lot older than I look."

I didn't add that I was sixty-five and old enough to be his father.

He looked me over again. Finally, he said in a lower voice: "Aren't you afraid that something bad will happen?"

He was wearing a tan and pale blue jacket and a deep blue shirt and I thought he looked totally edible and smelled like heaven.

Had. To. Have. Him. Simply *Had! To!*

"No. I'm just afraid that *nothing* bad will happen," I said.

That amused him. "Okay. You asked for it, kiddo."

"Yes, I did!"

"Ladies," I added in a louder voice as I tipped my hat and left.

All three were gone when I exited the men's room.

Marlene was there, however, and she was saying, "No. I will never go back there again! They are all monsters there now. Nazi monsters! And the rest are all zombies!"

The others in her group began to argue with her.

But Marlene held up her hands in their purple silk gloves, saying, "No. No. Never!"

I thought: She must know what's really going on in Germany. She really must know!

15

Hey! Hay Fever! had a surprise preview showing the day after it was ready, held at the amazing Fox Theatre in Westwood, with its huge, four-sided tower. Patrons who'd come in to see the Sunday serials and the children's show were given free tickets to the special showing to be held after most people's dinners at eight p.m. A huge poster for our movie, like the one I'd seen on Vermont Avenue, had been up on a nearby building for several weeks already, so we had a solid crowd show up, virtually all of them under twenty: our target audience.

Sue-Anne, Billy and Milly and I snuck into the movie house during the last fifteen minutes, and when the curtain went up, Thom Rafferty asked people to stay and meet the featured players. This had been my idea, as I'd thought it would be a more intimate way than filling out a form asking how you liked the movie, the usual way movies were previewed in 1935.

All but the edges of the loge and part of the downstairs had been closed off for this special showing, so of the six hundred people present, about twenty left, including a girl in the balcony who came to the edge and shouted down, "I love you, Christopher Hall. But I've got a curfew of nine-thirty." This earned her applause and laughter.

This unusual encounter of actors and audience had come about because a few days before, I'd overheard Rafferty talking about the sneak peek with Seiter and someone else from the Marketing department. I'd talked to Sue-Anne and then to our agent, and we two had of course reminded Frances about how bad the script had been and my role in rewriting parts of it. We'd managed to persuade Frances to ask for a post-production meeting for us at MGM to discuss our "role in marketing the movie to teens."

Her initial response to this was "Good luck, kids!" Followed by a game "I'll try. But I can't promise!"

It was unclear how much persuading she did, but it must have been substantial, as the meeting was indeed called and that afternoon our director and his assistant and then Thom Rafferty showed up and eventually so did an executive from Marketing named Lloyd Talmadge, who looked like he'd had his job when the studio first opened, several decades earlier, making silent two-reelers. They all tried to look concerned about this gathering and instead came off looking perplexed.

As per our plan, Frances led off, reminding them about the script rewrites and our roles in that and then reminding them that all of us in the room had a strong interest in the movie's success. She added that Sue-Anne and I wanted to continue to help its chances. Once the others were softened up, Frances gave me the floor and I asked how they planned to audience test.

Rafferty merely chuckled. He was slowly getting used to whatever I might come up with, which was certain to surprise. The others looked at each other, pretty much at sea.

"We'll pass out impression cards, like we always do," Talmadge said.

"What if, on top of that, we did something else?" I asked.

"What?"

"What if me and Sue-Anne and Mr. Seiter got up after the movie and asked the audience questions directly?"

"What kind of questions?" Talmadge asked, fiddling with his cravat—not tie—cravat, that's how old-school he was.

"Questions like 'How long have you been gay? And who buys those awful cravats?'" I wanted to say. But I restrained myself and instead said, "Well, I thought we'd ask questions that teenagers would ask each other. I mean, I believe we are going for a predominantly teen audience, right?"

"Right." He was acting like it was a trick question.

"So why don't we take advantage of having this self-selected sample of our key audience," I asked, unsure but hoping that "sample" and "key" were already existent in his professional lingo, "to find out what they really want to see?"

"Well, that could open the door to all sorts of…"

"To see in this kind of teenager movie," I interrupted to clarify.

"What kinds of questions?" Rafferty asked me. I turned to Sue-Anne, who had a short list we'd worked out.

They all seemed to ponder that and eventually Seiter spoke: "I see no harm in any of those questions."

"We might actually hear what teenagers are thinking!" the assistant director added.

"I think it will mean a lot to those teenagers," Sue-Anne now said, "if they see us right there, accessible to them."

"Well, that's hardly been the policy for the studio's actors," Talmadge began.

"Mickey Rooney and Jackie Cooper do road shows all the time," Frances argued.

"What if they are unfriendly? Aren't you afraid of criticism?" Talmadge asked Sue-Anne.

"No. I welcome it!" she said boldly.

Then Talmadge and Rafferty got up and left the room and evidently spoke together, and when Thom came back in he was smiling. "We'll try it. One time only. And Talmadge wants his people to rework those questions."

So here we were, actually implementing this strange request.

Talmadge's assistant in Marketing began with "How did you like the film?" which earned him applause. We'd gotten applause as the film had ended and when we actors marched in front of the proscenium, so we knew that already. Nice, if useless.

I'd tried to skew the questions a little more usefully, so that for example instead of asking what did you like or dislike, the Marketing fellow next asked, "Are these kids you'd like to get to know better?"

A resounding yes.

Which ones?

Sue-Anne and myself, first, of course. And, unbidden, the young audience began telling us what they most liked. "The way they talked to each other," one girl said, "was just like we talk to each other."

Applause followed that. "They seemed real," a boy said, and blushed deeply. More applause.

What could be better? Say, in another film with these characters? Seiter asked them, "More singing? More dancing?"

No, it turned out. They wanted more realistic stories.

"This one was fun and enjoyable," one very put together young lady said. "But we've got real problems too. We'd like to see those up on the screen too."

That very answer was why I'd demanded a Script department representative to be there. Even Seiter claimed to be surprised. So I asked that girl, "Even if the stories taken from real life are sad, or even tragic? Would you go still see that?"

The reaction among the teens was widespread, positive, and especially the older teens agreed. The boys began mentioning problems they had, and I copied them down quickly.

One girl charmingly said she thought "Billy and Milly were the funniest. But Christopher Hall was the *swooniest*!" This was followed by shouts of agreement and even a few wolf whistles.

We'd suggested that to "reward" our marketing audience that extra "cards"—little posters for our movie, the size of the announcement cards placed outside of the theater—be printed up, and we began handing those out and were surprised when we ran out of them, it was such a popular idea. We four actors signed the posters and a few of the patrons stepped forward and met us directly after that session was over and we heard even more useful comments from them, some of which we immediately asked them to repeat to the executives there.

We went to the local after-hours diner on Gayley Avenue afterward, a UCLA hangout, where more members of the audience came up to our big corner booth.

We remained long after it had emptied out, at which point I said: "To summarize: They love us, but…they want more realistic dialogue, more realistic stories, and more real teen problems."

The representative from Scripts said, "That's not going to be as easy as you think, you know. We don't know much about teenagers' problems."

"Well, we do! Sue-Anne and me and our friends," I said. "So maybe we should partner up with you people on the next script—from the very beginning. What do you think, Mr. Rafferty? That might work, couldn't it?"

"It might. But do you really want to do all that work?" he asked us. "You're young people. You're earning a lot of money. Wouldn't you like to go out and enjoy yourselves? You, Sue-Anne, don't you want to buy ball gowns with your earnings? Maybe get a horse of your own and all those riding outfits. And don't you want to go out dancing? I'm sure there's plenty of young fellows who would take you."

"Well, sure, but when I heard what some of those kids had to say, I don't really, Mr. Rafferty. I mean of course, I like all that, what girl wouldn't? But there's other things going on in the world too! And then, Chris is so good with my dialogue. I'm sorry, Mr. Herman, I know you people work hard and you try hard, but if Chris could write my lines from now on, I'll make as many movies as you want me to." Billy and Milly took up that statement and supported it. They all liked my dialogue far better than what they'd first been given.

"Christopher?" Rafferty asked. "That's a great deal more work for you."

"I don't mind, although I'm sure I've got a great deal to learn from you, Mr. Hermann," I said and I added, "You know, things are happening so fast nowadays, I'm not at all surprised that we four here are the only ones at the studio who really know what young people are thinking anymore. We're beginning to have our own movies. Soon we'll have our own music, and our own books and…"

So that's where it began, tentatively enough, and of course it was evident that the "grown-ups" would be looking over our shoulders every inch of the way, because after all, there was so much money on the line. But that's when it was first agreed to let us begin to generate the stories for our movies from then on.

As we were getting into cars to go home to bed, Thom took me and Seiter aside.

"You both understand that if this works as well as it seems from that preview that it will work, that we are all looking at a Schiller and Hall franchise?"

"Meaning how many films, on what kind of schedule?" I asked.

"It's early July. I'd say two, or maybe three more movies this year. That's a lot of work for you both."

"I don't have anything else planned. What about you, Will?" I asked.

"I'm free," he said, with a chuckle, "and if you and Sue-Anne are right, this could be some kind of youth sensation."

Talmadge couldn't be bothered to come to our preview, but his second in command, who was considerably younger, had grown more enthusiastic as the evening went on. "Those handout posters worked better than we thought!" he said. "I've collected a dozen names and addresses of kids who asked for one, after those were all gone."

"They'll put them up in their rooms and they'll tell all of their friends," I said. "Because that's what teenagers do."

"Let's hope so. You know, Talmadge didn't think this would work at all."

"What will you tell him?" I asked.

"Maybe I won't. Maybe I'll ask to meet with Goldwyn or Louis B. and tell him directly."

"You can take the credit for the idea," I said.

"Of course I can. It was my idea," he lied and stalked off.

Once Frances and Thom and Sue-Anne and I were packed into his Buick, headed back home, I said, "Blaine Anthony will begin the next scenario right away. I had an idea for a title: *Different Curfews*! He's a soda jerk and works after school in his dad's grocery or newspaper shop, and she's from a close-knit traditional family. Maybe even bring up religious differences."

"I like that," Sue-Anne said.

"So do I," Frances agreed.

"No religious differences!" Rafferty declared with finality. "Remember, this is a family studio…But perhaps we do *have* a basic plan."

Sue-Anne was quieter than usual when Rafferty dropped us off at her residence hotel. I saw her to her door at Miss Irene's and asked what was wrong.

"Nothing's *wrong*, Chris. It's just that until tonight, I'd never thought that we could, you know, make a difference in other people's lives. I guess I'm kind of surprised by what those kids said. I sort of feel that we have a responsibility to them. What if we do or say something wrong?"

"We do have a responsibility, Sue-Anne. But you're so wonderful you won't say or do anything wrong. You heard how crazy they were about you."

"And about *you*! Why, I think I ought to be jealous after how those girls were talking about you."

"Except…we don't have that kind of friendship, do we? I mean *off* the screen?"

"We don't? No, you're right, Chris, I'm sorry to say we don't."

"You're sorry, but not *that* sorry because you *do* like a friend of mine a great deal already in a short time, don't you?"

"Don't you dare say a word to him! Well, maybe a word."

"Done. But as soon as I'm done with the scenario for *Different Curfews*, you're going to read the whole twenty pages and discuss it with me in excruciating detail. Before I hand it to those jerks. Do we have a deal?"

I stuck out a pinkie, to seal it.

She joined me with her own. We twisted them together.

"Deal! G'night, Chris—*the swooniest*—Hall!"

At the Alsop House, Pops woke up long enough to say, "Your friend was here looking for you."

"Which friend? Don't you know I have hundreds, Pops?"

"The guy that first brought you here, in the middle of the night."

He meant Larry Allegre. The costume jewelry sales rep! I'd forgotten all about him. "I hope he left his number."

"It's here somewhere. There it is."

"I'll call him tomorrow. First thing."

16

Larry Allegre didn't answer the phone for the next few days, at least not whenever I called. The following week I called again and some kind of secretary answered the phone, saying she came in once a week, handling the calls for several desks, and that she would convey my message to Mr. Allegre.

Several weeks and then several months would go by before Allegre and I finally connected and actually spoke on the phone, and then, because he said his job had him on the road so much, it would be months longer before we could make a solid plan for dinner: My treat, as I'd said before. Although by then, much would have changed for me, and it would no longer have to be the "cheap dinner" that I'd first promised him.

Meanwhile, we five Alsop House pals continued to meet for breakfast at Anderson's Diner, no matter what else we were doing. It was there that Hank finally asked me about Sue-Anne and I said I thought she was very interested in him. It was there too that Sid Devlin told us that he had come up with this neat idea to rig up an old car to go over a cliff and burst into flames for the one gangster movie that MGM was planning to release that year. Sid said he would drive the rig himself. Within a year he would be heading up a new Stunts department and reviving a moribund Special (FX) Effects department. It was also at Anderson's that we celebrated Ducky Deutsch making the team of the Bulldogs, to play in September's first game, and also there that Jonah told me on "the q.v." (whatever that meant) that he'd gone to a "legit doctor" and gotten blood tests, and when those luckily came back negative for "The Syph and etcetera" that he'd "gotten together" with Frances Wannamaker. He'd be the first of us to spend nights outside the Alsop House too.

Still we were there Monday through Friday mornings come what may, hell or high water: it was our hangout, our clubhouse, our meeting ground, and people knew we could be found there every morning.

Hey! Hay Fever! opened and did great business and *Different Curfews* was written with a great deal of back and forth and because "those kids" were writing it, with almost daily interference by seemingly everyone at the studio but the janitor. Actually he might have been giving his opinion too, given how ignorant and illiterate most of them were. That film was then shot, went into post-production, opened in September, in more theaters than its successful predecessor, and it did even better business.

This meant that all of a sudden, one early fall day, Sue-Anne and I were "recognized" going about what had been our usual casual and easy-going day around downtown Hollywood, where, after all, we both lived.

The first time this happened, we were at the newly opened Citizens Bank of Hollywood, a sort of credit union that had opened in response to the crashing closure several years before of so many long-established banks. One of the fellows in Scripts—Rafferty declared they were "all Commies!"—had suggested that this was a "relatively conscionable place" to put our earnings, and so we had both gone and begun savings accounts there. We were standing in line, the two of us, heaped with various parcels, since I'd been book shopping and she had been stationery buying again, right across the street. I was trying to balance those parcels, my bank book, my bi-monthly check from MGM, a pen and deposit slip, and some scripts that had been tossed at me "for possible improvement" earlier that day when Sue-Anne said in a tight voice, "Don't look up too quickly."

"Because?" I whispered.

"Because I think we have a half dozen fans staring at us," she managed to get out, almost entirely without moving her lips.

I slowly looked up and directly ahead, and I did exactly as I'd been taught by the assistant at George Hurrell's photography studio a few days previous. I'd looked up and at his enormous and flattering camera lens, my eyes huge and "softly glowering" a bit, and even fluttering a mite. As I now did, I spotted three teen females inside the bank against the far end windows, and another six or so girls behind that window, and they were all saying something, communicating despite the glass, and pointedly staring at us. Sure enough, the ones inside headed right at us and those outside hastened indoors.

"Too late!" Sue-Anne declared and then we were surrounded and autographs were demanded, and compliments flew at us, and then other patrons in the bank recognized or pretended to recognize us and they too circled us and asked for autographs and I thought this might become very weird. Two executives from the bank approached and extricated us. They took us into a private room and sat us down while girls gathered outside the office doorway, and one of them banked our checks for us, and the other fellow said, "This can be done directly from your agent's office, you know."

We hadn't known, and we were very apologetic for the hubbub we had caused. The bank executive assured us that the Citizens Bank was thrilled with our business and they would even get us out safely through a side door, if we didn't mind waiting a few minutes until the crowd had thinned out.

"It's going to be even worse next week, when that story in *Screen Gems* runs," Sue-Anne declared wistfully once we were out on the side street, headed away from the bank. "And then there's the one of us in *Photoplay* too," she moaned. "With Mr. Hurrell's completely gorgeous picture of you, Chris. I've already got a copy on my dresser. I'll bet not a single issue will remain intact," she added, in an oddly predictive statement.

Those articles and the photo sessions had come about because of the greater success of our second movie and the success of *Hey! Hay Fever!* in the British Isles. That all had also meant that suddenly we began to have meetings with the Lion's large Publicity department. In no time Schiller and Hall had obtained our own very own publicity assistant, a young man named Sergio Hawkins. He was a soigné fellow with a Southern drawl who had worked with various other MGM starlets before and who said to us when meeting us for the first time, "You kids are moving faster than my granddaddy's chestnut did at the Preakness."

Our regular co-breakfasters at Anderson's Diner soon became aware of this evolving Schiller and Hall situation too, and they nicely enough ensured that autograph seekers never got in, or if in, at least not close to me. Nice guys, they protected me. Even so, we five friends moved from our usual table in the window back into the most hidden and secure corner, close to the lavatory and the rear door for a hasty getaway.

Shooting on the second film went a lot better than the first, partly because the script was about eighty percent Blaine Anthony. Billy and Milly returned for a special skit-like "comedy dance number" that me and Sue-Ann had worked out on our own, and on our own time. They were pleased to be in the movie. I played a "swoonier" role with Sue-Anne, aware that this would up the ante on my glamour outside the studio, with all the complications that would no doubt ensue.

So we set to work on film #3, *Traditions*, in which I would play an Italian-American Catholic kid romantically involved with Sue-Anne, who came from a strict Anglo-Methodist Midwest upbringing.

We'd managed to get marketing to pull in several "focus groups" of teens already loyal to our "franchise" to discuss this third movie. We fed them sandwiches and soda pop while Sue-Anne, I, and several adult actors listened to their comments of the story I'd written and which we'd read to them.

Later on all of them and their friends too were invited to the nearby

Hollywood Playhouse on Vine St. to see the film acted out before it was filmed. We played out all the key scenes from the script that I had ended up pretty much writing myself—with the usual comments from Mr. Hermann's office and this time from Seiter and Rafferty. At the last minute, I'd decided to end the film sadly, with the young couple *not* getting together. He would join the Navy, and she would secretly come to see him off as he left, despite her parents forbidding her. This would leave open the possibility that they might get together some time later on. It was taking a chance, we knew, to not have a happy ending, and we might have to change it. We were already prepared to reshoot the scene to a stupid, upbeat one, if necessary.

Our teen audience adored the staged reading of the script and they loved the ending as it was. Two girls mentioned similar experiences among people they knew.

They remained talking about it with the cast and producers, et al, for over two hours after the sneak preview. Finally someone was taking them seriously, they said. The adult actors had been about to leave but they remained out of fascination with the entire process. Afterward, Seiter said to me, "You've tapped into something important here, Christopher. Something we'd all do well to pay attention to."

And of course I would mention this and script ideas to Hank or Sid or anyone, to get their opinions, which I wrote down. Ducky said "put in sports," naturally, and added that he could tell me some stories—and he did. Hank finally opened up one night about his leaving home, and I asked if he would mind if we put in a character with his story in the fourth movie. I remember him looking at me so oddly that I said, "What you did was *courageous*, Hank. Look at your life now! Great friends. Good job. You're doing what you love to do and you are headed up in the world. You have a terrific girl interested in you. You could help some other kid who's wondering if he or she should stick around and take all the abuse, or wise up and get out of town, like you did."

Naturally enough, Jonah got into the act: finding me alone, he wise-assedly asked if I'd consider a story about a young fellow and an older dame (his words).

"I was thinking of calling it *Twenty into Thirty-Five*," he said.

"You mean," I shot back, "because 'How many times does Twenty go into Thirty-Five?' And the answer is 'As many times as humanly possible'?"

"Geez, Junior! You know everything!" he complained, but he seemed pleased.

Everything seemed to be going well, "peachy keen" in Sid Devlin's only half-ironic words.

So it was with some surprise that one morning I began hearing diners beginning to "grouse"—a term I'd only recently learned. I'd always thought it meant some kind of small land bird.

I looked around and realized suddenly that no food but only coffee and juice had been served for maybe fifteen minutes.

"Hey, Andy, what gives?" Ducky asked the diner's owner. You could hear the big guy's stomach growling all the way over in Glendale.

"Cookie took offense and left. Gotta close up, boys."

Now, Andy and Cookie were the most argumentative unmarried pair I'd ever come across, so the fact that Cookie had actually taken "offense" was odd, to say the least.

"You mean there's no food?" Ducky asked.

"There's plenty of food. There's no one to cook it."

A giant hubbub began in the place at this news. The spectacle of watching a dozen grown men sitting around threatening to riot because no one could fry an egg was utterly ridiculous. Then I recalled that I was living in an era in which the genders had and, more importantly, were *expected to have* very different kinds of competences, and that the only men who would or did cook in 1935 were professionals. Even backyard barbecuing wouldn't come around until suburban life after the Second World War. Seven decades after, in my time, those differences had merged. Women drove trucks and men embroidered. And I was sure I could do both of those activities with a little guidebook. I did know I could cook breakfasts. So I grabbed Anderson and dragged him into the kitchen.

"What's your breakfast menu? Eggs, ham, bacon, toast, griddle cakes, French toast, what else?"

"That's pretty much it."

"Omelets? What else?" I probed.

"Biscuits."

I checked the flour. "You're a little low here."

"Why that, darn Cookie! He said we had plenty."

"There's plenty of corn meal and enough flour, so listen, Andy, let me talk to my boys. Maybe we can help you here."

"Whaddya mean? You can cook?"

"Breakfast stuff? Yeah! Easy! But instead of biscuits I'll make cornbread."

"Holy moly! Cornbread?!"

"I was in the Merchant Marines." I trotted out the old-serves-anywhere-in-this-time-and-place excuse. "Get me an apron."

"Ya mean I don't have to close down and lose money?"

"Not this morning, you don't."

Anderson was about to hug me, bad-smelling, cheap cigarette and all, so I shook his hand and propelled him forward again saying, "I'll start on the cornbread, which will take maybe fifteen minutes to be ready. Send my guys in."

Ducky immediately picked up what I was aiming for. "I can help. But we get to eat too, right?"

"Right. You can nibble while you work. What can you do?"

It turned out Ducky used to help his mother with breakfasts back in Altoona, P.A., and he could do a lot with things like toast and cereal and even oatmeal, not to mention arranging plates.

Hank was amused but game. He said, "I'm a carnivore. Bacon and ham's my specialty." So I put him in charge of grilling those.

Sid Devlin said he was lowering himself but he admitted that he'd actually done some table waiting in his dissolute youth back in Brooklyn. I found aprons for all of us and we set to work. At first it was bedlam, and I had to keep telling Sid to keep filling up those coffee cups. But soon enough I had my cornbread in the oven and simple orders of ham and eggs and toast were actually being plated and served, and then the loud rumbling outside in the diner settled into more localized grumblings. In about two hours we managed to put together and serve some thirty-five breakfasts before Anderson locked the doors and pulled closed what passed for curtains and we leisurely cooked for ourselves and sat down to eat breakfast.

"You guys is princes!" Andy assured us. "And who would have thought, a big movie actor like you…?" He looked at me with what might have been tears in his eyes, speechless.

"First and last time!" I declared. "And if you ever tell anyone I helped here, Andy, you're a dead man," I said in my best Jimmy Cagney impersonation.

"Now, go apologize to Cookie. Because we are *not* making lunch," Sid said, then filled his mouth with cornbread slathered over with marmalade.

We toasted each other with orange juice and I said to Ducky, "You were terrific!" He'd not only made toast and cereal and plated the food, he'd helped make eggs and had helped serve. He'd seemed comfortable in the kitchen. All of us told him so.

"That was my mother's dream. You know, to open a roadside diner. Never happened, of course, not once the Crash came along. She'd saved up for it. But we had to spend all that just to get by, once my father lost his job and all."

"Maybe she'd want to move out here?" Hank suggested. "Plenty of areas out here could use a good diner. Around the studio, for one," he said and the rest of us agreed.

So we all hoisted our coffee mugs and toasted Ducky's mother's diner.

That day's shooting on *Traditions* had begun late and it went on into evening. I got home about nine p.m., and as no one was around at the Alsop House, I nipped up the corner on Hollywood Blvd. to the new Sardi's for a light dinner.

Jonah, Sid, and Hank were there, finishing meals, and as I came in they raised up a cheer, "Hip, Hip, Hooray," for me.

This brought me to everyone's attention, which had not been my intention at all, and the manager came out and, recognizing me, asked if I would present a signed photograph for the back wall of booths. For the first time I was embarrassed by all the attention. "Really, Anton? Do I have to?"

"We want this to be the place all the stars come when they're in Hollywood," he assured me.

That wouldn't happen as long as the Derby was still around, but I agreed to it.

"Is there anything you can't do, Junior?" Jonah asked once I sat down.

"Apparently I can't shut you up."

"No, you can't. I meant, anything in the world you can't do." To the others, he announced, "I present Mr. Christopher Hall, aged twelve. He sings, he dances, he acts, he writes scripts, he cooks breakfast."

I wanted to say, "and I seduce movie stars half my age," but I desisted. The fellows might ask for names. Instead I said, "That was a group effort! To all of us!"

Later on I said, "You know, guys, there's no reason why a fellow shouldn't be able to cook breakfast. Or in fact do anything," I said. "Anything."

"You mean Hoovering too?" Sid asked. He meant vacuuming.

"Hoovering too!"

"Head surgery?" Jonah asked.

"Well, that's a bit much unless you've studied how. But say piloting a small plane. Or racing an automobile or one of those speed boats they have. You know. Stuff like that."

"I can do that," Sid allowed.

"You're my hero," Jonah declared. "If I was a girl, I'd marry you!"

"Who said I'd ask you?"

"You would," Jonah said, and I had to admit, at that moment I probably would too: his confidence had been restored with work and steady sex, and he seemed better-looking, sleeker somehow. I knew that I would soon have to have a talk with Frances about taking him on as an assistant agent. She had too much to do now that Sue-Anne and I were in such high demand.

Late that night, Hank knocked on my room door, in his shorts and singlet, bare-footed, hair messed up, blanket under one arm, a pillow dangling from a hand.

"You don't mind?" he asked, groggily. "I can't sleep."

I gestured for him to come in. He zipped in and right into my bed, where he put himself under the sheets, a pillow under his head, blanket atop.

"Would you read to me, Chris? I'd like that a lot. Your voice is so calming."

Great! I had a gorgeous young guy in bed with me and all he wanted was a soporific!

"Move over, Seattle. How about some *Lawrence of Arabia*?"

"I don't care what," he said, and he was already yawning.

17

Finding the Scott-Grant house on Malibu wasn't too difficult. Unlike 2010, when houses there were four feet apart and formed an almost unbroken residential line from one end of the city at the ocean end near Sunset Blvd. to the other, some twenty-one miles up the coast beyond Point Dume, in 1935, the place was a lot more spottily built up.

The house was not even in the area already known as the Malibu Colony, favored by movie stars of the time as "weekend vacation spots." And, second surprise, it wasn't anything like the all-glass walls on the ocean and blank wooden walls otherwise, built-up-on-stilts style of architecture that would dominate down here on the sands later on. But instead it was a big Cape Cod, with a half second floor of balconied open rooms above the living room and dining room, and was complete with dormer windows, shutters, the New England cockerel weather vane: the works!

Nor was there a swimming pool tucked in between the house deck and sands. I mean, come on, people, you have the entire Pacific Ocean out there!

There was a little, mostly fenced-in, wooden back deck level to the sand—and a white picket fence to match the architectural style. And as the house was locked up, that's where I decided to wait.

I'd brought a book, Faulkner's totally over-the-top story of Temple Drake, a book I'd not read in forty-two years, not since a college course titled *Faulkner and the Southern Novel*. I'd also brought my MP3 player with its ear buds.

And my new 1935 bathing suit, which, while not a Speedo, was a lot smaller than the ugly, oversized board trunks most men sported in 2010, and thus wouldn't drag me down in the surf, although these days they wore their suits higher on the waist than I usually did. What's wrong with showing a little navel anyway? Everyone has one.

In fact, I'd been playing in the ocean almost until sunset—at 6:30 p.m., as it was now October and it was fairly warm, for the Pacific—and then I'd listened to an hour or so of a recording of a Jean-Baptiste Lully opera from a score not rediscovered until the turn of the twenty-first century. I'd also read pages and pages of Faulkner, whose descriptions of night were excellent, I thought.

As it got cooler, I covered up with my shirt and then with some old beach towels, lying on the beach chaise on the back terrace, and I'd at last fallen asleep.

Before that, however, I'd had a long enough time to just watch the sunset and think about what it was that I missed the most in being back in 1935, and what, if anything, compensated for it.

Oddly, food had turned out to be my biggest problem. I'd ended up going to the farmers' market for fresh fruit and produce several days a week. I'd also driven out to an almost brand-new shop in Venice Beach that had begun to specialize in "Health Food" in order to locate some of the food staples that I used to get regularly anywhere in 2010: yogurt, for example. Whole rolled oats, whole wheat in forms like bulgur and semolina and farina, not to mention brown rice. Nuts and seeds and beans like lentils and soya. Vitamins too. Various herbal teas. Forget tofu! I ultimately did end up finding some sold out of a giant can filled with tofu and water in colorful little Chinatown, across the corn field from downtown L.A. It looked freshly made, but how sanitary could it be? Fruit juices also were few and far between, except for the ubiquitous orange. Avocados, mangos, guavas, jicamas, and plantains were only found in a few rare Mexican food shops difficult to locate. As for dinners out, everyone who could afford to ordered steak. I ended up ordering fish and dictating exactly how many minutes and at exactly how high a temperature it ought to be cooked so I wouldn't get a piece of white or pink cardboard served on my plate. Doubtless, I developed a reputation among restaurateurs as a "problem patron" and "picky eater."

I'd gotten an early and unreliable sterno stove for my room, and all the other four had their fun with it, calling me "Doctor Zarkoff"—from *Flash Gordon*, then in movie theaters as a ten-part serial with the divine Buster Crabbe. None of them but Hank would even taste whatever I cooked on that. Sid called it my "wrist-radio-Sterno stove"—Yes, *Dick Tracy* comics were all the rage. The diner owner, Anderson, was more understanding, and he sometimes let me whip up something in his diner's kitchen, where Cookie had returned unchastened, and then had to humiliate himself by asking for my cornbread recipe, which breakfast patrons kept asking for.

To say that I missed computers and television and the Internet was completely true. But I'd known that would happen coming here.

One had to go out of one's house and into a theater to watch a movie. If you missed it locally, you had to go find a place where it was playing. Usually out in Monrovia or Pomona. There were no DVDs. There was no streaming video. To do the kind of research I could have done in a few hours via Yahoo and Google, I had to take my chances in the reference section of the L.A. Central Library.

Almost ditto with concert music or jazz. You would have to go to the Hollywood Bowl or the Wilshire-Ebell for classical and to the Wiltern Theatre or to the few jazz clubs that had started up on Central Avenue downtown for pop music, where it was live and cheap too. Big band stuff was popular, and all over town, but it was song-and-dance music and I had enough of that from work. Of course the radio—it was AM only, as Morgan had predicted—provided plenty of music, but again, you had to sit there to listen. I did enjoy Otto Klemperer conducting the L.A. Philharmonic and various guest conductors and soloists taking their shots with the Pasadena Civic Orchestra. Violinist Jascha Heifetz was at his height of fame, and pianist Artur Rubinstein too, and you could hear them playing. Also that anomaly Erwin Nyireghazi, once the European child prodigy who had apparently settled in L.A. somewhere, destined for a life of women, boozing, and being utterly forgotten—until he was in his eighties, when he was rediscovered briefly—and recorded, before dying. So I bought the best record player I could find, a German Braun, alas, sold in England and shipped to me with a His Master's Voice label pasted over it, and I played all my newly bought 78 rpm vinyl records.

Cars were beautiful, classically so, but mechanically…well, they didn't have power steering, windows, brakes, or power anything! Only the most expensive ones had easy-to-use ignitions and anything like easy steering. Once Jonah went to work full-time for Frances Wannamaker, on his way to becoming a talent agent himself, he bought the Willis-Knight sedan off me entirely. He needed it all the time.

My income ballooned considerably by movie number three, however, and I got myself a sporty new Ford Model B "Deuce" coupe, and then after a few months of being fatigued with all the manual handling required in driving that, I traded it in for an Auburn boattailed roadster, in cream and tan. That had a manual transmission too, but one that was as fluid as shaking a hand. It also had tight steering, powerful brakes, and a zero-to-sixty speed to take most other cars on the street.

I'd had a radio installed too, a rarity except in limousines, with a big whiplash antenna. That was what I'd driven in out to the beach house, with the rag top down, listening to the Dorseys.

In addition, I was sometimes at a complete loss for words when someone said something I didn't understand and realized I should have known or understood. But rather than make a fuss about it, I would usually shrug it off, or make a joke about it, and then just move on. I'm sure some folks thought I was faking it.

I never lost that sense of never quite being able to pick up people's signals. "Do you mean...?" I would have to ask. "Whaddya think I meant?" people would ask back, and I'd say, "Let's not go there." "Go where?" "Wherever that question will lead us," I'd have to respond. By which time they were pretty well confused. Talk in 1935 was for the most part grounded and specific, not metaphorically high flying, allusive and abstract as even the lightest chatter would become later. I sometimes longed for the latter and had set my cap on connecting with a few of the intellectuals of my time and place: Aldous Huxley, Christopher Isherwood, Franz Werfel, and Arnold Schoenberg all lived in Los Angeles, and I knew I had to meet them.

Where I ended up being the most improvisational was in trying to work within my sexuality without causing too much of a stir: a big deal for someone who'd been out from the age of twenty-two, which by 2010 was forty-three years. By contrast, Billy Haines's career—and his wasn't the only one—was a clear case of what could and what would happen if you didn't publicly play the heterosexual game in 1935. But my life in that quarter almost seemed set up from the beginning: Sue-Anne and Hank moved very slowly together and never in public unless I was there too. She seemed to need me as cover of her real intent as much as I was using her as a "beard." People expected us to be together in public, anyway: I wondered if anyone actually saw Hank was there too. That was a dual role that the two of us could play for several more years, before anyone noticed the ubiquitous other guy.

All that was fine, and having a few carefully selected (mostly older) people know I was interested in other men seemed to be fine too, since everyone in the movie business was very quiet about that. But at least among my growing set of I guess you'd have to call them older, successful men, there wasn't that secret and closeted life that as a youth in the 1960s I had first entered into and then watched dissipate and then vanish in the harsh glare of us coming out with Gay Liberation. No, it seemed that level of closeted-ness would only come later on, after the Second World War, and probably partly as a result of gay servicemen fraternizing and needing instantaneous code words and euphemisms. After all, they would have so little time to get to know each other for a one- or two-night hook-up before they were shipped off to another theater of war and possibly death.

With Randolph Scott, I openly flirted and he'd openly flirted back. Based on what I'd seen at the Haines/Shields party the one time I went—Rafferty never let me go again—that was pretty much how it was done, and nobody really seemed to notice or care. Pops had warned me not to be surprised at any gay action I came upon in the Alsop House showers and johns, but either it wasn't there or I just missed it every time I stepped in the door. Did Hank rub up against me sensually in his sleep? Absolutely, and I let him. Were Ducky and Sid doing stuff together in their bed they didn't talk about? I'm guessing yes, since neither of them took a single room when one came available. Did anyone care? Not that I was aware of.

Women who easily had sex with men were sluts or rubber-heeled (falling backward easily) or at best called "divorcees." With that kind of a double standard going on, they were hardly in a position to call a man a queer if he didn't sleep with them. And no adult female would think of approaching a man of my apparent age of eighteen. They wouldn't dream of it, no matter how available they were. This despite the rumors going around of at least one male "child star" who was known to passionately go after older women stars. Was there a male-on-male casting couch in Hollywood at this time? Sure. For example, everyone seemed to know about Howard Hughes's residence hotels for good-looking younger actors on Fountain Avenue in West Hollywood; but so what? He was an eccentric millionaire! And didn't he also have one on De Longpre for good-looking younger actresses?

Only those busybodies who'd formulated the recent Code of Decency in Movies seemed to care, and they were easily blackmailable for other reasons.

As for other changes coming back here? Morgan had said it would be quieter in '35. It was. With only a few thousand cars and trucks plying the roads, the air was a lot fresher. I'd expected both of those. Smog wouldn't arrive until after the Second World War, with increased automobile production and sales. In this era I'd found myself in, public transportation via streetcars ruled L.A., and it was predominantly clean-fuel electric.

What I hadn't really counted on was how much simpler people were. For every shark like Rafferty, there were thousands of people who would never even suspect the kind of games he played or who understood his internecine politics. At least in America. True, a bunch of Germans had left their own country and come to Southern California, writers, actors, theater people, musicians. But they tended to hang out with each other and it would be years before they allowed others to know exactly what they had left back there—partly out of shame, just pure shame!

That bothered me. Sure, it would keep Americans out of World War II until more horrors had happened in Europe and Asia, but then it would mean more drastic measures would be needed to end both wars.

So the simplicity was something I hadn't quite counted on; how naïve pretty much everyone was about motives and scheming and how really bad other humans could be to each other and were actually being to each every day in faraway China and Germany.

As for setting my guns on Randolph Scott, hell, as I said before, he'd been one of my early idols in the movies, along with another drop-dead handsome star of questionable sexuality—Alan Ladd.

What I'd known of Scott as a fan and what I'd strongly suspected were closely related. He'd been a college football star and then his wealthy Carolinian father had made a connection to Howard Hughes and Hughes had brought Scott to L.A. in 1929, put him up in one of his residence hotels on Fountain Avenue, and groomed him for the pictures, getting him bits in various movies.

If that wasn't suspicious enough, the facts also said that Scott married Marion Dupont in 1936 when he was thirty-eight years old, but then she moved East and he and Grant lived together on the beach for over four years, until Dupont eventually divorced Scott. When Scott remarried after World War II, in 1944, it was to his agent/manager Patricia, and he was already forty-seven, long in the tooth for a Hollywood matinee idol, and to add to the ambiguity further, the couple adopted two boys but never had children of their own.

One could easily read both of Scott's unions as "lavender marriages," typical of the time. The agent/manager would be "safe."

Scott wouldn't even have to sleep with her. We knew the kids weren't biologically his.

But what had convinced me to go after Scott was what had happened to him in later life. He'd become a star in 1935 first with *Roberta*, and then with *She*, based on the H. Rider Haggard book, and originally intended as a vehicle for the shapely if stiff Helen Gahagen. In 1936, Scott had gone on to play the most gorgeous of all Deerslayers in *The Last of the Mohicans*. In 1938, alongside Shirley Temple he'd done *Rebecca of Sunnybrook Farm*. 1939 saw him in *Jesse James*; 1940, in another Western, *Virginia City*; and then in 1942, he had opposed John Wayne for Marlene Dietrich's attentions in *Pittsburgh*.

He'd had seven solid years of big box office, and while Scott was forty-five, and thus too old to enlist in the armed forces by the time Pearl Harbor came around, he did work with the U.S.O. and even worked with a few film units in the European Theater before returning home to make more Hollywood movies.

After that, while his body still looked great, Scott's face began to change: he was no longer the sunny, open, handsome Southerner, but instead he'd become gaunt and haggard-looking, distinctly older than his real age, almost a character actor. He had not seen action in the war, unlike, say, Tyrone Powers, who had been totally freaked out by it—so that couldn't be the cause.

No, more than likely, it was the choices that Scott had made in life—playing the hetero game, making the lavender marriages—that he realized too late also came with a price to pay at the end. He looked haunted and maybe he was: by his choices, now seen as mistakes that he could no longer go back and change.

Everyone had noted it by 2010, fans, biographers, admirers, and critics alike. It was what made some of those later films where Scott played the role of a once-promising loser and now a bitter criminal so believable and so devastating: in *Ride the High Country*, for example. Jimmy Stewart and Bill Holden would have to work at being a villains later in their careers. Not Randolph Scott: he was instantly credible.

Scott had also become a real estate speculator and was worth hundreds of millions of dollars by the time he died. He'd become conservative politically, one of the biggest and earliest donors to his sometime buddy Ronald Reagan's bid for the governorship of California, and then, later on part of his core support group for the presidency.

When he died at eighty-nine, it might have seemed to Scott that he'd had taken the worst possible road and made the worst possible choices in his life.

And I felt that it was up to me, newly placed in 1935, to get him back on the right path. My duty and my right too.

It was that sense of purpose and the fresh air and the cuddly beach towels that got me to sleep.

When I woke up, it was because Randolph Scott's big face was leaning down into mine and saying, "C'mon, kid! Wake up."

I did and pretended I couldn't.

"You can't stay out here all night," he argued. "You'll catch cold or something."

So I let him lift me up and take me indoors, and as he put me into a bed he began to put a blanket over me. But once there, I grabbed him. I'm guessing that at that moment I looked totally adorable, hair all tousled, salt-tinged skin, mostly unclothed, half-asleep.

Meanwhile he looked like a big golden cat, and after all I was big game hunting.

"I happen to know that despite your roles, you are completely legal," Scott said, possibly asking me to deny the fact.

I wanted to reply that I was old enough to be his father and I knew exactly what I was doing.

By then I had his shirt opened and all that golden chest hair to play with. So instead I asked: "Are we going to talk all night? Or are we going to give this beach shack's reputation something to live up to?"

18

Coffee had been served all around Louis B.'s office, and once the secretary had left the big room, everyone looked at the floor and then at Mayer. I knew several of the others were nervous and desperately wanted to smoke cigarettes. Their hands kept going to their pockets, then remembering that he wouldn't allow it, they moved away again, fingers empty. Mayer kept a cigar going on his desk ashtray but he seldom puffed on it, and only out an open window.

Finally Mayer asked, "Did everyone read the script?"

The script in question being one I'd penned myself under the pseudonym Blaine Anthony that I'd been using, but the script was unlike anything that I or anyone else had ever done before, titled *American Boys*.

It was a warm April afternoon in 1936, a full year after I'd arrived back in Hollywood again. Santa Ana winds had been predicted but only arrived late and at half-force. I, however, was a much stronger force, and without a doubt one to be reckoned with at the studio, having established a youth market for the Lion, solidified my and Sue-Ann Schiller's joint stardom, and then produced very healthy box-office grosses for our six youth movies, the last of which had just opened to the best opening take of any of them. Slowly but surely, I'd taken on as much control as I could of the movies as one succeeded (in all ways) the previous one. First with the dialogue, then with providing stories, then writing the entire scripts, and even moving on to casting. As our names and reputations rose in the still quite little industry, as my box office increased, so had my grasp, which was more important to me than the money I was earning. These days, Rafferty, Seiter, and I were a team. I was an equal among equals inside the offices, and other executives who'd ignored me before now called me by name and greeted me. Rafferty had even recently reported that Mayer was overheard at an industry party boasting about his two *wunderkinds:* Irving Thalberg and Christopher Hall.

Copies of my script sat all around the room, several on Mayer's desk, others upon coffee tables, a few on people's laps. None were being held closely—which I took as a bad sign: they were distancing themselves from it.

There was a general murmur among the others. The director I'd been working with for all of my movies so far, William Seiter, even touched his script, as though acknowledging its existence. My usual producer at MGM, Thom Rafferty, tapped his script three times with stiff fingertips.

"Well, I read it," Goldwyn answered, as though daring the others. "Anyone else?"

"I read it," Thom Rafferty said. "It's…very, very sad, Christopher, what it says about…this country…and all," he trailed off, afraid to speak up.

"It's all completely accurate," I defended. "Taken from life. Based on interviews with twenty-five boys and young men that were arranged for me by various physicians, thanks to Dr. Weissman, here at the studio."

"And then, after I read it," Rafferty added, "I couldn't get to sleep until four a.m."

"And of course I have to mention," I paused, "that a few of the scenes are based upon what I myself witnessed and experienced as a youngster. But some of you may have already known that."

Rafferty and Seiter acknowledged with mumbling that they heard something.

No one else spoke for a while and then Mayer burst out, "My wife read it before I got a chance to. She was intrigued by the title, she said, and she just grabbed it off the pile on my desk. She was in hysterics afterward. Crying for hours. I had to call in a doctor to sedate her."

"I'm sorry to hear that, Mr. Mayer. But the truth is, I sugarcoated everything."

"Sugarcoated it?"

"It made me cry, Christopher. Me? 'Rhinestone Willy'!" Seiter said, using the nickname people at the studio had given him for directing any film for money. "The last thing I read that made me cry, I was six years old. Six!"

"Does young Sammy have to die…?" Rafferty began.

I quickly answered, "Yes. Boys out there on the road died."

"I was going to say, quite so horribly?" Rafferty asked.

"They died more horribly than that," I said. "What's important is that our hero Joe lives. He makes it all across the country and here to Los Angeles," I added, by way of amelioration. "He makes it to the Wonder City of the West."

"You didn't give it to Sue-Anne to read?" Louis B. asked, suddenly concerned.

"I did, Mr. Mayer. She reads all of my scripts. I want her opinion."

"I dread to think what that poor girl thought," he said, shaking his head.

"Well, Mr. Mayer, you know that Sue-Ann was also kicking around a bit on her own. Actually, she thought it was my best script ever, her exact words. And she also thought that if I got anyone else to play Lois, you remember her, the young woman who helps the boys at her own cost? Well, Sue-Ann said she'd never speak to me again."

"That role will ruin her career," Rafferty said.

"Her career as a teenage star, yes. She's aware of that."

The look of consternation on the other's faces was obvious: was this the death of a franchise?

"She made me promise to not offer the role to anyone else. Of course, *I'll* play Joe," I added. "And," to Mayer and Goldwyn, I added, pointedly, "naturally, I'll defer my salary as screenwriter and actor until the film opens and earns it back."

No one had ever said that to Louis B. Mayer before and he gawked at me, simply sat there open-mouthed.

"Wannamaker and Wolff will contact you with the details of what we're asking to be deferred," I added.

"It won't be cheap to make," one of the other suits in the room said. An accountant named Wilberson, who had signed off on the increasing expense of the Schiller and Hall movies. "It's got locations. It's got a big cast. Costumes. Vehicles. It'll be double the budget of the last two."

"I'll be exec producer on it," Rafferty surprised me by saying. "If we make a realistic cost-out, I'll bring it in within budget."

A shark with a heart? Or just very canny?

Goldwyn now turned to Seiter. "You wouldn't want to direct this, Will? Would you? It really doesn't seem your kind of thing."

"No, it isn't. Not really. It really is Christopher's project. But I'm willing to try my hand on something different. For the first time, as I read the script I was suddenly seeing scene set-ups, two-shots, even some lighting cues. If you want, I would do all the expensive stuff in the movie. Then Christopher and I can work out the more intimate scenes together."

"Really, Will?" Mayer asked, surprised.

"Really, L.B. In an ideal world, George probably would direct it. Or Victor Fleming. Couldn't you talk to one of them about it? What are they doing, anyway?"

"Fleming's up to his ears with projects and Cukor's over in Liverpool shooting exteriors for that film with Hepburn and Brian Aherne."

"*Camille*? I thought that was Garbo and Taylor?"

"It is. And that's another one Cukor is signed up for." Turning to Wilberson, "What is it, Walter? That's right, *Sylvia Scarlett*!" Then to Thalberg, who'd snuck into the room, unobserved until then, "Irv, what's the status on *Romeo and Juliet*?"

"It's in post-production, L.B. It looks great!"

"And Rathbone worked out?"

"He's great. Norma, of course, will carry it!"

"Sure, she will, Irv." A pause and then Mayer turned to me: "Is that what you want, too, Christopher? Co-directing? On top of everything else?" he asked. "Wouldn't you rather wait for Cukor? He'll be done with everything by the middle of '37."

"Mr. Mayer. I think the time for this movie is now. So we can get it out at the end of the year. The choice of Will as director is fine with me. We proved that we work together well. But as he said, I'd really like to be there for every scene."

"By the way, Chris," Goldwyn asked, "is that a dolly shot? You know, when the boys begin jumping out of the darkness at the moving train? Is that a *four-minute dolly shot*?"

"Three minutes and ten seconds. For two hundred and twenty feet," I said. Letting him know I'd done the technical preparation too. "It will be twenty-six boys jumping for the train. Jumping for their lives, really! It could look amazing at thirty feet high on a movie screen."

Louis B. stood up and faced the window. We all waited.

He began mumbling and the rest of the room was quiet enough that I heard some of it.

When he turned to face us, I thought for sure *American Boys* was dead.

"I'm a Republican. Damn it. I'd have to be completely out of my mind to approve this picture."

"Then why do it?" the nervous Wilberson asked.

"Because my wife'll never let me into the house again if I don't."

❖

American Boys opened in early December 1936. We had targeted the same audiences that had come to the six previous Schiller and Hall movies by handing out at those shows advance theater cards for the new movie. We showed lengthy coming attractions to them, with just enough footage of what the film was really going to be about to make an impression.

We then checked our "impression cards" at the end of that week of coming attractions, asking what they thought of this new movie they had not yet seen. The kids' comments were extremely favorable. *At last, the real deal!* someone had written. *I'll go if it kills me* a girl had neatly printed.

Finally, by Halloween, we had most of the film shot and put together and Rafferty said it was now or never: we had to have an MGM executives-only showing.

The rushes had been powerful as they'd come in and the first full edit was, as I had hopefully predicted, amazing, even without all of the music. The scene with all the boys suddenly coming out of hiding and leaping into the open boxcars as the train takes off, leaping from darkness and into almost bleached-out light while Joe fights off the railroad yard guards to distract them, was gorgeous, and it packed a real punch.

I had talked Sid Devlin into playing Sammy as the wisecracking, over-mature young man he actually was, and I'd annoyed and harassed him personally before each of his scenes. As a result, Sid had come across onscreen at his prickliest and most entertaining. But even to me, not to mention to all who knew the script, the death of his character in the last fifteen minutes of the movie came as an unexpectedly emotional surprise. It provided the sense of personal loss that I hoped every audience member would also experience.

We shot Sue-Anne like an Angel of Mercy, and her murder was equally horrifying; she was left lying in the barn like a discarded doll, like a Christ without his cross, sunlight burning down through the open hayloft.

The other boys' safe but filthy and bedraggled arrival into a transcendental Pacific Coast sunrise was done in extreme close-up, hair and shoulders cropped close to concentrate on their faces in harsh light. We slowly panned each individual face, so they resembled a gallery of portraits you would never forget.

Joe's last speech to them, almost a minute long, set against the newly built Broadway bridge from Chinatown over Sunset Blvd. and then into downtown L.A., sounded to me like a sermon and a rallying cry combined. Seiter had backed me on its length at this late place in the story and he'd outdone himself with every angle and every shot. In an interview later on, he would say that until this production, he'd merely been "moving people around a set," but that having to deal with all of the challenges of *American Boys* had turned him into a movie director.

All sixteen of us at the executives screening filed out of the studio room after the film without saying a word.

Outside everyone lighted cigarettes and pipes. I chewed gum. No one said a word for a long time.

Then Goldwyn turned to me: "I'll say this for you, Christopher, and you, Seiter, and Rafferty, too: You're not in the junior league anymore."

"I think we've got a monster hit!" Seiter said, enthused.

"*Frankenstein* and *King Kong* were monster hits," Goldwyn assured him. "This could just as easily be a monster, period."

Despite that sobering estimate he managed to convince Mayer to open the film as big as possible, with every bit they could harness of studio support. That of course told me that they wanted me to remain a featured actor under contract no matter what happened to what I believe they considered an "experiment" of mine.

At the premiere at the Carthay Circle Theatre several weeks later, everyone was dolled up and sparkling, no one more than Sue-Anne and me.

We arrived last, in a gigantic, two-toned Pierce Arrow Brougham limousine, dressed in the highest of formal wear. She wore her hair up, signaling that her youth was over, as well as a diamond choker and a white ermine chubby. I wore a shiny ebony tuxedo with lapels sharp enough to maim, and white tie: my accessories were eighteen karat gold, signaling I was grown-up and successful. All of what would later be called "re-imaging" of us former teen stars was Frances Wannamaker and Thom Rafferty's idea (with a little help from me), and the actual costuming and accessorization took two days to complete.

Everyone came to meet us, from Louella and Hedda to George Burns and Jack Benny. On the red carpet in front of hundreds, we spoke into giant radio mikes and it was neat, a lot of fun. There had been no previous audience full-film screenings and so there was only an indication of what we were going to see. Some word had leaked out of the studio that this film would be different and superior to the usual Schiller and Hall picture, but that too had been carefully controlled, and just enough had been leaked to titillate the gossip mavens, who fell beautifully into line. Louella asked Sue-Ann, "Don't you think that after this movie screens you'll be compared to Virginia Grey and Paulette Godard now?" And to me, "Rumor has it, Christopher, that now that they've lost the late and great Irving Thalberg, the Lion's top brass believe you might be able to take over some of his projects at the studio." All of which we very graciously denied.

Several other MGM actors of the day (the studio's motto was "More Stars Than There Are in Heaven") had already arrived, including the young Eleanor Powell and Spencer Tracy and the older favorites Edmund Gwenn and W.C. Fields. They welcomed us warmly in a special section of the lounge as we entered. Expectation misted the air.

Once everyone had found their assigned seats, Sue-Anne got up in front of the crowd before the lights went down and before the movie would begin.

First, she explained that there would be no cartoons or coming attractions or shorts at this showing, which earned her restrained boos. Undaunted, she read my little introductory speech.

"Seven years of the worst depression in modern times has broken families, torn children from their parents, ripped apart homes and dreams, and ended promising lives. It has also left a large unformed army of children wandering the great American land, from cities and villages to deserts and swamps, and across mountain passes. Hungry, ill, abandoned and in need, innocent prey to every wrong that is possible in human life. This is the story of several of them. This is *American Boys*."

Ten minutes into the film, I got so nervous I had to leave my seat.

Even that wasn't enough to calm me down, and I left the theater altogether.

I wandered among all the parked limousines, chatting with the drivers. I was far too nervous to think about what was going on inside that hall where nine hundred people were experiencing the first piece of art I had made here and now, back in time.

I knew the film was good, I knew it was true. I also knew I had pandered to the taste of the time somewhat by making my boys heroic and their persecutors diabolical. And I also wondered if Sammy's death would be viewed by later times as sentimental mawkishness.

And then, just as suddenly, I knew the entire thing was a disaster. It had to be. No one could accept this vision of America.

I'd been a fool, a fool filled with hubris yet, to even begin it. What had possessed me to think anyone could care? That anyone would want to share this horror? My career was over. My new name was eternally besmirched. My new life was over only a year and a half after it had begun. Where could I hide? How could I get away? Maybe, if I turned and walked calmly, the opposite of what I actually felt, up San Vicente all the way up to Wilshire Blvd....? All those empty nighttime streets! I could see the newly installed tall lights on Wilshire from here, and I could calmly remove my white tie as I went along and I could mess up my sleeked and pomaded hair and then take off my tux jacket, and maybe toss it casually over one shoulder, and maybe, just maybe I could pass for anyone else coming out of one of the two or three theaters located up there.

Who would think to stop me? There was enough traffic there at night that I could find a cab and pay to get me the hell out of town as far as my money would go. How much cash did I have with me, anyway? $100, $110? How far could that get me? To a train station and then maybe up to San Francisco and beyond. Why stop there? Why not Chicago? New York, even!? I began walking away.

"Mr. Hall! Mr. Hall!"

I turned, about to say, you've got the wrong guy, buddy. Lay off. Leave me alone.

It was Wilberson, the accountant for our movie from MGM. He looked confused.

"Where are you going? The theater's this way."

He circled a fleshy arm around my shoulders and turned me around and firmly walked me into the outside circle of the theater where news and magazine photographers had huddled, and where a spate of flashbulbs suddenly went off all at once, photographing me, and thus confirming my last moments of any remaining grace or style or dignity. Then another Suit found us and together the two of them all but dragged me into the theater lobby.

Not a soul could be seen. Where was all the theater staff?

The two all but dragged me over to the porthole-windowed double doors that led from the lobby into the orchestra section of the theater, and at last I understood that I could not escape, that I must in fact undergo an utter public humiliation.

They each opened one of those double doors into darkness and flickering light from the screen. The ushers and all the rest of the theater staff were there, popcorn and soda sellers hidden by the doors under the overhanging loge, closely packed into the upper aisle, all watching the movie.

It was the last frames: Joe on that bridge, with the sunrise behind him, as he looked up, a sun-drenched statue in Seiter's bleached-out, almost Graeco-Roman photography, defying the black universe as Joe had come to know it.

The music rose and rose, and then Joe turned away, and he walked along that bridge and into the big city just coming to life at morning, and he became smaller and darker and darker and smaller until he was gone.

The End came up on the screen.

"Oh God! It can't end *yet!*" one chubby candy counter cashier cried out, and then shushed herself with a hand over her mouth.

There was silence, silence, and then from above us, from the huge balcony above where all the young people, our audience, all of our Schiller and Hall kids, had been seated, all those loyal followers of all those decreasingly frothy six movies, began a rumble that slowly grew, turning into thunder, and I realized that they were stamping their feet.

The accountants shoved me forward into the auditorium's totally exposed central aisle as the credits rolled and rolled and the house lights began to come up.

I turned around and looked up at the young people, and they were standing and stamping their feet in the otherwise utter silence of the huge theater. They sounded and, even more so, they resembled soldiers on the march.

One girl pointed down at where I was, and she called out: "There he is! *That's* Christopher Hall!" and the teenagers on that big balcony exploded into foot-stomping applause and screaming, hanging over the railings, snapping photos with Brownie cameras of what must have looked like a completely astonished me. Suddenly, the rest of the seemingly hypnotized audience around me stood up and began to applaud.

I could see MGM people dashing up the aisles, speaking excitedly to each other, while gossip columnists and known reviewers for the papers and magazines and radio stations charged up the aisles behind them, men and women both blowing their noses and drying their eyes as they stumbled around and past me, not even seeing me.

Sid Devlin found me. He was almost unrecognizable with his slicked-down ginger hair and dressed in his tuxedo. He grabbed me by the shoulders and he screeched, "I was good, wasn't I, Junior? I was good up there! Geez! Who'da believed it!"

Suddenly it seemed like everyone I'd ever met surrounded me, congratulating me, shaking my hand, kissing me, and after that I remember nothing at all that happened for the next fourteen hours.

❖

The Academy Awards were held that year at the "Biltmore Bowl" in the downtown Biltmore Hotel. The nominations had been announced the last day of December and the winners announced at the end of January and we met to celebrate on March 4, 1937.

Luise Rainer won featured actress role for *The Great Ziegfield*, and Paul Muni for featured actor role in *The Story of Louis Pasteur*, but Sue-Anne Schiller edged out Gale Sondergaard's misbehaving society girl in *Anthony Adverse* and Sid Devlin slipped past the previous favorite, Basil Rathbone, in Cukor's *Romeo & Juliet* to take a supporting actor Oscar. Among the total of twenty-four awards available that year, *American Boys* swept best picture, best original script, best cinematography, best director, and best assistant director (me). Its total of seven awards, a ten-year high, edged out a pretty good field of movies that year, consisting of *The Great Ziegfield*, *Romeo & Juliet*, *San Francisco*, *A Tale of Two Cities*, *Mr. Deeds Goes to Town*, *The Charge of the Light Brigade*, and *The Story of Louis Pasteur.* Among the most interesting awards that year were those for assistant director, three short film awards including one for color short, and the Oscar for dance direction, given on alternate years to Busby Berkeley and Hermes Pan. Why was that one ever dropped?

So the only suspense was halfway through the convivial and increasingly alcohol-fueled awards celebration evening at the Biltmore among five hundred people, when the screenwriter Blaine Anthony was announced to come get his award for writing the screenplay to *American Boys* up on the little dais.

No one, no one…then l stood up and went onstage.

I could hear Roz Russell saying to Spring Byington as I passed their table, "What a nice boy! He's getting it for the writer."

So when the cursory applause died down and they were all expecting the speech explaining that Blaine Anthony wasn't there and I was accepting it for him, I amazed them all by saying quite distinctly, "I thank the members of the Academy and all who voted for *American Boys*. I am Blaine Anthony."

That was the second example of thunderous applause I received, although from only half of the people who'd been at the premiere.

19

The restaurant that Larry Allegre and I finally met at for dinner was located in Santa Monica Canyon, where the Pacific Coast Highway met Channel Road, a seafood restaurant, naturally, being right at the ocean's edge. It hadn't been there in 2010, long replaced by a gas station.

Larry Allegre had set dinner for nine p.m., late for this place, and it emptied out completely during our meal until we, one waiter, and the manager were the only people in the place by the time the entrées arrived.

I recognized Larry's two-toned Chevy Six coupe from our first (and until now, only) meeting. Even though I was staying just up the road, I was a little late, and drove up and parked right next to it in my Auburn boattailed roadster.

In 2010, the few examples of that model Auburn still around would cost a quarter of a million dollars if any came up for auction. I'd gotten mine new for a cool $2250, f.o.b.—exactly my new bi-weekly salary at MGM. I planned to hold on to that car and to add a Cord Sedan, then a 1940 Packard Super 8 Convertible, and then more... I thought vintage autos could become another casually profitable collectible area for later life.

Allegre was in a booth by the window and he waved at me. He looked exactly the same as before, with the curved-down hat brim and everything, although his overcoat was off and he was in a dark suit jacket.

He'd ordered a beer and I ordered lemonade.

The waiter called me "Mr. Hall, sir."

After we'd clinked glasses, Allegre said, "The soft-shell crab here is pretty decent. The fish and chips too."

I ordered both entrees, explaining that I was "still a growing boy."

"I'm not going to embarrass us both," Allegre said, "by asking how your stay in Los Angeles has been, Christopher. Also, it's extremely evident that you sensibly failed to take my friendly advice and not go into the pictures."

"Don't tell me you've seen any of the monstrosities?" I asked.

"One doesn't have to actually see them to be *aware* of them, you must know," he riposted. "But of course I saw *American Boys*. Everyone has, no? Everyone in America?"

"And England, and France, and Mexico and Japan and…"

"As I said, you're all over the place in one way or another. You are almost ostentatiously present, one might say," he concluded.

"While you, Mr. Allegre, are just the opposite, not to mention strangely difficult to get hold of," I replied. "It's been quite a while."

"I'm a jobber. I travel…" Allegre began.

"Sure, you do," I said.

"Do I detect a wisp of disbelief? Why? Just because you can't reach me?"

"That," pointing to bits of fog coming across the Pacific Coast Highway toward our window, "is a *wisp*," I explained. "I'm talking about something a little more…substantial."

He was amused. "Meaning…?"

"Meaning that there is such a thing as a private detective that one can hire, Mr. Allegre. You've heard of that profession, I take it? After all, half of RKO and Republic Pictures movies in the past year have utilized them as protagonists, I believe."

"You hired a detective to find me?" he asked, unable to hide his surprise.

"I'm a well-off man, Mr. Allegre. I hired *two* detectives."

"Why would you do a thing like that?" he asked, sipping his beer out of a glorious old side-handled Stein.

"Well, because you were so hard to find. At first."

"At first…?" he said. "And at second?"

"At second, because your flat in the Alcott Arms appeared to be unlived in for weeks at a time, and then suddenly there you would be, living in it, with no one ever figuring out how you came and went. Since you aren't the Invisible Man. Or are you, Mr. Allegre?"

When he didn't answer, I went on, "No, you aren't, since that is a fictional work by H.G. Wells and a successful James Whale movie of a few years ago. And thirdly, because no one, including your telephone secretary, knew how to reach you. Not ever."

"I'm a jobber. I travel."

"He explained unpersuasively," I commented aloud. "Since I happen to know that your little coupe there," pointing to it, outside the window, "which you said you used while traveling, instead tended to go into storage inside a garage on Sixth Street, off Harvard Avenue, with a canvas cover over it, whenever you were not at your flat and whenever you couldn't be reached by telephone or telegraph."

"Leading your detectives and yourself to conclude?" Larry asked, now quite amused.

"Well, you completely befuddled them, I'll admit that. After several months of watching you as closely as he could, the smarter of the two actually said to me, and here you won't mind my imitation, 'He's gotta vanish into thin air, Mr. Hall. Thin air!'"

"I see."

"But, Mr. Allegre...that's not your real name, is it? I happen to myself and quite personally know of a way in which someone *can* suddenly appear out of thin air and into Los Angeles of, what's the date now, February sixth, 1938?"

"Indeed, and you know this how?"

"Because I did appear here suddenly myself, Mr. Allegre. On April twelfth, 1935."

"That's right, on a corner of Laurel Canyon and what was it? Sunset Boulevard," he said, not taking the bait I'd thrown him.

I ignored that. "And the longer I'm here...in Los Angeles," I qualified, "the more I feel that you already knew that particular fact. And also that you yourself are not from...*here*...either."

He laughed. "Keep in mind, Christopher, that it was *I* who thought *you* seemed lost the minute I saw you. But then again, look how wrong I was about your arrival here. Why, I never encountered a young fellow who fit so perfectly into a new..." He settled for the word "town!"

Our appetizers arrived. Shrimp cocktail: giant Pacific shrimp, luscious and pink. He looked at his the way I suspect a child molester looks at a six-year-old pageant beauty.

"And now what?" Allegre said, for the waiter to hear. "You'll be acting in more movies?"

"Acting in more of them. Writing more of them. Co-directing them. Louis B. said my instincts are so good, he wouldn't be surprised if I began *producing* them before too long."

"Nor I. Well then, I couldn't have been more wrong in my advice to you back then, could I?" he said as he attacked the shrimp ruthlessly.

The waiter was gone.

"Now that I think on it," I said, "it was *you* who brought me to the Alsop House. Wasn't it?"

"It was. But remember, Christopher, I wanted to take you to Father Flint's church. Or was it the YMCA? You wouldn't go to the first and we couldn't get in the second because of the hour."

"And it was at the Alsop House," I continued, undaunted, "that I fell in with my bedmate Hank and his three pals, all nice guys, talented guys in their own right, and they were all unemployed and working as movie extras. Trying to break into the pictures."

"Your point being?" Allegre asked.

"They're not unemployed now, are they?" I asked. "No, they're all working. In fact, now that I think about it, it was me that got them all jobs."

"Well, then lucky for your friends that you came along! It seems as though I inadvertently did all of you all a great big favor that night. Here's to me! Wonderful me! So...tell me again...what exactly is the nature of your problem with me, Christopher?"

Red sauce mixed with clam juice shamelessly stained his chin, which he was imperfectly cleaning. He seemed to be eyeing my appetizer, barely touched so far, and I pushed it toward him to finish it off. And I swore he was going to add, "And that's not your real name, either, is it?"

"Bear with me a minute longer," I went on. "Okay, so I went with them the next morning after I arrived in...town here...went with them to be an *extra* too, and there I was pulled out because I was too young. But then, somehow, I ended up with Sue-Anne and at MGM being a *player* and eventually a *featured* player...The rest is history," I trailed off, having lost my precise train of thought.

He was looking at me in an odd way.

So odd that I suddenly said, "Tell me, Mr. Allegre, where *do* you go when you aren't around your office?"

"Oh, all around. I'm a jewelry jobber, you know. All around Southern California."

"Right. But we've established that you don't take your car. The reason I ask is that I'm all of sudden thinking how *all of that* happened a little too neatly. Very quickly too. As though it was a...as though it was some kind of *set-up* that only needed someone to fill it."

"Well, Christopher, if you believe that, then here's where I ask for your money or your life." He sipped. "Actually, I'd settle for that Auburn I saw you drive up in. Gosh, that is a honey!"

His attempt to change the subject fell astray, however. Because his last statement was so of the time and place that it sounded all wrong to me. As wrong as I often sounded to myself at times: a stranger in this time and place using language of the time that didn't somehow belong to me.

And now I was furiously thinking as our salads arrived—ghastly things, a wedge of iceberg lettuce, a few sliced cucumbers and sliced tomatoes with a gunk of a white dressing, one step beyond mayonnaise.

Once the waiter was gone again and I could see the booths on either side of us were empty, leaving only a seascape studded wall as company.

So I decided to go for it. "Tell me something, Mr. Allegre. You wouldn't happen to have one of those little three-dimensional, hand-sized screens that connect to the National Mint in Denver that Mr. Morgan once showed me, would you?"

I thought for a moment he was going to ignore my words or ask what I was talking about.

Instead he said, "Oh, dear, are we going to have *that* conversation already! As a rule it takes three or four meetings before it comes up. Well, Christopher, since you ask, what I have is not *exactly* what you described."

He looked around and then, holding a tall menu up next to his hand, he opened up the crystal on his Bulova wristwatch and handed me a tiny plastic thing resembling a wireless speaker bud that I could see fit into an ear.

"On!" he said, and the watch immediately projected a hologram maybe six inches high off the watch lens, first of Mr. Morgan, my uphill neighbor from 2010, along with Ralf, waving and saying "Hello," and then of a woman about the same advanced age, who said, "Hello, Mr. Hall. We're all *extremely* pleased with you and with your progress."

Allegre kept checking that no one could see what I was seeing. But the place was empty.

"My progress?" I asked in a low voice. Then, "And you are who?"

"My name's unimportant. I'm the International Minister of Other Times, of course. We cannot converse too long. We do have your best interests at heart, Mr. Hall. But also our own interests and our own situation."

Whatever that meant. "I'll just bet."

"And that situation is very dire indeed. Please listen to Allegre. Everything we wish for you to do there is moral, it's legal, and it's good for you personally *and* professionally. That's the truth and it is all really that I can say. What's the appropriate sign-off?" She turned half-away and seemed to be asking someone off screen. "Oh, yes, that's right!" And to me, she said, "Good-bye now."

The watch was normal once again, the ear bud was silent. I handed them back to him, he put down the menu, and we finished our salads.

The soft-shell crab and fish and chips arrived and I dug in. Allegre had a tuna steak, rare—"I've heard so much about tuna. None around for us, of course. Or if there is, too difficult to get to. So many nice things gone."

"Gone from 2061, you mean?"

"No. That was Morgana's time. Ours, the Minister's and mine, is ahead several hundred years from that."

"The future time of a 'dire situation,' she said," I clarified.

"Yes. Believe me. I'm here *and now* as often as I can be—or at least, *not there and then* as often as I can be."

"Go on," I prodded.

"One reason is because I'm one of the healthiest people alive.

Most would look like cripples or appear deformed today." He removed his hat, and he was completely bald. Odd in one so relatively young.

"Solar radiation is mostly to blame, unstopped now by any thick atmosphere or by magnetic fields. Those shifted several times and then seem to have shifted away altogether. All of North America, by the way, now consists of four completely partly underground, domed cities. One is approximately here in Southern California, although inland a great deal, and not far from your town of Banning, stretching up to about Victorville and down to around Julian. A second one comprises San Antonio to about Austin. A third city is in the highlands of what had been Guadalajara, Mexico, and the largest and southernmost lies in the hills around old Puebla. The total national population is seven hundred thousand and dropping. All of our food production and manufacture is within the cities themselves, as outside our domed cities is completely hostile to life. What atmosphere does exist there is very thin, and of course very frigid."

"That's the United States?" I asked to be sure.

"That's the United States of North America. Europe consists of three underground cities, one near Gibraltar, another at Messina, Sicily, and a third in north central Greece."

"So it's a full ice age, then, like the one of a hundred thousand years ago?"

"No, Chris, that was a *small* ice age. This ice age is far more severe. Africa and Australia are iced over. South America is ice up to what used to be Caracas and Cartagena. Asia is reduced to Greater Madras, Sri Lanka, Rangoon, Bangkok, and Singapore. That's the world capital now, and our largest city. It's three times in size what it is in this time because the oceans are so much smaller."

"Didn't California freeze over? Morgan told me it was icy in his time."

"That was the Little Climate Shift, as we have come to call it. When the second or Big Climate Shift took place, the ice and glaciers dropped directly down the center of North America, gliding over the Great Lakes and the Great Plains but leaving whatever was south and west of the Rockies ice-free. New Angeles, more or less replacing this town, is where I reside. Alaska too is ice-free but no one lives there at all. It was depopulated centuries ago."

"Continue," I prompted.

"The total world population is maybe nine million and dropping. Less than any time since the time of the Classical Greek civilization, circa 500 B.C. Most of the people alive are much older, three to four times my age. Population replacement is at a rate of below minus sixty, meaning that one child is born for every sixty who die, and few are born healthy. At that rate, we can last maybe another four more generations or ninety to a hundred years. Then we'll go out—like a light. Extinct."

"Dire." I agreed.

I finished my lemonade and wanted something stronger. The picture he painted was beyond bleak.

"Not to be an egotist, but where do I fit in to all this?"

"About ten years ago, and after some thirty-five years of research, the Ministry of Other Times was able to finally focus on those times and those places where it all changed for the worst."

"In the 1960s, right? We were aware of it then."

"Actually, it changed before you were aware of it, Chris. Before you were even born. You all had the right idea, your counterculture generation, in the 1960s. But you were simply too late. Because it actually all changes *now*, in the next few years. It changes in seventeen places around the world, and it does so very clearly. Also, it requires forty-seven people to prevent it from happening."

I was beginning to put it together.

"One of whom was…who, exactly? Someone who I replaced? Is that what you're saying?"

"Exactly, Christopher. Someone who never made it to the Los Angeles YMCA the night that you arrived, April twelfth, 1935. And because he never arrived, he also never arrived at his already planned job interview with an oil company the following morning at a downtown office building just off Wilshire Boulevard. And because of that, he never took a job there, and he never rose to an executive position, and as a result of that, he never okayed research into certain procedures and techniques which as a result never got developed, so that…well, I don't need to get technical. But don't worry. He was totally unharmed. He was in an 'accident' and he was projected forward. He lost some memory, but he's doing fine. He's in a different field where he will rise to the top. Someplace where he is safe for all of us."

"Wow" was all I could say.

"You understand that once we were able to pinpoint the when, the where, as well as the who, we felt utterly compelled to go into action and stop that from happening."

"Okay. Granted. I'd do the same thing. But *I'm here* because why…?" I tried, "You needed to fill his time/space with another body?"

"Yes. A body of approximately the same weight, height, size, and age, yes."

"I see. Then there was nothing personal about it. Morgan saw me walking up the hill and he what, calculated what I'd weigh at eighteen years old and…?"

"I'm afraid it's not quite that simple, Christopher. We had our eyes on you way before that. Remember how suddenly that house on upper Crescent Heights went on the market? Don't you recall how you were *just* able to afford it, despite thinking it was out of your price range?"

"Yes. But that wasn't for another eleven years after that that I met Morgan! Which," I stopped myself, "is, of course, meaningless to the Ministry of Other Times! So he was chosen. So was I. Why me?"

"Because you had accomplished. Because you were already. effective!"

"So effective that I was broke in 2009."

"You would have come back in 2011 or 2012. Really! But anyway, you were a high achiever. Anyway, what tipped us off that you were a PTR was your unusual method of death. Because it was approximately your size and build, the body that was found was *assumed* to be yours. No one looked into it closely."

"No, Morgan explained that's how it would work. You used the term PTR. What does that signify?" I asked. "Potential Time what?"

"Potential Time Repair."

Repair—not Repairer. "You mean I was like a swab of glue?"

"A bit more complex than that. At any rate, history says that in 2010 you went away on a car trip to visit friends in Paso Robles. Am I correct?"

"Yes. Morgan said he'd arrange it so that my burned-out car would be found driven down a ravine in a flaming accident with a skeleton too charred for recognition."

"That's exactly how history says your death happened," Allegre confirmed. "You have no idea, do you, of your reputation later on? I'll show you sometime. You changed the world in your own time in two distinct areas. How many people do you think do that? So…we figured you could be relied upon to do the same in this time."

"Be a high achiever here and now also?"

"Yes. *That* was why you were selected."

That was a great deal to absorb. I chewed and chewed and only partly absorbed it at the table.

Then I said: "Okay. Now that we're totally in the clear…what next? You calmly explain to me what needs to be done, and I will do… what?"

"That's the ever-loving beauty of it, Christopher." Allegre laughed. "We don't have to explain *anything* to you. In three years minus a few weeks, you are…already…doing it! On your own! No prompting needed."

I was stumped. "By making movies for teenagers?"

"Yes. You see, you can't escape your instincts for changing the world and for making things better and also for making art of some kind. Also you can't escape your competency, nor your abilities, nor your flexibility. Qualities that you take for granted and which were needed to achieve in your own era, which was one of generally high competency for excellence. Qualities which are rarer and needed at *this* time and place, where they are in somewhat shorter supply. You barely think about it, but you're a sensation, Christopher! Shirley Temple is cute. Mickey Rooney is darling. But you're the toast of the town because at twenty-one—that's the official fake age now, right?—you're a triple threat. And because you have already effected change in this new timeline."

What Allegre meant was—as the result of *American Boys*.

The film had in fact opened many people's eyes to what had happened and what was still happening all across the country. Our well-off teens in Westwood and Carthay Circle and Santa Monica and Hancock Park, teens we had carefully cultivated for and through our movies, actually began to effect change themselves. After they saw the movie, they wrote to us at the studio in droves, asking how they could help. So we went out and met them at their schools and churches and synagogues and said they had to help. They had to organize, they had to form charities. They knew what they wanted to do already: to build shelters and safe homes for those kids who we had shown to be in such peril. They would do it first in Southern California, then all over the state, and then eventually all over the country.

Sue-Anne had said to them, "I will personally help you do that. I will be your leader."

As a result, half of them signed up on the spot and another third filtered in later on; an amazing number. Teenagers became the face of L.A. Cares because for one thing, our young victims had learned to trust only young people: each other. So our teens went out on bikes and on foot and in busses and in cars and they talked to homeless youth all over the city, handing out food, telling them about the shelters and the free rooms and board. The rooms were small and simple and only two young people fit in each one. But the shelters were guarded by other teens and safe. Dr. Weissman gathered a team of physicians and dentists and oculists, and every weekend they met at the shelters and treated any kids who came in. They gave everyone physical and dental and eye exams. They put them on special regimens of food, vitamins, and medication. No child or teen or young person was forced to remain or to do anything to earn these benefits. Soon those shelters were full, and they were building extensions and new shelters, usually in the iffier parts of town because that's where the kids in peril were. Anyone at the shelters who wanted to help build them or work got training and paid work helping to build new shelters. Soon L.A. Cares had a good-sized contingent of helpers, aides, and clients, and sometimes who was who or what became all mixed up…delightfully.

Sue-Anne went to the White House and met Eleanor Roosevelt and she told her all about it, and she got help there too.

We'd also been getting phone calls and letters from other actors and people in the film industry, asking how they could help, and so we formed Hollywood Cares. Free movies, free school classes, free art supplies, donated pianos, and musical instruments and typewriters and people to show how to use them all arrived, and soon the kids and some stars were mixing. If any young person had a dream or a desired vocation, we tried to locate someone to help them toward that goal. Soon, Hollywood Cares was joined by Broadway actors when we opened up East Coast shelters. It became the thing to do for all the popular actors, from Carole Lombard to Laurence Olivier, to get involved when they weren't shooting a film or promoting it. This of course meant lots of young people would learn all the various crafts involved in filmmaking too.

"I suppose Sue-Anne was another PTR," I asked Allegre. "She's placed here too, like me?"

"Actually, not at all. She is a link we found for you. She was pretty much sitting around twiddling her thumbs, waiting to be useful. But because of all of you, the youth movement of the 1960s that you originally lived through, Christopher, and were a part of, well, now that will happen in the late 1930s and early 1940s. It will be national and then it will be worldwide. An entire generation of youth will raise their consciousness about politics, and social injustice, *and* then about the environment."

"Great! But what if we inadvertently change something and it results in me not being born at all later on and therefore…"

"We're monitoring your parents, of course. Not to worry."

"Well, what if I change something and someone else isn't born?. Say Jonas Salk?"

"Salk and Sabin are already here. We watch their timeline carefully too. Remember, Christopher, you are not the only PTR we are dealing with. There are forty-six other…repairs." He suddenly changed his tone of voice. "Tell me if I'm wrong: you're already thinking about a film different from any of the ones MGM has planned, aren't you?"

"Don't you already know?"

"No!" he insisted in a whisper. "We *don't* know. We *cannot* know. Don't you see, Christopher, because now we are *changing* the timeline altogether! We *have* to change it, otherwise…"

"Otherwise it becomes the 'dire situation.' No, I get it."

"Good. Now tell me about your idea for the new film," he insisted.

"I don't know…It's just a fantasy right now. It's going to be really, really, hard to pull it off for all kinds of reasons. This studio system is great when it works. But Lord, with all the egos involved and all the money needed, it's elephantine. It takes manipulating, not to mention ass-kissing and…"

"That never stopped you before," he said.

"No, it hasn't. Well, my new idea is about," I lowered my voice,

"World War Two! And, by the way, won't *that* nasty bit screw everything up for you and your PTRs?"

"Not if it doesn't happen, it won't," Allegre said.

"Not if it *what*?!" I couldn't believe my ears.

"Not if someone with the media power of Christopher Hall in the new timeline of 1938 or 1939 makes a movie about it, predicting it, say, or…"

"Wait. Wait. Wait. That's not my plan at all."

"What is your plan, then?" he asked.

"Well, something a lot smaller. You see, I want to write and direct and produce a movie, a full-color movie, an expensive movie, filled with stars—about a Jewish family living in Germany," I said. "They'll be kind of ordinary. Nice people, with ordinary, recognizable problems and joys. I'm calling them the Golds. There's a mother and father and unmarried aunt who lives with them. Grandparents who live in another town. Three boys and a girl…But these ordinary people who will end up guess where? In exile. Beaten to death by Nazi thugs. In concentration camps. In Nazi ovens at the end of the picture!"

I waited for him to say, you can't do that.

Instead he said, "If they are alive today in Europe, isn't that exactly where the Golds *will* end up? In those awful places?"

I tried to absorb what he was saying.

"Yes, they will. And that's what I want to draw attention to: what's happening over there already with all the anti-Jewish laws. And what can and will happen."

"Not necessarily *will* happen," Allegre said. "Remember that you've changed the timeline. You and Sue-Ann and *American Boys* and your teenage fans."

"Do you mean to tell me that the Holocaust *doesn't* have to happen?" I asked. "Really?"

"Remember, Christopher. There are forty-six other PTRs…"

"But Hitler's already in power in Germany. Tojo has the Japanese emperor under his thumb and his armies are halfway across China. Mussolini's Brown Shirts are in Yugoslavia and all over northwestern Africa."

"Yes. But recall where they all end up, Christopher."

"Defeated. Dead."

"Exactly. *How* they end up is set in stone. But not *when* they end up there," Allegre said. "Frankly, we would *prefer* that World War Two did *not* occur."

I was stunned.

"'We' at the Ministry of Other Times?" I asked.

"Yes. World War Two is *very messy*. Millions killed. Millions displaced. Economies shattered. Worse, it's very *distracting*. It will end the same way it did in your time, eventually, but it will bring on almost a decade of destruction, not to mention distraction from the real problems: the ones that lead to *our time* hundreds of years from now. But if the war doesn't happen at all, well, so much effort can be applied to the problem of world health, to hunger, disease, to renewable fuels, to desertization, to deforestation, to water and land conservation."

"You mean if I make a movie about the Gold family ending with them in the ovens?"

"If you make it so that your political predictions inside the film begin to come true, Christopher. And people begin to see them come true!"

"I see."

"If you do that, important people will then meet with you. You already have a toehold in the White House thanks to Sue-Anne. You will meet people and you will explain the crucial moment so that it the crucial moment *doesn't happen*."

"This is nuts. The crucial moment being what? The Anschluss with Austria? Isn't that later this very year?"

"Yes, but the crucial moment is further along."

"Munich? Chamberlain and Daladier appeasing Hitler at Munich!" I tried.

"No. Even that can occur."

"Wait. I remember. The Annexation of the Sudetenland. Wait, no. That was an accord too. The crucial moment would be *after* that, it would be when Hitler invaded the *rest* of Czechoslovakia. The non-German part?" I said. "The part that *didn't want to be annexed*? Am I right?!"

"Bingo!"

"So in the new plan, what happens?" I wondered.

"France, the U.S., and Britain go into a state of high alert and already begin to arm. As soon as Germany invades, the Allies declare war on Germany in defense of Czechoslovakia, and get this, they do so in September of 1939."

"I see! One month before Hitler actually started the war in my time."

"In the timeline change, the Allies have an air force all ready in France and Belgium to counter the German buildup. They immediately begin to bomb Germany from the Ruhr to Berlin to Danzig and across the militarized south of the country," he said. "That happens while the Nazis are focused upon annihilating Poland and invading Denmark."

"I see," I said. "So Mussolini is forced to step down in when? Earlier? In '39? Ditto Franco in Spain in '39 or '40? Then what? We then have one of them, say Ribbentrop himself, reveal the Brest-Litovsk secret pact with Russia. That's an excuse to declare war on the Soviet Union too, launching our combined air forces from newly acquired bases in Germany and Poland? And…?"

"And," Allegre went on calmly, "the Allies assassinate Stalin and his cohorts. Do you see how they all fall into place, just like dominos, Chris? After Europe, everyone then goes after Japan. That way nuclear weapons are not fully developed, nor do they have to be developed at all, as that's another great waste of time, personnel, and resources."

"But rockets already existed by then—by right now, possibly."

"Yes, but they are rockets with non-fissionable payloads. Good for outer space exploration. We'll need those for harvesting future minerals. For air. Water. Methane. Our abandonment of space in your time-era was another major error, leading to our future's dire situation."

Our desserts arrived. For me, Nesselrode pie, a treat from my childhood, its recipe all but totally lost by 2010. For him, another shrimp cocktail.

"Can that happen? Really?" I asked.

"Asks the disgruntled, solitary sixty-five-year-old man from the year 2010," Allegre said, "who is busy and thriving in the mid-1930s, where he is the number-one teen movie star in the country."

"I see your point. But…who'll listen to me?"

"First, your friends. Who will help you make the film. The ones from Alsop House. Who by then will have the power and the places and the ability to help you make the best film ever seen. A film so startling and tragic that everyone must see it in the free world. Then your teenager audience, who will listen to you as to no other person before you. And then their parents. And I'm told the First Lady loves to meet talented young people. Arrange a private screening of *The Golds* at the White House."

That was more than I could absorb.

I sighed.

I ate pie.

I yawned.

I ate more pie.

We ate the rest of our desserts in silence. The place was empty but for us and the manager, counting cash in a far booth, listening to the radio, turned low.

Finally I asked, "What happens to me?" I wanted to know. "What about me now? A doctor said I had a heart flutter. I never had that before, and at this young an age."

"If the plan works, Ministry pre-analysts believe that stem cell research is in full force by approximately 1960. Two and a half decades from now. You'll certainly be able to afford it, even if it's still experimental."

"In other words, no problem?"

"The Ministry of Other Times takes care of its friends."

"And my personal life? Won't that…get in the way of all this fame and influence you seem to believe I'll require? I'm not changing anything, you know."

"No reason to. You will continue to be discreet, as you are now, and others will busily cover for you until your work on *The Golds* is done and it goes all over the planet. Anyway, the Ministry predicts that in the new plan, tolerance of other's races and sexuality also leaps forward in time: racial integration could begin in the '40s; sexual tolerance in the '50s. Perhaps you'll take part in those movements again."

"You have all the answers. At the Ministry, I mean, don't you?"

"No, Christopher. What we have is forty-seven young people who have lived and who, like you, abhor what has happened, and what *will* happen if they *don't* interfere."

Outside, shortly after, with a bag of uneaten fish I was taking home for Randolf wrapped in newspaper and stuffed into a brown paper bag, I said, "Poor Mr. Allegre. All that work and no Auburn for you, huh?"

"I'm a jewelry jobber." He shrugged. "I drive a Chevy Six."

"And you'll keep in touch? Just so I don't screw up. Right?" I asked.

"I'll keep in touch," Allegre said and got into his car. "Don't worry!" he added. "And don't drive that damn thing too fast and get yourself killed."

20

It's possible that nothing further would have come of that very strange conversation at dinner. But not a few weeks later, on one of those surprisingly summery, hot L.A. days in late February, I found myself in the backseat of Jonah Wolff's new Lincoln V8 Phaeton convertible, not quite squashed between Sid and Hank in the luxurious, special pony leather upholstery of the backseat. The car had been built by LeBaron for Mae West, who had unaccountably thrown it over for a Dusenberg S.J. Jonah heard of that contretemps at the MGM Commissary while visiting me and Sue-Anne, there and he had swooped in and picked up what was a relative bargain.

Ducky was in the front passenger seat, replaying the Bulldogs game of the day before, which Jonah had missed, an extremely notable game because Ducky had unexpectedly caught a flubbed pass to another receiver and had run it across the field, turning every few seconds to wonder why no one was chasing him. They couldn't believe he could run, that's why—and so he'd made a seventy-yard touchdown, to the loudest, most thunderous noise and celebration that I'd ever heard in my life.

But today was Sunday and all of us were—surprisingly, given our busy schedules—at leisure.

We were also all of us moved out of the Alsop House. Yes, an era had ended. Further, we were all spread out, so it was a job getting us together for breakfast.

Jonah had moved with Frances Wannamaker into her oversized Mediterranean in Hancock Park with its many columns and even more numerous awnings, gardens front and back, a *porte cochere*, and a barely attached solarium.

Sid and Ducky had moved out and bought a single-story cottage together in back of Norma Talmadge's film studio on Cynthia's Lane, in what would later become West Hollywood. Here Ducky could cook to his heart's content in the big, wonderfully tiled kitchen and serve his constantly hungry friends. Here Sid could bring his new string of girlfriends, as the house had two bedroom suites separated by the more public rooms. Even so, more than once I'd gone in to use a lavatory and found only one bedroom looking at all lived in, and only one bed unmade, and I guessed they still slept together whenever Sid felt lonely. And if I noticed others must too, no?...Apparently not.

Hank and Sue-Anne and I too had all moved into an all-but-hidden-from-the-street-by-banana-and-ginger-bushes, four cottage and central alley complex within walking distance of MGM, off Overland in Culver City, on a "temporary basis."

I knew this was a blind for the two of them to be together, and I rented the third little house in front for myself and also the fourth cottage, which became my writing office and Hank's private design and sculpture studio. Sue-Ann also took over a few rooms for her L.A. Cares work. I made certain to appear at the cottages whenever there was company or an event for the charity or an outdoor barbecue or a party all of us shared.

By now, I was mostly living in that Cape Cod Malibu too, and that had turned out very interesting indeed. If any of the others knew where I stayed most nights, or what I was doing and with whom I was doing it, they never once breathed a word.

Surprisingly I'd been home that Saturday night, as Randolph was away on location, spending time up in Chatsworth filming a forgettable Western, the final film in his current studio contract with RKO, when Sid phoned me to make up this Sunday plan and then also again this morning when he'd come to pick up me and Hank, and here we all were.

We'd even stopped at a place on Venice and Motor for breakfast, like we used to do all the time at Anderson's Diner on Selma in Hollywood. Here too we read the Sunday papers, with Sid doing the voices of all the characters in the funnies, and then complaining that Ducky only got "one stinking paragraph" on the sports page and threatening to sue the *L.A. Times*.

Jonah meanwhile sighed over the news of the signing by a rival of a hot new actor that he and Frances had wanted, guy named Tyrone Power. Hank sketched my blank face and very detailed hair—I'd let it grow long and hadn't much tended it lately as I wasn't shooting anything—over and over on his pad. When I saw what he was doing, I yelled "Stop!" and tried hand-brushing it.

Hank knocked my hand away, aggrieved. "Leave it alone. It's beautiful! Beautiful! Just the way it is!"

Sheesh! I tried to finish a crossword puzzle.

Ducky "watched" our meals in the kitchen, meaning he made them himself, unsatisfied with the cook.

Not an hour later, we were at the Venice Pier and then under it and on the sand.

I'd turned Ducky and Sid onto my health food store nearby on Rose. This area would soon become Muscle Beach!

"What is this place?" Jonah groaned once he was in the health food store. "People don't actually eat this stuff, do they, kid? This grass and…Geez, what is that?" Until he all but fell into the display of honeycomb and discovered he couldn't get enough of the sweet stuff.

The beach had not been populated that day as it might have in the summer or fall. The warm weather was unexpected, and so few people had planned for it. We'd spent most of the afternoon there, swimming, surfing, wrestling on the sand, playing a game of catch with an old football Ducky had brought. Eating, and in general having a great, exhausting beach day.

It was now five p.m. and already the marine layer was advancing and would soon cover us.

After a shoreline walk, Hank and I had returned to where we'd parked the car—i.e., right up against the sands (no paved parking lots)—where there was still some hazy sunlight.

As soon as we'd arrived back, Sid and Ducky and Jonah had taken off for their own stroll.

Sid broke off from the others, having been spotted by two young ladies who'd seen him in *American Boys*. He hunkered down on their beach sheets to chat, and then knelt down, and then sat between them.

I didn't know anyone who enjoyed his celebrity more than Sid Devlin. Partly that was because he didn't quite believe it. Before shooting, he'd read his own parts in my script but no other parts and so, when he'd seen the whole film of *American Boys* at the premiere, he'd been surprised and impressed by it—that was the word he used: "I'm impressed, Junior. I'm really impressed."

Meanwhile, Sid knew that his lifetime in films wasn't destined to always be in front of the camera for many more years, or if so, then in a limited capacity. So he was enjoying it while he could. Of course he had signed up with Jonah, at the renamed Wannamaker and Wolff Agency.

On the beach earlier he'd whined: "They send me parts only good for a Dead End kid. What do I look like? Don't answer that, wise guys!"

"What did you expect?" Jonah had asked. He was Sid's agent. "Hamlet?"

"Well, I hear they're making this other play of Shakespeare's. What was the name, Junior? A Summer's Dream or something?"

"*A Midsummer Night's Dream.* Do you mean the role of Puck?"

"Rooney's already got it," Jonah said, unfazed and immovable.

Sid would fade back into Special Effects and Stunts, I figured. He was already a whiz at both of them. From certain angles he filmed a lot larger than he was, especially alone onscreen, and he was utterly fearless, more so than I was, and would try any stunt once, no matter how crazy, a half century before the Jackass movies came along.

What Sid didn't know was that I'd already pictured him in my mind as Randolph Scott's sidekick in my next project. I'd written Sid's part into the first, rough version of the script for *The Golds*, my so far pie-in-the-sky dream. Sid would play the part of "Brooklyn" and he would be the few minutes of comic relief in the film whenever he appeared, especially when the two G.I.'s sneak into Germany via the Austrian Alps and attempt to rescue Scott's pre-war love, Marlene Dietrich. Who knew? Sid might even get another Oscar!

I could see Jonah and Ducky trying to get Sid moving again, then give up in disgust and move on ahead without him. After a minute, as they walked on, Ducky draped an arm over Jonah's shoulder, one of his absolutely typical, almost unconscious "pal" gestures. I could see Jonah's entire body flinch slightly before he let Ducky keep holding him like that. Jonah had intimacy issues and also male-male issues, which Ducky was completely oblivious to. Earlier in the week, I had put a flea in Jonah's ear about someone doing a college football movie based on some of the gridiron experiences that Scott had told me *après-sex*, and our up-and-coming agent was looking for talent to be in it.

Hank had gone into the water again and a few minutes later he headed back to our makeshift base, toweled off the sand he'd picked up, chugged some watered-down hooch out of my silver flask, and then collapsed onto the beach towel.

I'd been leaning against a towel-pillowed Lincoln front bumper, reading a John O'Hara story in *The Saturday Evening Post*, and after a while, Hank turned around and fell backward, his head square into my lap. He made himself comfortable there and I thought he was going to go to sleep. But after a while, he pushed the magazine away from between us and, pointing ahead, said, "Look, Chris!"

I looked at the beach; a fog bank drifted slowly toward us. Behind and above it was one of those ultra pink and aquamarine skies, shot through with cantaloupe, raspberry, and chartreuse, that defined a West Coast sunset. At the very edge of our vision we could see Jonah and Ducky walking, little figures arm in arm, the smaller gesticulating to the larger. Closer by was Sid on the blanket paying cards—Old Maid?—with the two young women. They were wrapped in sweaters, he in his porkpie hat and singlet, a towel curled like a scarf around his neck.

"There's no one, but no one on the beach but us," I said.

"It's perfect," Hank said.

Odd that he'd say that, since I would think that he'd want Sue-Anne to complete the picture.

"Pretty close," I admitted.

"I wish...I wish *nothing ever changes*. That we can continue to be like this and come here and do this for...Well, for the rest of our lives," Hank said with his usual utter sincerity.

He was expecting me to say that we could, don't worry, Hank, we *will*, and it *won't* change. But I knew better. I knew that across the Pacific, plans were already being hatched in Yokohama for the bombing of Pearl Harbor, and in Berlin plans to take over all of Europe were in advanced stages, and that soon all of my friends would be in one theater of war or another, destined to probably never return to this beach: or if they did return, then never entire again in body or mind.

"Me too," I said then. But it didn't sound convincing to Hank.

"You're not planning to go anywhere?" he asked.

"No. No, Hank. Not at all. I'm staying right here."

"Good. I never had a friend like you, Chris. Never. I don't know how I'd get over not having you as a friend."

"I said I'm not going anywhere. What this all about, anyway?"

"I don't know. Aw! Yes, I do. Those sets I'm drawing following your descriptions. Those war...camps...what did you call them? Concentration camps? Death camps? For the new script you're working on...*That's* what it's all about?"

I wanted to tell him that plans for them already existed in 1938.

"The more real, the more horrible you draw them, Hank, the better."

"I'm getting the heebie-jeebies out of doing that," he admitted. "It's really scaring me."

"Don't worry. You're safe. We're safe."

"'Work Will Make You Free'?" he asked. "Would people put that up at the front of a place where they intend to work you to death and starve you to death?"

They would; they could; they will.

"Don't think about it. It's only speculation, I told you! Like *Weird Tales* or *Amazing Stories*. It's just science fiction, Hank."

"It seems awfully real to me the way you described it and all." He shuddered. "What a nightmare."

"Don't think about it."

"You know, for a wonderful fellow, you've got some...I don't know...some really bad ideas inside you."

"Forget about it, Hank...Think about this perfect beach day and all of us. It's only a bad dream, a bad dream."

I began reading aloud the story in the magazine.

After a while I could feel my voice calming him as it always did when I read to him, and I could feel his head drop in my lap and he was asleep.

I picked up my book to read again, but I couldn't concentrate on these Main Line suburbanites and alcoholic attorneys in Pennsylvania.

All I could think about was what a great place it was now here, what a great time it could be if we fixed some stuff like racism and tolerance. So why *couldn't* it last, why *couldn't* we all be here five, six years from now? Maybe not young and perfect and innocent like now, but…Yes, innocent, because that's what they were, my friends, and most of our life was pretty innocent too, and our country was too, even with the Great Depression. I was sure we would forever lose that innocence in 1941 with Pearl Harbor's treachery, then even more so in 1945 when G.I.'s (possibly including one of my friends) stepped into their first Nazi death camp and saw what they saw, and heard what they heard, and then slowly taught themselves to believe it. But right now they were all so innocent.

There would always be a lingering question for me of how it was that I had found and then fitted in so well with these four young men. I was already working with three of them, and perhaps would also work with Ducky. He was moving his mother out to L.A. to open that diner, their long-deferred dream, and the rest of us had told him that we would invest in it and patronize it. So it looked like we would all be together as friends—at least for a while yet. I'd realized that was one of the things I'd missed about not being young anymore: the ease with which younger people came together. Would I ever be certain that somewhere in the Ministry of Different Times they hadn't arranged it all? Not really. And suddenly I didn't care about that. Because I had a much more important decision to make.

"It's not a perfect life, but you know what, it is close, Hank," I whispered into his sleeping face. "And I promise you to make it last as long as I can."

Having said that, I knew what I was going to do. I would move heaven and earth to write, direct, and produce *The Golds*. I would make it if it destroyed my career, I would make it if it bankrupted me, and I would make it if it killed me.

He stirred a bit and I whispered again into his unhearing ear:

"I promise you, Hank. I promise you and everyone I know. In fact, *I swear it!*"

EPILOGUE

To: A. Lewis Folteroi
School of Film
U.C.L.A.
Westwood, CA

June 13th, 2014

Dear Dr. Folteroi,

As per your request, we are forwarding to your office all and any documentary evidence found among the rather sparse remains of Christopher Hall's house at 2251 North Crescent Heights Blvd.

As I mentioned to you by e-mail, the house was one of four upon that road and on that side of the hill that were affected by a large storm and a resulting mudslide on February 22nd of this year. Because of the apparent damage, it was the task of this office to investigate the property and assess structural integrity and compromised living conditions. Those having been found to be completely substandard, the house at 2251 has been condemned and is slated for demolition, at a date and time to be determined by this office.

Aside from this manuscript, discovered upon what appeared to be a coffee table in an upper room apparently unaffected by the slide, very little else was found. This was found in a sealed plastic box, within a leather binding with a slide clasp for the pages, exactly as you are receiving it. It was addressed to you. In your e-mail response, you expressed surprise at this, saying you had only met Mr. Hall one time, some years ago when he was a guest lecturer at the school. Nevertheless, here it is. The accompanying note reads, "Hi Lew. You might find this interesting."

No trace of Mr. Hall has been located. He had sold and or donated all properties before Christmas of 2013. If I recall, you mentioned that he was elderly, possibly ninety years old. Those areas of the house under the mud have been probed and carefully scanned. No body showed up. We did find a shallow grave for a small Bedlington terrier that seemed to have died of natural causes recently.

Naturally, given the neighbors' concern for Mr. Hall, we instituted a complete search of all of Mr. Hall's financial records and found a will, of which your school is a beneficiary, as well as checking and savings accounts. All credit cards, and we also understood from a discussion with a bank officer, all of Hall's investments, appear to have been cashed in sometime in the fall of 2012.

I wish this office could be more helpful.

Tawana Earl, Supervisor
Dept. of Housing, Los Angeles, CA 90012

CHRISTOPHER HALL LEGACY
ON DISPLAY DECEMBER 15TH, 2015
AT THE POWELL LIBRARY
U.C.L.A., WESTWOOD, CA

As was previously announced in *The Daily Bruin*, the papers and many other articles of memorabilia of famed Hollywood actor, writer, director, and film producer Christopher Hall left to this school will be on display beginning on December 15, 2015.

Hall, a major figure of the film industry's much vaunted "Golden Age," was active in film from 1935 to 1955. Among his most noted accomplishments are the Academy Award–winning films *American Boys* (1936), *The Golds* (1938), and *Before I Wake* (1948). As an actor, Hall began as a teen idol in a series of films with his professional colleague Sue-Anne Schiller. They formed a team known as Schiller & Hall, equal in popularity during that decade to Rogers & Astaire and Rooney & Garland.

The young Hall, however, soon moved into more serious fare, and his epic of our nation's forgotten youth who were destroyed or lost to the Depression was a socially conscious movie with a heart and a head. It gave rise to the L.A. Cares youth shelter movement and its various outgrowths. Had Hall accomplished only

American Boys as a film, he would have been seen in the same light as the creators of *Boystown, Mr. Smith Goes to Washington,* and *The Grapes of Wrath,* films that now define the beginning of our nationally raised social consciousness.

By then a matinee idol and movie star in his own right, Christopher Hall's second epic, *The Golds,* ended up having an even greater impact, indeed an enormous one. Written by Hall, directed by George Cukor, starring Hall, Schiller, Randolph Scott, and Marlene Dietrich and a huge, star-studded supporting cast, Hall's eerily predictive, amazingly accurate film might be said to have raised the political consciousness of an entire American generation and then helped ensure worldwide freedom for decades to come.

Most commentators say *The Golds* led to the secret treaty of the governments of the U.S., France, and England in early 1939 to mitigate German power, and their secret arms buildup that led to the declaration of war against Hitler once his troops overran Czechoslovakia. Revelations of another secret alliance by Hitler and Stalin led to the Allies overrunning the Soviet Union, and eventually to the new European, All-Americas, and Anzac Union Forces taking on Emperor Hirohito in Asia. Scores of millions of lives and an entire generation are believed to have been preserved.

After two more films based on the classic novels *Bleak House* (New York Film Critics Award) and *A Sentimental Education* (American Film Critics Award), Hall turned his attention to the problem of American racism in his explosive film of Ralph Ellison's novel *Invisible Man* and his controversial film about sexual tolerance in his adaptation of James Baldwin's *Giovanni's Room.*

Hall took on the ongoing capitalist exploitation of our natural resources, leading to his third Oscar-winning movie, the enormously influential *Before I Wake,* a film that is said to have defined and then thrust into the limelight the Save the Earth movement, which has become an international project of the greatest significance, as may be seen on the U.C.L.A. campus today.

Hall himself helped guide that and other social movements for the next twenty years, aided by his staunch cadre of famous actors, directors, and writers, among them Cary Grant, Carole Lombard, Gene Tierney, Randolph Scott, Marlene Dietrich, John Huston, and many others.

Hall only fully retired when his health required more treatment in 1970. He had been out of the limelight since then, and he appeared in public only once more, along with his famed 1930s costar, Sue-Anne Schiller-Streit, in 1984, to receive the AMPAS Jean Hersholt Humanitarian Award.

The actor/writer/director did, however, remain open to hobbyists of various kinds for many further years, being an avid and talented collector of books, films, film posters and art, animated film regalia, popular and jazz music, sports memorabilia, and automobiles. Most of these collections now occupy entire museums, collections, or rooms in major museums and library-archives.

An *Inquiry* Concerning
the Irregular Occurrences and Anomalous Circumstances
Including but not Limited to the Disappearance of
Mr. Neal P. Bartram
at the Once Privately Owned now Foundation Owned
and Operated Estate of Chester A. Ingals, Known as

INGOLDSBY

The Junction City Intelligencer

★ ★ ★ ★ SATURDAY, APRIL 21, 2001 ★ ★ ★ ★

UNEXPECTED TIME CAPSULE DISCOVERED IN BANK RUINS

OPENED VAULT OF OLD FULTON FIRST SAVINGS BANK YIELDS "TREASURE TROVE" FROM 1940 MAYOR QUIMBLY EXULTS

By Caspar Lockhead

Fulton's Point, WI— When he jackhammered the solid-looking cornerstone of the old Fulton Savings Bank, the last part of the venerable ruin of the old building located at the corner of Main and Branch and the one remaining structure on the block of what is to become downtown Fulton Point's fashionable new shopping district, the last thing Herb Mahony expected to find was another vault.

Weeks before, the Myers DeConstruction Co. crew had removed the two huge standing metal vaults installed on the spot more than sixty years before.

"That took two days and derrick and winch equipment so big we had to rent it," Thommy Myers, Jr., co-owner of the company with his father and two brothers, admitted. But with nothing else to the grand old bank left standing higher than your ankle, there was still that cornerstone, a giant granite stone, and the first piece to be inserted into the old bank when Ford's manufacturing plant was the area's biggest employer and Ella Fitzgerald had the country's number one hit record.

A plaque from that plant some two miles to the north—recently reopened and converted into manufacturing Hyundai sports coupes—and a copy of that record—a single-play, two-sided, red vinyl 45 r.p.m disc on the Bluebell label—were among the "treasures" that Herb Mahony found when he reached into the two foot by three foot metal vault with a legend "not to be opened before the year 2000" incised on its front door. "It took some prying," Herb and Thommy admitted, but then it sprang

TIME CAPSULE, continued on Page 5

FELICE PICANO

UNEXPECTED TIME CAPSULE DISCOVERED IN BANK RUINS

TIME CAPSULE, from Page 1

open and they looked inside and were astonished, and delighted.

Besides the Ford plaque and Ella's LP, they found the latest women's fashions in kitchen aprons—a polka-dot yellow on pale green, wrapped in a cellophane package—an eight-ounce green glass bottle of Coca-Cola, among the first carbonated soda pops, that looked as though it still had some fizz in it, a *Good Housekeeping* cookbook for brides, a copy of the *Junction City Intelligencer*, dated sixty-one years earlier than this one, and, according to Mayor Quimbly, who was soon called to the scene of the discovery, "many other marvelous and delightful objects of everyday use."

Quimbly promised that the contents of the vault will be put on exhibit in display cases between the mayor's office and the post office in the Town Hall as soon as all the contents have been catalogued, and care has been taken to ensure that the items are historically cared for against contemporary germs, molds, and even bugs. "We've called in an expert from the university archives who's in charge of such matters," she assured the *Intelligencer*. "He'll know what to do to ensure this unexpected and remarkable cache of life from our grandparents' generation long ago, will be available for all to see and study."

"Time Capsules themselves are as charmingly archaic as any of the objects they may contain," said Professor Aranda "Randy" Chananbranda, from the university archives. "Our ancestors had a wonderful optimism about the future, and equally a wonderful faith in what they surrounded themselves with. Thus their desire to send them to what they saw as a certain, and wonderful, future." Chananbranda pointed out that most such Time Capsules stopped being sent around the year 1960, while the earliest yet opened was from the year 1905.

With the vault opened, its contents removed, and the vault itself to be put on display, the ground is now thoroughly cleared and ready for the Fulton's Landing Fashion Center to rise. On the site of the old bank will be a Gap Clothing Store, an Armani A/X Botteghe, a Payless Shoes, and Geree's Sports Equipment and Guns filling up the block. Already across the street, the old Fulton Theater has been restored in part and then converted into a film multiplex housing fourteen smaller cinemas, surrounded on either side by a glass-enclosed food court with favorite eateries like Ruby's Retro Diner, Taco La Rica, Hamburg Hell, Pizza Hut, a sit-down and take-out branch of local favorite, The Wen Young Chinese Food Outlet, and one of the county's best known eateries, Snyder's Inn.

The Junction City Intelligencer

Sports Final—   —25 Cents

The Junction City Intelligencer

★ ★ ★ MONDAY, APRIL 30, 2001 ★ ★ ★

BAFFLING MANUSCRIPT FOUND IN TIME CAPSULE

"TREASURE TROVE" FROM 1940 CONTAINS JOURNAL POLICE CHIEF CALLS "SUSPICIOUS," TIED TO STUDENT'S SUMMER DISAPPEARANCE

By Caspar Lockhead

Fulton's Point, WI—Admitting that he didn't know whether it was "a joke or what?" Police Chief Abner Estes told the *The Junction City Intelligencer* yesterday in a special interview that a journal found inside the Time Capsule recently opened for the first time in over sixty years appears to "not belong with the rest of the items." But that it does appear to be connected to the disappearance of a graduate student last August 30 at the nearby historic Ingoldsby estate.

"It's both handwritten and computer-print generated," Chief Estes said of the journal found amid memorabilia of the year 1940. "Impossible for that year. Someone must have slipped it in, as a prank." Although he couldn't say how.

A tasteless prank, at best. Last year, local police and the Portage County Sheriff's office sent ten officers who for two days combed the entire long-closed estate buildings and the extensive nearby grounds, searching for Neal P. Bartram, the student who'd been hired as a groundskeeper for the famous site. He had been reported missing on August 31 by A.J. Torrington, attorney for the Ingoldsby estate in Chicago, who had hired the young history student.

Bartram had been employed both to ready the grounds of the historic site for a potential opening as a museum and to watch that squatters and vandals stayed away. An honors student at Northwestern University and a Ph.D. candidate in

BAFFLING, continued on Page 5

BAFFLING MANUSCRIPT FOUND IN TIME CAPSULE

BAFFLING, from Page 1

American History, Bartram was called "rock-steady" by Torrington, and thus unlikely to simply run off.

After some weeks of fruitless search with no clues, the hunt was called off, and the mystery of Bartram's disappearance has remained unsolved.

But this is by no means the first mystery to have surrounded Ingoldsby, home of renowned financial wizard Chester A. Ingals. On the very same date in 1940 as Bartram's vanishing, Ingals reportedly perished along with his minor ward and closest friend in a freak fire in the much-photographed, architecturally noted house built especially for him only a few years earlier.

Rebuilt to be as it originally was, by terms of Ingals's will, the estate was to have opened to the public, but until last year, it had enigmatically remained in the private hands of the enormously wealthy Ingals Foundation. The estate is shunned by some Fulton's Point residents who claim the place is in some way "out of whack," and even haunted.

Mr. Torrington has not returned inquires from the *Intelligencer* reporter.

The Junction City Intelligencer

STATE of WISCONSIN
District Attorney's Office
Government Center, Building C
120 State Street
Madison, WI 53711
Wayne G. King, Assistant D.A.

To: Detective-Sergeant Annabella Conklin
Wisconsin State Police, Cold Case Department
Eau Claire, WI 54701

May 7th, 2001

Dear Det.-Sgt. Conklin,

Pursuant to our brief phone conversation yesterday, I am enclosing the surprising new material (two articles from *The Junction City Intelligencer*) sent to this office by local authorities regarding the disappearance of Neal P. Bartram, August 30, 2000, on the grounds of the Ingoldsby estate. As this falls within your purview as a recent but closed and thus "cold case," we are also passing along that locality's request "in the light of the discovery within the 1940 Time Capsule of a ms allegedly written and signed by Neal Bartram," along with this office's sanction, to fully and immediately reactivate the case, as a grade gl2, with financial resources commensurate to that designation.

Although a further, smaller, item in a later issue of *The Intelligencer* called the new-found journal a patent fraud, this was official persiflage, and by no means the truth. We wish to bring this evidence to your attention, along with several other pieces of evidence related to the as yet unsolved disappearance.

Fulton's Point Police Chief Abner Estes has prepared a full list of materials previously collected which are enclosed for your attention. We encourage you to work up further, corroborating, or non-corroborating evidence, at your discretion.

We are confident you will be able to make some sense of all this. The D.A. is especially interested in the case as he is a second cousin to members of the Ingals Family, not unrelated to the foundation upon whose property this unpleasant predicament occurred.

Cordially,

Wayne G. King

PORTAGE COUNTY, WI
FULTON'S POINT POLICE
39000 Rte. 18
Fulton's Pt., WI 53908

Enclosed find all items collected by this office, catalogued by Officer Jeremy Schaeffer, signed off by Chief Abner Estes.

1. Initial request made by telephone and backed up by e-mail of one A.J. Torrington, on noon of August 31st, 2000, from his office in Chicago,

IL, regarding the disappearance of Neal P. Bartram, employed May 20th, 2000, as watchman and groundskeeper at the Ingoldsby estate. The gist of the request was that Torrington was Bartram's employer and had been trying to reach him for close to twenty-four hours and had failed to do so. He'd then phoned a local who'd then driven to the site and who also failed to locate Bartram.

2. Secondary request, by letter, and e-mail by A.J. Torrington, officially requesting that the F.P. Police step in and locate the "missing person" Neal P. Bartram.

3. Official Report of Officer Jeremy Schaeffer, dated September 1st, 2000, following his preliminary investigation at the Ingoldsby estate, made in response to the above official request.

4. Follow-up report of the expanded investigation and search of the Ingoldsby estate and Environs by Chief Abner Estes and Officer Shaeffer, dated September 3rd, 2000.

5. Request by Chief Estes to the Portage County Sheriff's Offices for a 10-man search squad to help locate Bartram, dated September 3rd, 2000. Signed by Chief Estes.

6. Depositions taken by the Portage County Sheriff's Office/Fulton's Point Police of known associates of Neal Bartram, regarding his habits and possible whereabouts. Including affidavits by the following:

A. Fulton's Point Pharmacy owner: Mr. Joseph Weyerhauser
B. Fulton's Point resident: Dr. Rodman Stansbury, M.D.
C. Fulton's Point Public Library employee:

Mrs. Antoinette Noonan
D. Fulton's Point resident: Amanda Ettrick
E. Fulton's Point resident: Ashley Sprague
F. Fulton's Point Post Office Manager: Mrs. Beverly Freneau

7. Report by Portage County Sheriff Griffith A. Angeles, following the search, depositions, and investigation, dated October 1st, 2000.

8. Final Report by Chief Abner Estes. October 13th, 2000.

Date   Signature

Date   Signature

1.

PORTAGE COUNTY, WI
FULTON'S POINT POLICE
39000 Rte. 18
Fulton's Pt., WI 53908

Received today, August 31st, 2000, 12.15 p.m. by Operator Anita Nichols, transferred to Officer Jeremy Schaeffer, a telephone call from Mr. A.J. Torrington, Attorney of the Ingals Trust in Chicago, IL, asking that this office drive out to the Trust owned estate known as "Ingoldsby" and conduct a search for the person of Mr. Neal P. Bartram, the groundskeeper and night/day watchman of the estate.

The reason given was that Mr. Bartram had not responded to Mr. Torrington's repeated phone calls or e-mail over the past 24 hours.

Complainant further noted that he had this

morning phoned Fulton's Point Pharmacy owner, Joseph Weyerhauser, and asked him to drive out to the estate. That Mr. Weyerhauser had done as requested but had not located Neal P. Bartram.

Action taken: Officer explained that a formal report/complaint of a Missing Person could only be made forty-eight hours after he/she has gone missing. Officer advised Mr. Torrington to make such a complaint.

Date   Signature

2.

The Ingals Trust
123 North Dearborn Ave.
Chicago, IL 60602

To: Chief Abner Estes,
     Fulton's Point Police
     39000 Rte. 18
     Fulton's Pt. WI

September 1, 2000

Dear Police Chief Estes,

This letter, sent by e-mail and also via registered letter, is a formal complaint and report of a Missing Person, as per my phone conversation and e-mail with Officer Schaeffer to your office yesterday. I hope this makes it official now that the Ingals Trust employee Neal P. Bartram, groundskeeper and watchman of Ingoldsby, located in your jurisdiction, is missing and we wish him to be found.

I've tried phoning him now for over forty-eight hours. I also sent a representative, Mr. Joe Weyerhauser of the local pharmacy, out to the estate to look for him. He reported that he did not see Mr. Bartram anywhere. Bartram has never been out of communication so long.

Mr. Bartram is a Ph.D. candidate at Northwestern University here in Chicago in American History, a solid and reliable young man with the best possible record of employment and credentials. Up until yesterday, this office had no reason to doubt that he would complete his term of employment—to September 10th, 2000—competently and without problems.

As you may know, Ingoldsby is an important American architectural landmark of the past century, and it has been the Ingals Trust's intention to seek full state landmark status for it and possibly open it as a museum. Toward that end, and to ensure that any representative from the Landmark Commission was guided about, we hired Bartram, who has provided invaluable service. He's given us no reason to believe he would simply walk away from his responsibilities. Mr. Bartram is an intelligent, resourceful, and personable young man. We are personally concerned for his whereabouts and for his well-being.

Please institute as full and thorough a search of the estate buildings and grounds as are needed. Joe Weyerhauser has a spare set of keys. And please let us know what we can do to help in this search.

Cordially,

A. J. Torrington

3.

PORTAGE COUNTY, WI
FULTON'S POINT POLICE
39000 Rte. 18
Fulton's Pt., WI 53908

Preliminary Report on Missing Person: Neal P. Bartram

Pursuant to the complaint/report filed September

1, 2000, Officer Jeremy Schaeffer drove to the Fulton's Point Pharmacy to get keys to Ingoldsby from Joe Weyerhauser, whom the complainant, A.J. Torrington, assured us had a spare set of keys.

He did and told the officer he'd been at Ingoldsby the previous day on Torrington's phoned request and had "looked around" for over an hour but "had touched not one thing" and had not found the M/P Neal Bartram.

Officer Schaeffer drove to the estate. One key opened the smaller door on the side of the sliding metal main gates between the brick walls that lead into Ingoldsby. Weyerhauser told us that the M/P lived inside the brick gate-house, a two-story structure similar to the brick walls and housing a garage with lawn and grounds equipment. Above it, a two-room apartment with bath in which the M/P had resided while employed there.

Apartment seemed lived in, and had various personal items in the bathroom and bedroom apt for a student. Clean and neat. No sign of a break-in or violence. Laptop computer open but turned off on main table amid school texts, notebooks, pens, etc. No signs of a struggle.

Officer drove around gate-house. Nothing looked out of place. Officer drove the half mile to the main house and garages. All doors were locked. No signs of break-in or violence. Footprints made by basketball shoes around various doors-to the extensive garage, main entry of house, side doors, etc.-exactly matched sneaker sole Officer found in apartment belonging to M/P. Nothing unusual.

Officer entered garage, an extensive structure containing 12 antique automobiles. All neat, swept, polished, well kept. No sign of break-in or struggle.

Officer entered main house. Most rooms are empty or contain a few pieces of furniture covered by sheets. All sheets are sealed beneath with tape. Officer searched for any not sealed or looking odd or newly sealed. None found. Officer opened every cabinet, closet, refrigerator, freezer, etc., door in the house. No signs of break-in or struggle. No sign of M/P.

Officer walked around main house in widening circle through bushes. No signs of violence or struggle. No sign of M/P. After four hours Officer concluded M/P was not in main buildings, garage, nor central area of property and that there were no signs of struggle.

Dated   Signature

4.

PORTAGE COUNTY, WI
FULTON'S POINT POLICE
39000 Rte. 18
Fulton's Pt., WI 53908

Follow-Up Report on Missing Person: Neal P. Bartram

Pursuant to the complaint/report filed September 1, 2000 and following Officer Jeremy Schaeffer's Preliminary Investigation and Report, Police Chief Abner Estes drove to the Fulton's Point Pharmacy to get keys to Ingoldsby from Joe Weyerhauser, and heard him repeat what he told Officer Schaeffer the previous day.

As did Officer Schaeffer, Chief Abner Estes drove to Ingoldsby and checked the gate-house and attached garage, then to the main part of the estate, including the multi-car garage and main house.

Found no signs of break-in, violence, or struggle. Chief Estes did a walking search of the area around the estate and failed to find the M/P.

Action taken: as the general area surrounding the house is close to fifteen acres, some of it brush, forest, and scrubland, we believe a general search party will be needed. Meanwhile, this office will call on six people known to have associated with the M/P tomorrow and begin taking depositions from them.

Date   Signature

---

5.   PORTAGE COUNTY, WI
FULTON'S POINT POLICE
39000 Rte. 18
Fulton's Pt., WI 53908

TO: County Sheriff Griffith A. Angeles
    Portage County Sheriff's Office
    172 Elm Street
    Portage, WI 53901

RE: Reports on Missing Person: Neal P. Bartram

September 3, 2000

Dear Sheriff Angeles,

Enclosed please find copies of a complaint/ report of a missing person along with reports by myself and Officer Schaeffer after preliminary and secondary investigation of this M/P.

Bartram is a Ph.D. candidate at Northwestern U. in Chicago, and there appears to be no earthly reason why he'd just vanish. No reports of hitchhikers on any interstate or intrastate highways fit his description. He seems to have lifted off the face of the earth.

We're taking depositions of six locals who knew Bartram in the two months or so he was in Fulton's Point or rather at the estate known as Ingoldsby. He seems to have made a good impression but no real friends. Naturally, as he was to leave in one week to return to school.

We'd appreciate your office sending a full search of the grounds of the estate, comprising fifteen acres. It's more than our two-man office can handle. Keys will be made available to you. There is a small pond and a drag-net may be required. Otherwise it's all on-foot or via ATVs.

Should we learn anything of import to end the search during the depositions, you will hear of it immediately. The Ingals Trust is admittedly pretty big and important in the state, but it's only because of how total and sudden a disappearance this is that we're making this request. Foul play is of course assumed.

Date   Signature

I owe you one on this, Griff!
—Ab Estes

6-A. PORTAGE COUNTY, WI
FULTON'S POINT POLICE
39000 Rte. 18
Fulton's Pt., WI 53908

<u>DEPOSITION</u>

Mr. Joseph Weyerhauser, Fulton's Point Pharmacy,
3300 Rte. 81

Yes, I do swear. I first met Neal Bartram the afternoon of May 24th this year when he came into the pharmacy and asked for the keys to Ingoldsby. Mr. Torrington had phoned me two days before to say Neal would be coming for the keys. I wasn't very busy at that time of day, mid-afternoon, on a weekday, so I left my mother in charge of the cash register, infirm as she is and elderly—sixty-nine this November—and I drove over to the place, with Neal driving behind me.

Showed him how to use the keys and what they opened in the gate-house & the garage beneath filled with lawn and estate equipment he'd be using. I'd a few days earlier aired out the apartment and dusted it. Drove him to the main buildings and garages and gave him a guided tour. My grandfather worked at Ingoldsby when he was a young man and so I know a great deal about it.

As far as I know, everything went all right between Neal and the estate until three days ago, when I got the phone call from Mr. Torrington telling me he could not raise Neal on the phone all the previous day nor that morning. I tried locally and couldn't raise him by phone either. So I drove over and looked for him. I found the little apartment as he'd left as though to go run errands. Same thing with the estate, which remains fully closed up, but ready to be opened at any moment if need be. I didn't touch anything at all in either the gate-house or the main house.

There's not much to do in this town and Neal began coming into the pharmacy around one p.m. most days, for lunch. You and he must have passed each other once or twice. Nice-looking feller, Neal is, strongly attracting the girls and well aware of it. Especially as he dressed more freely than most of the men around here, with small shorts and little, tight-fitting guinea-tee shirts, and on hotter days, nothing but shorts and those flat little sandals with thongs on 'em.

Even so he's a well-brought-up, intelligent, courteous, and all-around good person. Able to speak on a variety of topics. Aside from how he dressed-or rather undressed-I never heard a negative word about him from any person in Fulton's Point. Although it is true that he kept to himself mostly as he was preparing a book-length work for his Ph.D. I believe in mid-twentieth-century American History.

WITNESSED: A. Estes-TRANSCRIBED: A. Nichols, 9/4/00

6-B. PORTAGE COUNTY, WI
FULTON'S POINT POLICE
39000 Rte. 18
Fulton's Pt., WI 53908

DEPOSITION

Dr. Rodman Stansbury, M.D. 34 Aspect Ave. Fulton's Pt., WI

I so swear. I met Neal Bartram on Memorial Day Eve, May 28th of this year, in the pharmacy. I'd heard from Joe Weyerhauser that Neal had come down from Chicago to mind the house and grounds at Ingoldsby. We'd gotten word a few months before that the Trust was planning to make it into a local historical landmark, possibly a museum. Big news in a town this small and sleepy, especially in summer.

So was Neal Bartram news to the town, according to Mrs. Stansbury. His arrival doubled the available bachelors in town, and the fact that he was a healthy, good-looking, and a usually exposed-to-the-skin specimen of young manhood certainly made waves around the feminine side of town, according to the Missus. Tonia Noonan at the library and Bev Freneau at the Post Office apparently vied for his attention. But younger teens also followed him around the main street or gathered at his Cavalier coupe whenever it was parked in town. Nothing better to do.

I have no idea what, if any, kind of relationship Neal ever developed with either woman or any woman or girl here. Or in fact with anyone. But since apart from Joe himself there was no real romantic competition for Neal, I doubt that has any bearing on the matter.

As for myself, I played cards with Neal twice weekly, along with Joe Weyerhauser. Mostly at the pharmacy, on those "cafe" tables Joe's recently put inside; and once or twice at Neal's gate-house apartment.

Neal Bartram did come to me in a professional capacity a few weeks after he'd moved into the gate-house. While he was sound as a drum, he was complaining of night noises and other unlikely disturbances that were keeping him awake at night. Sometimes the country is too quiet for city dwellers. I prescribed a light sleeping medicine, Diphenhydramine Hydrochloride, similar to what you can buy over the counter, but in a 50 mg dosage. After that he had no further complaints.

Neal did become interested in Ingoldsby and its history. But that was only to be expected, being as he was in and out of it and around it daily and it is a fascinating place. Me and Joe told him what we knew, including when he asked about the tragedy there in the spring of 1940 when Chester Ingals and his guests died in a freak fire inside the house. There wasn't much to tell. I think Neal looked up more himself.

After that, his questions about the place were pretty specific and even pointed. Joe and me humored him. Neal's an ace Rummy player and a super guy. We hope you find him soon and unhurt.

WITNESSED: A. Estes-TRANSCRIBED: A. Nichols, 9/4/00

6-C. PORTAGE COUNTY, WI
FULTON'S POINT POLICE
39000 Rte. 18
Fulton's Pt., WI 53908

DEPOSITION

Ms. Antoinette ("Tonia") Noonan, Librarian, 9 Drake Rd. Fulton's Pt., WI

Yes, I do swear to tell the truth. I met Neal Bartram on the Saturday of the Memorial Day weekend. Was that the 29th of May? The library was closed on the holiday. Neal sort of wandered into the building, and as it is much cooler than the near hundred-degree temperatures we were experiencing, he immediately put on his T-shirt.

He looked surprised to find a library at all, never mind one so handsome as ours is and so well kept. Of course now that we've brought in the three computers, all as search engine/catalogue files and also for Internet use, the library is updated, so it's used by youngsters in addition to retirees and other regulars who came in.

Neal had been having trouble linking up to the Net from Ingoldsby and had been referred to me. As he always was, Neal was polite, courteous, and well spoken. After he'd received his e-mail and answered it on the library's machine, we spoke a bit and he told me about himself. I offered to subscribe to *The Chicago Sun-Times* if he wished–it's a paid service of the library. But he said he could read it online.

He came into the library after that once or twice a week, and I also encountered him at the Pharmacy's lunch counter. Although he was reading quite specialized books for his thesis, he occasionally leafed through a current auto magazine or a *New Yorker*.

As you know, it's been an exceptionally warm summer with few rainy days, and Neal dressed as people did at Northwestern and in Chicago, which some older residents in town found shocking. I saw nothing wrong with it, as he was a healthy-looking, well-behaved young man.

People have gossiped that Neal and I went out together. That's simply not true. We did have several long conversations at the Pharmacy cafe, and Neal seemed to be a genuine young man, sensible, and sensitive, yet practical too. Although he found his new home odd at times, he also loved living in a historical site. We spoke about "the good old days." I told him what I'd heard about it from my grandparents.

A month after he arrived, Neal began borrowing and reading about the history of the town and estate. He also drove to the Junction City library and got books there.

I do not believe Neal Bartram would leave of his own volition without fulfilling his employment obligation. I believe something was not quite right in his life, but I couldn't broach this matter with him. I feel harm has befallen Mr. Bartram and I pray to God he is found safe.

WITNESSED: A. Estes-TRANSCRIBED: A. Nichols, 9/4/00

6-D.

PORTAGE COUNTY, WI
FULTON'S POINT POLICE
39000 Rte. 18
Fulton's Pt., WI 53908

DEPOSITION

<u>Ms. Amanda Ettrick, 27 Wausag Drive. Fulton's Pt.,
WI</u>

Sure, I'll swear on it. But whatever happens, *you've* got to swear that you won't ever tell my best friend Ashley what I'm going to tell you about Neal Bartram or she will have six fits and absolutely die... Yes, I do realize this is an official investigation and no information will leave this room. I'm making sure... I'm thirteen next month.

Okay, so this is what happened. Ashley and me first saw Neal when he came to the Post Office a few days after Memorial Day. He was picking up mail for himself and for Ingoldsby. Bev Freneau, the postmistress, told us when we asked. He was by far the cutest male in town in five years, ever since Jake Holloway had to move to Idaho, and he wore like nothing! A teeny little pair of shorts so thin you could see everything, and no shirt. Of course it was hot out. But my best friend Ashley almost died right there in line at the P.O.

I said hello and he was really friendly. He was always friendly to me, whenever he'd drive into town in that little red Chevy coupe of his. So Ash and me took to hanging around him or his car. He never seemed to mind. We knew he was too old for us and all, still you never know.

Well! This went on all summer. We'd see him in the pharmacy, or at the pizza place. We saw him at that multiplex over on Route 18, with Bev. She's older than him and I guess they got along. And that would have been "it," you know what I mean, two girls hoping, *except* Ash thought we could see him without any clothing if we went to Ingoldsby. There's a pool and we knew he'd been a swimmer. Maybe he'd swim nude.

Well! We biked out there even though it's a trek and it's got a reputation for being haunted and all. We saw him at the pool. He wore a gorgeous white and purple Speedo, so Ash, who's never seen real dick, was disappointed. He stretched out and all and never knew we were watching. That's when we saw him talking to himself. Or rather to someone else, maybe two someone elses, on the terrace. Except there was no one there!

Well! You can imagine! Ash said, "Maybe he's rehearsing, like for a play, or something." Sure. A play! *I* think they were ghosts!

So! To make a long story short, even though she'll deny it up and down, I think that absolutely gorgeous as Neal Bartram was-is, you've not found a body, right?-that living at Ingoldsby all alone with those ghosts there, he just snapped one day and killed himself, and I guess you'll find the body sometime soon if you look really hard. Which is a shame because he's like the most beautiful guy in the county.

WITNESSED: A. Estes-TRANSCRIBED: A. Nichols, 9/4/00

6-E. PORTAGE COUNTY, WI
FULTON'S POINT POLICE
39000 Rte. 18
Fulton's Pt., WI 53908

DEPOSITION

<u>Ms. Ashley Sprague, 11 Wausag Drive. Fulton's Pt.,
WI</u>

What-*ever*! Yes, of course, I'll swear on it. But
in turn, you have got to promise that you don't
ever let my best friend Amanda know what happened
between me and the Divine Neal Bartram, because
she is like a total child, not a grown-up, though
she thinks she is… Oh, great! So…like nothing I
say can ever leave this room? Terrif… So this is
how it goes. We meet Neal in town at the P.O. and
he's drop dead gorgeous and we're stupid girls and
immediately get ideas, right? Right! But I mention
him at home at dinner that night, and my dad he
makes this weird little thing with his mouth like
he just ate a rancid nut or something, and he says
to my mom, "I thought you told me they'd never have
another caretaker at Ingoldsby after what happened
to that guy from Ohio?"

This is something I totally do not know. So
while my mom says, "You read that article in the
paper. The Trust is turning it into a museum and
landmark and all so they need someone out there,
I suppose." To which my dad makes another one of
those faces and so does she.

Later on that evening I ask my mom what happened
to the other caretaker at Ingoldsby, and she tells
me what happened when she was my age, around 1979
when they were planning to do something with the
estate, remodel it or open it to the public or
something like that, she wasn't exactly sure.
Her dad (my grandpa) and my Uncle Matt (by my
grandpa's first wife) owned this landscaping and
garden business and they were hired to do major
work out there at Ingoldsby. According to them,
at the end of summer this guy whose name my mom
didn't remember who'd been hired from out of state
just disappeared. So the Trust closed Ingoldsby
down again and only her dad and my uncle ever went
out to Ingoldsby anymore from the town and they

only went by daylight and always remained together whenever they went.

So I asked my mom what happened to the guy and she said that his body had never been found. And she said that her grandmother had talked about Ingoldsby as being weird when *she* was a little girl. So that's a long time ago. Was it haunted? I asked. And Mom said the way she understood it, it wasn't so much ghosts and all, as just there was something *wrong* with the place. According to her family, who's lived here in Portage County a hundred and twenty-five years, there's been something wrong with the land on which the estate was built right from the beginning. Which was why no one outbid Frank Ingals when he first got it in 1901 and why his son Chester Ingals had been forced to hire a county construction team from outside Portage County to build the place.

At any rate, my dumb pal Amanda gets some idea in her head that she can seduce Neal Bartram, as though a stud-muffin like him would look twice at a skinny infant like her! But to keep her out of too much trouble, I agree to bike with her out to Ingoldsby one day. We see Neal using the pool, swimming laps, then he's on the deck drying off and then, well suddenly it's like he's talking to people—people who aren't there. You know, gesticulating and all, all totally natural. I'm sure he wasn't onto us hiding and trying to freak us out.

Amanda, however, was totally freaked out, saying that Neal is talking to the Ingoldsby ghosts and all. But I remember what my mom said about the original Indians who lived on that land, how she told me that they believed there were strong spirits on the property. I figure if anyone would be cool enough to talk with spirits it would be Neal, since he was so smart and virtually a history professor already, getting his doctorate in American history, according to Miz Noonan at the library. She told me that he and she talked a lot and from the way she spoke of him, I think she kind of also had a crush on Neal.

So Amanda is freaked and we get out of there, and she's like crying all night, saying how will Neal ever escape these awful ghosts and all. Real weepy and a complete child! For the next few days all I hear from her is Neal this and Neal that. So I decide on a plan.

We both know Neal has lunch most days at Joe's Pharmacy lunch counter, so the next day as me and Amanda are waiting for him at his car, I slip a note into his hand when Amanda's not looking and it says to meet me at a certain time. Well, later that day I get a phone call from Neal at my home and he says we can't meet secretly because I'm underage and all.

So I tell him it's not about me or any gooey crap like that, it's about Ingoldsby and I know a lot about the place, so he does agree to meet me. We meet after dinner behind this very office right here, and I tell him what my mom had told me about Ingoldsby and he takes notes and all, and he thanks me and when I ask him to, he gives me a kiss, which is lovely. He also asks for my grandpa's address 'cause he wants to visit him and also ask him questions about Ingoldsby.

A few days later Neal phones me again and thanks me again and he says he's found a lot more information about Ingoldsby and about that caretaker who disappeared from old newspapers he's dug up at the Junction City Library. I've been really invaluable and a true friend, and if he ever publishes an article about the estate, Neal will be sure to give me credit along with my mom and Grandpa, which is how really nice Neal always is.

So I was feeling really good about it, and even though I was curious, I was also afraid to ask him who he was talking to and all. He never seemed in the least bit afraid, or upset, and I never got the idea that he thought anything was out of his control at the estate. So you can imagine how like totally bummed I was when I heard that Neal vanished too, just like that caretaker from twenty years ago. I just hope you find him okay.

WITNESSED: A. Estes-TRANSCRIBED: A. Nichols, 9/4/00

6-F.

PORTAGE COUNTY, WI
FULTON'S POINT POLICE
39000 Rte. 18
Fulton's Pt., WI 53908

DEPOSITION

Mrs. Beverly Freneau, 11 Lakeview Ave. Fulton's Pt., WI

I do swear it... Actually, I was born here in Portage County, over at the hospital in Monroe, and I grew up here in Fulton's Point and went to school here, graduated high school and even dated Joe Weyerhauser before I met my husband Jake and we moved to Madison, where he was finishing up at the University there. Our son, Josh, was born in Madison. And I got work in the Post Office in Madison while my husband did his internship and residence there, since we needed money to live on, which was how it was that I managed to get work in the P.O. back here after Jake died and I returned here. Janet Martin was retiring. That was about two years ago that I came back. Hodgkins lymphoma it was. Went through Jake in five months. One day he was exhausted, next day he had this horrible diagnosis. It seemed like there was nothing inside

Jake at all to stop it… No, I'm okay. Just every once in a while I naturally think about how…you know, how unfair it all is.

I met Neal Bartram I suppose the first time the P.O. was open after Memorial Day when he came in for his mail and for any mail going to Ingoldsby. I could see the old ladies were frowning and scandalized and the younger girls tittering and excited just because he'd taken his shirt off and had strung it through the belt loops of his shorts. Neal had been on the swim team as an undergraduate and he still swam and kept in shape, so clearly he was the best thing to hit Fulton's Point in years according to some women. Tonia Noonan at the library for one. She was completely ga-ga. But me, I've been married and saw naked men, so I guess I wasn't either so easily scandalized nor so excited either.

Over the next few weeks Neal and me got to see each other more often, either at Joe's lunch counter or at the P.O. when he came in, and we chatted if there was no one else waiting. Even sometimes at the library, and my opinion of him changed a lot. For one thing, the attention he paid to his body, which could be seen as superficial and just vanity. Turns out that when he was twelve he had one lung collapse and as he was recuperating, the surgeon who'd helped him survive told Neal that if he exercised and kept his abdomen and torso hard and rigid enough, that it would keep him alive should he ever have a lung collapse again. Also the swimming helped build up his lungs.

Despite the way Neal dressed, which I'd characterize as Big City college imitation Hip-Hop, Neal Bartram was a serious young man, more serious than any I'd ever met, and that included my husband Jake. Neal was intelligent, thoughtful, and even philosophical. And in point of fact, it was Joe himself who threw Neal and me together to go see some older foreign movies playing once a week at the multiplex on Rte. 18 headed toward Junction City. We'd have dinner after at Wen Young's place there and talk about the movies and about, you know, all sorts of things.

Neal didn't fit into the town very well, and he felt he didn't fit into our time and place very well either. He was always talking about how much better this country had been thirty, forty, fifty years ago, and how much better he thought he'd fit into that time, that America. He did seem very discontented, even though there was no outward reason for that. He expected to be done writing his doctoral thesis by the end of summer and he was pretty certain he'd do well defending it, that would be around Thanksgiving, and that he'd receive his Ph.D. by Christmas. So no worries there. He'd begun looking into teaching positions at some Wisconsin and Minnesota universities that were on track to lead to tenure and he'd gotten some solid offers already. Even so, he wasn't completely happy. I always felt he was miles away.

I felt that more and more as the summer went on. He began to become interested, even a little obsessed about Ingoldsby. Every once in a while he'd begin asking me odd questions about the place I couldn't answer. That I don't think anyone could answer who's alive today.

I know other people have been in here giving depositions, including Ashley and Amanda, and I'm sure they told you their suspicions about Neal and myself having an affair. It's true. We did have an affair. It was my doing entirely, and I think Neal was pretty surprised by how aggressive I was at first, but after all he was a healthy twenty-four-year-old man and I don't believe I'm so terrible to look at.

The terrible thing is, I thought it would bring us closer, and it ended up doing just the opposite.

Neither one of us wanted it to be public knowledge. Me because Josh would be starting kindergarten soon, and also because people in town here had always assumed that now that I was back in Fulton's Point that Joe Weyerhauser and I would take up again. You know, high school sweethearts and all that bunk. And Neal, well Neal because that's the way he was, very considerate of others, and also very private about himself.

So once we started sleeping together we no longer saw each other during the day except when he came into the P.O. for his mail, or if we happened to run into each other at the food mart or pharmacy or video store, and we cut these meetings short. We stopped going to the movies or Chinese restaurant. It's really all my fault. You know how word gets around small towns. Neither of us wanted my reputation hung out to dry.

In a sense I believe I failed Neal exactly when he needed me most. I knew from the way he'd begun asking me questions about Ingoldsby that something had started to happen between him and the house. I don't know how else to put it. It wasn't as though it were haunted. Not exactly. But you know, growing up here in town, I naturally heard all kinds of things about the place, true and mostly false, and it did have a weird reputation. When I was a teen, guys would dare each other to stay there overnight and stuff like that.

Not one of the guys I grew up with ever brought up the name of Ingoldsby without meaning to cause a shudder. And it always did. Except not for Neal. He treated it as a special place, but never with any sense of fear or revulsion or anything like that. Incomprehension at times, but also an abiding curiosity to find out more about the place and the people who'd lived there. Especially during the past few weeks he was dropping hints just before we'd fall asleep or just as he had to leave in the morning before Josh woke up, and I got the impression that Neal was being drawn more deeply into the house somehow, into its past and its secrets, and that he wasn't in any way unhappy by that. Only he wanted to understand it better.

So it's ironic that just when we got physically closer to each other, we drifted apart personally, me and Neal. Of course, from the beginning I knew I'd never be able to hold him. That was a foregone conclusion from the very first time we met. You see, I handed him an official letter of some sort from the State Teaching Board, certifying him, I suppose it was, and it had his full name on it, Neal *Percival* Bartram... You don't get it? Percival was the name of one of the Knights of the Round Table. He was the noblest and purest Knight of King Arthur and he went out in search of the Holy Grail. The composer Wagner called him Parsifal and wrote an opera about him. And Parsifal, or Percival? He alone found the Holy Grail.

In some strange way I believe that Neal found his own Holy Grail and that it has something to do with him vanishing into Ingoldsby. You see, Chief, I believe that although we can't see him, that Neal is in Ingoldsby somewhere...somehow. That's something my so-called woman's intuition tells me for certain. That he hasn't fallen into harm of any sort, but that he's in a place we cannot ever find him any longer. And that he's content somehow. I don't know where exactly and I don't know how. And I guess I don't know how to search the right way to actually find him.

Or maybe that's what I want to believe because he's gone and I'm alone without the loveliest young man I ever met and I'm just saying any old crap.

WITNESSED: A. Estes-TRANSCRIBED: A. Nichols, 9/4/00

7.

PORTAGE COUNTY, WI
Office of the County Sheriff
172 Elm Street
Portage, WI 53901

RE: Missing Person: Neal P. Bartram

October 1, 2000

<u>Report on Missing Person: Neal P. Bartram</u>
Pursuant to the complaint/report filed September 1, 2000, by A.J. Torrington of the Ingals Trust in Chicago, received by Officer Jeremy Schaeffer, investigated by the same on September 2, 2000; with a follow-up investigation by Chief Abner Estes of the Fulton's Point Police Department, and following no sign of apparent foul play nor of the M/P.

<u>Action Taken</u>: September 4, 2000, Chief Estes requested this office to utilize a large number of personnel to conduct a full sweep of the property surrounding the main houses and garage at Ingoldsby. To this end, County Sheriff Griffith A. Angeles did call on six experienced men in addition to the four working for this office, deputized them for the period of the search, repeated instructions as to what we'd be looking for, and we drove in four vehicles to the estate to begin a full, clean sweep of the entire fifteen and a half acres. This lasted 11 a.m. of September 4th to 7 p.m.-nightfall; 11 a.m. through 4 p.m. of September 5th, 2000.

<u>Results:</u> Neither M/P Neal P. Bartram nor any of his personal belongings or clothing were found on the property except where he had left them inside the estate's gate-house caretaker's cottage. We did find sneaker prints closely marked around the house at various locations, mostly windows, terrace stairs, and doors, that matched the pattern of

M/P's shoes. But no other such prints. No signs of struggle or violence. Nothing out of the ordinary at all on the property.

Sheriff and his team then entered the garages and main house and conducted a thorough search of the interior until 7 p.m. Again we found no signs of the M/P or any of his personal belongings.

Conclusion: The disappearance of Neal P. Bartram is not connected in any material way to the Ingoldsby Estate. Any further investigation must be focused outside the estate and its grounds.

Date   Signature

Hey Ab -- this conclusion should
make you and the Trust happy.
It's off to the D.A.'s
office now — Griff

---

8.   PORTAGE COUNTY, WI
FULTON'S POINT POLICE
39000 Rte. 18
Fulton's Pt., WI 53908

TO: Madeline Eiche, Esq.
STATE of WISCONSIN, District Attorney's Office
Government Center, Building C
Madison, WI

October 13th, 2000

Report on Missing Person: Neal P. Bartram prepared by Chief Abner Estes with additional reports

<u>(enclosed) by Portage County Sheriff Griffin A.
Angeles</u>

Dear Ms. Eiche,

Enclosed find all generated reports on the Missing
Person. Although both this office and that of
Sheriff Angeles will continue to pursue all and
any new leads as they may happen to develop, at the
moment there are no further possible procedures or
lines of investigation to follow.

We are however requesting that your office put
this case at the head of the line in your national
hotline so that should any leads develop out of
state we can receive information immediately.

Upon your validated, dated, signed return of a copy
of this report, this office will forward all of
the M/P's property left behind to the Ingals Trust,
which shall handle it thereafter.

Regretfully,

Abner Estes, Chief

cc: G.A.A / A.J.T. records

Felice Picano

WISCONSIN STATE POLICE
Cold Case Department
Linklatter Mall, Bldg. E
Eau Claire, WI 54701
Detective-Sergeant Annabella Conklin

TO: Wayne G. King, Asst. D.A.
STATE of WISCONSIN, District Attorney's Office
Government Center, Building C
Madison, WI 53711

May 17, 2001

Dear District Attorney King,

In re. your letter to this office of May 13th, 2001: I received all of your materials <u>except</u> the journal noted in the newspaper reports and allegedly written by the M/P Neal Bartram, and while they tell a disturbing story indeed, we can't really proceed <u>without</u> that journal. In order for this office to work toward settling what appears to be so unsettled, please send a complete facsimile, or better yet the original of the journal to this office a.s.a.p.

Also note that this office rapidly accessed the National Police Network System and has already received a "strike" on the name of the M/P Neal P. Bartram since his disappearance. It appears to be in some way connected to a bank ATM card of the M/P found in the possession of another person detained and then apparently let go. Will get back to you with more when that data is processed here.

Also note that in light of the extreme mystery involved re: the M/P, this office has taken what might be seen as an correspondingly extreme action in requesting the M/P's name from all and any official, state, interstate, and national records going back in time to the date of the Time Capsule. I don't expect anything but…just checking. This may all take some months.

WISCONSIN STATE POLICE
Cold Case Department
Linklatter Mall, Bldg. E
Eau Claire, WI 54701
Detective-Sergeant Annabella Conklin

TO: Wayne G. King, Asst. D.A.
STATE of WISCONSIN, District Attorney's Office
Government Center, Building C
Madison, WI 53711

May 22, 2001

Dear Mr. King,

I received the material sent from your office re: M/P Cold-Case, reopened as Case #324-01. In other words, the alleged journals of Neal P. Bartram. I glanced them over and will read it in greater detail with notation.

One thing is for sure, the part that was printed on typewriter paper was <u>undeniably</u> printed out by a computer printer. Our in-office expert confirmed it was a Hewlett-Packard Deskjet, probably a 500 to 600 class printer. Further, the watermarking on the paper confirm that it is Williamette brand, 8 1/2 by 11 inch white "letter-sized copy-paper." The paper is widely sold around the U.S., and Williamette confirmed that the sample of paper we sent them "cannot be over eight years old or it would curl at the edges and yellow" as it is a very inexpensive paper, usually sold by the ream.

Our expert also confirmed that the lined notebook pages of the some of the journals are contemporary: They come from National Brand: it's Science and Laboratory Notebook #43-571, 128 numbered pages, pale yellow with green lines. Although this has been in National's catalogue for over four decades, the numbers printed on the upper outer corner here match the Verdana typeface, which National informed him only began to be used in 1998. These notebooks are sold primarily through university bookstores.

Enclosed is a copy of the report we received from the Sheriff's Office of West Hollywood, California. This was the only "strike" this office has received from the National Police Network System, although the M/P's name remains current. The findings are ambiguous. Who knows who the Caucasian Male was? Can we get another, color photo of M/P?

As per my last letter, inquires have been processed to a dozen different agencies of the U.S. Government re: Neal P. Bartram.

City of West Hollywood
Sheriff — Dan P. Bellardo
2900 San Vicente Blvd
West Hollywood, CA 90046

RE: Suspicious Person: 4:30 a.m.

November 24th, 2000

Report:

While on ordinary midnight to eight a.m. patrol, Officers Rob Adkins and Mario Gutierrez noticed Caucasian Male approximately 20 years old behaving oddly at three ATM windows of a Washington Mutual Bank set somewhat apart from a strip mall at 8100 Sunset Blvd.

Officers drove around a curving block onto Crescent Heights Blvd. and pulled into parking lot from that street and continued to observe C.M. attempt to use the ATM. Officers theorized that C.M. was probably inebriated, which would explain why he was unable to utilize card.

Officers pulled up to bank and approached C.M., asking him to step away from ATM window.

C.M. was surprised by officers' approach, but complied. Tall young gentleman, dark eyes, dark hair, pale skin, well-dressed, well-spoken with an American accent not from California. Officer Adkins asked what the trouble was. C.M. said he was unable to get money out of the bank for some reason. Could we help? Held out typical ATM card toward us.

Officers approached more closely. As C.M. was wearing a close-fitting leather jacket and black denims with dark cowboy boots, there was no reason to expect a revolver. Even so, Office Gutierrez remained apart with one hand on his weapon. Officer Adkins looked at card, which read Chicago Union Bank, confirming C.M.'s accent and being a stranger. Card was in the name of Neal P. Bartram. Officer asked if card belonged to C.M., who said that was him, Neal. P. Bartram. When asked for other ID he produced a wallet with one VISA credit card, library card for Northwestern University, but no driver's license and no picture ID. C.M. told officer this was his "second wallet." The "other one" was where he was staying, a block away, 1765 Havenhurst.

On closer inspection, C.M. was not inebriated. As he was courteous and in need of aid, Officer Adkins sought to help him. First ATM machine was not working at all. Second and Third machines, when accessed using card, replied "Sorry! We're Out of Cash" on screens. C.M. asked, "How can that be? They're a bank, aren't they?" We explained that on holiday weekend like now, Thanksgiving, ATMs often ran out of cash since many people access them. We suggested he try again after the holiday. His reply was "Well! I guess I'll just have to."

Officers offered to drive C.M. to where he was staying. He replied, "I'll walk. It's such a lovely, balmy, night. Don't you just love Los Angeles at night? I never guessed it would so amazingly wonderful!" C.M. walked off in correct direction toward Havenhurst Ave.

Officer Adkins noticed from balance receipt left by C.M. in his possession that the total balance for both of C.M.'s accounts was substantial–six figures.

STATE of WISCONSIN
District Attorney's Office
Government Center, Building C
120 State Street
Madison, WI 53711
Wayne G. King, Assistant D.A.

To: Detective-Sergeant Annabella Conklin
Wisconsin State Police, Cold Case Department
Eau Claire, WI 54701

May 28th, 2001

Re: Case #324-01

Dear Det.-Sgt. Conklin,

As per your request, enclosed find copies this office has on file, previously sent to us by Portage County Police, of M/P Neal P. Bartram's ID viz.:

1) His Illinois driver's license

2) His Northwestern University graduate student/faculty ID

Note that both documents show Bartram to be five feet six and a half inches in height, with "light brown eyes." On his DMV's ID "blonde hair" is listed, while on the school ID it's listed as "light brown" hair. The two photos xeroxed here confirm that coloring.

He hardly sounds like the "Tall young gentleman, dark eyes, dark hair, pale skin," of the West Hollywood Sheriff's Department report. Also, the large sum of money involved now gives us another alibi for potential foul play against Bartram. Especially as the person stopped was trying to access the money and possessed the ATM code. It is, however, odd how cavalier he was about not getting it, although he might be a consummate actor, not wanting to throw further suspicion upon himself.

Please look into those Chicago Union Bank accounts belonging to the M/P.

Wayne G. King

CHICAGO UNION BANK
24 South Wacker Drive
Chicago, IL 60606
Government Liaison Office

Detective-Sergeant Annabella Conklin,
Wisconsin State Police, Cold Case Department
Eau Claire, WI 54701

June 3rd, 2001

Re: Your Case #324-0 — Our Acct: 2770979913

Dear Detective-Sergeant Conklin,

Confirming our telephone conversation of May 29, 2001. As I told you then, the account of your Missing Person, Neal P. Bartram, was accessed by a person or persons using his ATM number. In fact, right after Thanksgiving of last year—the date of your forwarded West Hollywood Police Report—$500.00 was withdrawn. But just before the end of the year, December 29, 2000, we received Wisconsin State's notification of Bartram's Missing Person status, and we immediately sealed his accounts.

Until that date the account had been accessed as follows:

Withdrawals:

October 5, 2000	—$500.00	ATM, Madison, WI
October 30, 2000	—$800.00	ATM, Reno, NV
November 12, 2000	—$600.00	ATM, San Francisco, CA
November 26, 2000	—$500.00	ATM, Los Angeles, CA

Deposits:

| October 17, 2000 | —$12,000.00 | The Ingals Trust, Chicago IL |
| December 18, 2000 | —$250,000.00 | Anders Escrow, Fair Oaks, IL |

Attempts to reach next of kin on Bartram's 1994 application were returned, stamped "deceased" by the Post Officer of his hometown. They confirmed that his parents were killed in an airplane crash in April 1999, outside Missoula, Montana. The first deposit is a direct payment for his caretaking duties. Before this, Bartram received two checks for sixty-five thousand dollars each for each parent's loss, as insurance payouts. The last deposit shown above was from the sale of the Bartram home, of which he was sole heir. This is an interest bearing account. We would appreciate any help your office can provide locating Mr. Bartram's heir or heirs.

Georgia Dimaggio-Wilkes

STATE of ILLINOIS
Bureau of Records
Richard J. Daley Center
400 East Adams
Springfield, IL 62701

Detective-Sergeant Annabella Conklin
Wisconsin State Police, Cold Case Department
Eau Claire, WI 54701

June 8th, 2001

Re: Your Case #324-01
Our Case #98-230-2310

Dear Detective-Sergeant Conklin,

A codicil to the Last Will and Testament of Neal P. Bartram was received
by this office on September 30, 2000, drawn up by Ralph J. Elysious,
Atty at Law, 65 Station Avenue, Junction City, WI, on September 29th,
2000, and witnessed by two persons known to the decedent.

In his codicil, Mr. Bartram asserts that he is of sound mind and body,
and explains that he is revising his will of September 14, 1996, in light
of the death of his parents, as well as in the partial receipt and expected
full receipt of insurance monies pertaining to their death.

He states that he continues to wish that his maternal cousins, Dean
and Daryl St. Clair of Bellington, WA, receive monies—now in the
amount of $20,000—apiece to be held in trust for them by the Chicago
Union Bank until their 18th birthday. He leaves the "bulk of the estate
to my dear friend," Anthony Jackson Kirby of Milwaukee, WI, and Los
Angeles, CA.

Although this office is empowered to give over those monies once this
will has been properly probated according to Illinois state law, we did
not possess any exact address for Mr. Kirby until January 12th, 2001,

when he phoned this office and provided one.

I hope this answers your questions. A copy of this has been sent to Ms. Dimaggio-Wilkes of the Chicago Union Bank.

Office Mgr. — Ruby Tobias

THE JOURNALS OF NEAL P. BARTRAM

(parts handwritten in notebook/and otherwise transcribed to computer C-drive under Microsoft Documents: "What The...?")

June 2, 2000

Had a start yesterday, which became a mystery. Don't know what to make of it.

Was on the big John Deere machine, which I finally figured out how to baby to stay working without it shutting itself off every five minutes. I was mowing the lawn on the south side of the house at Ingoldsby. It's such a boring job, I'd brought my headphones and portable CD player, and was listening to REM when I happened to look up and saw two people standing on the deck, off what I thought might be the dining room.

It was a bright sunny day—really hot again; close to 90°F—and there they were! Young man and young woman, dressed all in white, yet oddly. He was tall, and not really thin but broad one way slender the other, with a shock of dark brown hair and dark eyes. She had light brown hair or blond hair, was much shorter, with pale eyes, but I couldn't really make them out due to the shadows. She wore a sort of flimsy sundress I guess you'd call it. Very thin material of some gauzy sort that caught and lifted with every breeze. She was slender—amazingly attractive in that outfit—her hair was short, and cut close around in back to her lower neck, yet kept long around the sides and front, and very curly. She was very pretty. I couldn't stop staring. He was very pretty too, if you like guys.

They looked as though they were talking intently about something. He leaned down to insist on something. She put a hand on his arm—he wore a white V-neck sweater (in this weather?) over a long-sleeved white shirt and pants of some thin material and white and brown wingtips. They looked like they belonged in a play, but were too far away for me to hear what they were saying. All of a sudden, he leaned down and kissed her lips. She didn't pull back or anything, but she kept him from doing it a second time.

I came to my senses and shouted at them, something like "Hey! You there! This is private property! What are you doing here?"

They looked at me. He said something to her. She squinted at me and half smiled. They turned around and went inside the house.

I shifted to neutral, engaged the brake, jumped off the mower, and ran to the house.

The terrace was empty and the door they'd just gone in through was solidly locked. Looking inside I couldn't see anyone or anything.

I walked around toward the living room windows and entry and saw no one, only covered furniture inside, as usual. I doubled back and tried the windows, headed toward the kitchen and pantry. No one inside there either. Hopped on the Deere and zipped around to the bedroom wing and looked in there. No one. Every door of the house locked up as it usually is. Where did they go?

Went back to mowing but I kept checking around. Didn't see any strange cars or vehicles and I didn't see the two again. Where did they come from? Where did they go?

What the...?

June 4, 2000

Was cleaning my teeth last night before going to sleep. Had a long and pretty exhausting day, first clipping and trimming those bushes alongside the north side of the house at Ingoldsby, and then reading more of Morrison and Ledrick's texts, taking more notes for my last few chapters, then going to town (!) for some food shopping. So I was good and ready for bed, there in the little bathroom, flossing away, when I heard music through that little pebbled glass window I've been leaving open for better circulation.

It sounded like old jazz music, I don't know, maybe Tommy Dorsey, Glenn Miller, something like that. That kind of old instrumental sound, lots of winds and brass and a piano, instruments doubling up for solos.

Tried to place where it could be coming from. There's nothing in the south until you hit town some seven miles away. Nothing west until Junction City, some twenty miles away, nothing to the north and west except Ingoldsby.

I finished flossing and was brushing when I had an idea: What if those kids I'd seen before had come back to the house to hang out and brought a boom-box with them?

I was still wearing shorts and a T-shirt, so I put on sneakers and went out. Sure enough, once I was outside, the music sounded much more like it was coming from the house.

This time I was smart enough to stop in the gate-house garage and pull out two big rings of keys for the house. Then I loped over the little rise over to the house.

Ingoldsby was dark as soon I was in view of it, say a football field away, and it was silent too, but with a conscious kind of silence, as though someone could see me coming, although I don't know how. I was wearing dark clothing and it was a clouded-over night.

I ran quietly to the house. Totally dark. No one there. I used my keys to go into the dining room terrace door, then when that proved empty, through the pantry door, around and into that door to the bedroom off the swimming pool. Place was empty, dark, noiseless.

I almost expected to hear the music start up again soon as I gotten back to the gate-house, but it didn't.

I am <u>sure</u> I heard that music. I am <u>sure</u> I saw that couple.

June 5, 2000

In town at Joe's Pharmacy having lunch. He and I and that older guy, Dr. Rodman or whatever his name is, were shooting the breeze and I said something about hearing music at night, but not being able to find the source. Dead silence, then the both of them had a fast answer. Joe said on still nights out here on the plains you can hear sounds from twenty miles away. The doctor said it might have been someone's car radio as they drove by, or parked to make out. That makes more sense to me.

Was in the library a little later and that Miss Noonan, the librarian, the one who wears all that lilac scent on her that's like dust and powder whenever she moves, kind of smothering you, she was being friendly and asked how I was liking living out "in the sticks" after the big city (i.e., Chicago). I told her about the music I'd heard. She too had an answer: said she read about it somewhere, how the mind makes up sounds in the quiet so it can be comforted, and not afraid. Yeah. Right, Miss Noonan!

June 7, 2000

I had no intention of keeping a journal until this stupid business at the house began, but now that I have, well, I guess I want to write about Bev Freneau, the postmistress (does that sound dirty or what). She's about twenty-eight and not really my type ("What type?" Bobby G. would ask. "When you're horny?") and slender but not skinny and with really nice breasts, pointy, and nice hips, though her rear is a little flat for my taste, and long dark hair she's keeping wrapped up high around her head in the heat wave we're having and she is pure s.e.x. and she knows it and she knows I know it too. So I was surprised when she moved over from the counter to one of the "cafe tables" in the pharmacy lunch counter today and began talking to me. Those olive green eyes, and nice skin. I mean, she's no kid, and I guess she thinks I am. Well, I was about to leave, was paying and Bev said she had to get back to the P.O. when Joe said, "Hey, Bev, maybe Neal here would wanta see that old movie." Turned out they were planning to go to the multiplex up on Route 18 but she wanted to see a French film made during World War II, I think she said, playing one night only, and Joe wanted to see the new James Bond, and so I said sure, I'd go with her. So we have a date, I guess, for the weekend.

Don't want to make too much out of it, but even though I knew it would happen out here I find I am missing sex, especially as all the women in town (!) from twelve to a hundred look me over like they want to eat me alive, and with this heat, believe you me, I am giving them everything to look at short of public lewdness, but not a damn one of them except the little girls will even say hello. Oh, except Miss Noonan at the library who makes me sneeze. But it's not like school where I had two or three women who'd drop by a week including Connie (with that mouth!) and it was so easy meeting women around the school when I had my bike.

June 8, 2000

Nothing happened. Sexually, I mean. We met at her place, the downstairs of a two-story house, not sure who lives upstairs, but whoever it was was looking after Bev's son Josh, who's going to be five next month. We drove to the movie, which was crowded on a Saturday night, with five theaters full. Didn't see Joe Weyerhauser, but nearly everyone I'd ever seen in Fulton's Point was at one or the other movie houses because they were milling about before and in the lobby getting popcorn and sodas.

The movie we saw was set in Paris in the middle of the nineteenth century and it was, well, what can I say, it blew me away. Totally unexpectedly and at the end as Garance in her carriage was swept away from her actor lover by the ocean of celebrating crowds, it just broke my heart as though I were the guy himself, and when the lights came up I had tears all down my face and so did Bev. We weren't alone either. It had been over three hours long and it just went by like nothing, like the wind, like life, I suppose.

We strolled a bit—she'd taken my hand as we left the theater. On the other side of the huge parking lot were a few restaurants, including the Wen Young Chinese Food Outlet, so we went in there to eat, both being hungry by then, even though it was after eleven. Bev said this was the site of the original—they're a chain— and we had a pretty good meal, so maybe I'll try the take-out one in Fulton's Point.

She told me the movie we'd seen had been made during World War II in France and that after the war the female star, Arletty, whose connections with a certain Nazi officer had helped the film be made underground, was deemed a traitor and had her head shaved and all. Amazing, though, that it could be made in secret with all those extras in the movie and the sets and all. So we had plenty to talk about, me and Bev, and when we got to her place, she said they were showing another good one next week and maybe we could go. I said if it were half as good as this, sure, and she kissed me on the cheek real soft and went in.

During dinner she told me about her husband and kid and all. She's had a pretty hard life for someone so young. I was already shaken up by the movie and I told her she'd gotten a raw deal and deserved some happiness. I meant it. And she knew I meant it.

June 9, 2000

I <u>said</u> I'd seen people and heard music at Ingoldsby. Yesterday afternoon, the weather changed to cloudy and cool. The gate-house flat was still warm, so I wandered outside with my Ledrick and thought I'd hang out on the bedroom terrace where the pool is. Torrington at the Ingals Trust said I could fill up and use the pool as long as I kept it clean. I've been swimming there on and off, usually in the early a.m. And I've pulled one of the wooden chaise lounges out of storage in the big garage.

So yesterday I mosey on down there in the afternoon, and what do I see? Three chaise lounges out and covered with pillows, as well as a matching low wood table, and there on the terrace, with the bedroom door open, were the guy and the girl I'd seen before. This time they were dressed a little differently. He was in one chaise, reading, and she was busily watering plants I'd never noticed before, three big geraniums on stands and a few hanging white petunias. Both wore old-fashioned retro sunglasses, almost round.

The guy noticed me first and shouted, "He's come back!" Not to her so much as to someone inside the bedroom. This other guy came out wearing a pair of strange-looking bathing trunks and a paisley bathrobe mostly open. Tall guy with lots of reddish brown hair, still wet from his swim, big pale blue eyes, big nose, big mouth, big smile. Introduced himself as Chester Ingals, and asked who I was.

I told him I'd been hired for the summer to watch the place and keep the lawns and bushes trimmed. Introduced myself. Said I didn't know anyone would be using the house.

"We're just down on a whim!" he admitted. "But it's so hot in town we decided to stay a few days." He introduced me to the girl, who is pert and pretty as I remember—did half a curtsey meeting me—name of Cecilia Nash, "My ward," Chester said. The other guy was "Anthony Kirby, my best friend since childhood."

Very easy-going folks, although clearly they've got piles of moola. Or at least Chester does. Not sure about the others. I said I'd been using the pool and was that okay, and he said sure, anytime.

So I stripped down to my Speedo—the violet one with the white stripe—and they made a big fuss over it. "Hubba hubba!" Chester said. Tony and Celia asked what it was made of and Tony sort of grabbed the material and said it felt like rayon. I thought everyone knew about Speedos. Guess not. "That Speedie going to stay on when you dive in?" Tony asked. Chester explained the physics of how it gripped my glutes and when wet would presumably grip even more, doing it all very scientifically. They're both funny guys. Meanwhile I could tell Celia was trying not to look at my package too much.

I dove in and did my usual ten minutes of laps. Chester joined me afterward and Tony, without a bathing suit—Celia said she was "shocked. Simply shocked!" and went indoors. The two guys started rough-housing and I got out and found her coming out again, dressed less casually, and she reminded the other two that they had an appointment to visit Chester's grandmother a few towns over for lunch, so they got out and said I could stay but I put on my shorts and sweatshirt and took off.

I guess they were out late, because I heard that old-time jazz music playing again late last night. So I'm <u>not</u> crazy after all.

June 9, 2000

I <u>said</u> I'd seen people and heard music at Ingoldsby, I can't quite put my finger on it, but there's something not quite... I don't know what I'm writing here!

Wait. For one thing, this guy Tony, he's as queer as anyone I've ever met. Certainly queer as Nate, as in "Gay Nate the gay roommate" I roomed with two years undergraduate at Chicago. Yet no one seems to notice it. He looks at me at times like he could swallow me without chewing, then the next minute he's all over Celia being stupidly romantic.

Meanwhile, I'm still trying to figure out all of their relationships to each other. Chester said that Celia was his "ward." I looked that up in the O.E.D. and he seems too young to have a ward, unless that's their way of saying she's his girl. His "paramour," Celia would say, blushing. She blushes at everything I say and half of what the others say, and I actually believe her. Then there's Chester himself. He's obviously in charge of the place. It's his house, he's told me that. But is he doing Celia? Or is he doing Tony? Or is anyone doing anyone? Or are they all doing each other? Like I say, I can't quite figure it out.

And some of the words they use! I mean, where do they dig them up? The other day Tony said that surely "a healthy young fellow like yourself must know at least one round-heels in town."

At least one <u>what</u>?

So Tony explained, surprised that I didn't know the term: it means a "woman who falls backward into bed easily, as though her heels were rounded."

Is that nuts or what?

Still, they're nice folks, easy-going and fun to spend time with. Chester and Tony have known each other since they were little kids, and Celia has known them almost as long. Oh, Chester took me aside and said I should call him, much hesitation, I should call him by his nickname. I waited, wondering what it could be? "Penis-breath"? "Hung-stud"?

Suspense, then—"Bud!"

Well, it's better than Chester. And he sort of looks like a Bud. Not quite fully formed. A big boy. Oh, and once they all heard I was writing my Ph.D. thesis they were like suddenly very impressed, and it was "shouldn't you be studying?" or "shouldn't you be busy writing?" until I cleared that up. I do that here at the gate-house apartment.

But Celia? Well, she is very, very pretty, sexy-pretty, and she knows it, and she flirts all the time. It's all I can do not to have a chubby when I'm around her. Then I remember if I do, there's always Tony checking me out.

But hey, at least I'm not bored anymore.

June 14, 2000

They must have brought their own furniture and stuff or gotten some of it from out of storage nearby, because when I stepped into the bathroom—"the water closet," they call it—looking for a towel, I noticed the bedroom was filled with things, a bed, big reading chair, tables. They were playing music and it was coming out of a console built into this long wall in Bud's bedroom—the place is filled with built-ins, hidden bureaus, etc.

Bud showed it to me, and it was this ancient and really handsome blond-wood record player, playing these old, long-playing 78 RPM records! So I checked out the rest of the collection—in an adjoining built-in cabinet, natch—and it was all Billy Holiday and Louie Armstrong, Arturo Toscanini and Arthur Nikisch and stuff like that. In the old original covers, which are in great condition too. Totally retro. Very cool, Bud!

Oh, and the retro theme is throughout the bedroom. On the table that's cantilevered out of—you guessed it—the built-in headboard of the bed, I found all these cool old magazines from like the 30's, <u>Vanity Fair</u>, <u>Punch</u>, an old <u>New Yorker</u>, and this nifty old issue of <u>Popular Mechanics</u> that had this futuristic drawing of a streamlined car on the cover, and it read "Oldsmobile's Big Breakthrough—The Hydromatic Transmission!"

How cool is that?

Have to borrow one of the magazines some day. Just love that old Americana.

While the others were busy doing something, I let Celia touch my "Speedie," as all three of them call it. She said it was soft as a Siamese cat. Mee-oow! A chubby and a lot of blushing.

June 15, 2000

Glory Hallelujah! I finally got laid! What's it been? Three weeks or more? A record for me going celibate. But the long dry spell is over. And I must have sensed it was going to happen because just before showering to go out with Bev last night, I beat off, just so I wouldn't be too ready.

After the movie we went to the Chinese place again and talked again. This time she asked me about myself but I kept moving the conversation back to her, asking about her kid and her family and what it was like growing up here in Nowheresville. As much to keep her on topic as because I don't really want to talk about myself and my lately extremely stupid life. And it paid off.

Seeing her into her doorway, I began kissing her and she pulled me deep into the doorway and she was like all over me, so I turned the key she'd put in the door and opened it and pushed us in, and she said, "Yes, yes, no one should see," and from there it was the old Bartram smoothness in control, of course along with her being really hot and hungry, I mean her husband's been dead, what, three years and he was sick the last six months and what if she hasn't, you know, in a really long time?

So by the time we got into her bedroom, most of our clothing was off and I was eating her out, then pushing her down on me, then BA-BANG. Even with having come earlier I was hot enough for three pops, no pulling out, finish one, go for the next. She popped a minimum six times, she was all wet, grabbing me like a crazy woman. I got away when the old lady upstairs caring for the little boy came down, calling "Is that you, Bev?" Snuck out the bedroom window. Round-heeled woman, huh?

June 16, 2000

Wait one minute. Wait just one minute. Something happened yesterday at the house with the three of them, and I may be crazy after all. I mean seriously fucking nuts. Maybe losing my folks and staying with the thesis despite that and then coming here away from everyone and everything I know really did unhinge me more than I thought, because what happened yesterday afternoon was...

Let me tell it step by step. Ever since the heat wave broke, the weather's been lousy here. Cool, damp, stormy looking. Yesterday was no exception. So after my morning work I walked over to Ingoldsby to use the pool. They're all there, wide awake, as I strip down for a swim. When I get back out and put on my sweatshirt, they're talking about this mystery novel Tony's reading by one Raymond Chandler, <u>The Big Sleep</u>, which sounds familiar and he's making fun of it, reading examples of really bad purple prose. Bud says, "Tony could write better, of course." Celia—who's wearing this short-sleeved sky blue sweater and no bra under it—says, "It's the hit of the season. Can fifty thousand readers be wrong?" And they're arguing, while I'm wondering wasn't that the name of a movie with Bogart and Bacall? Detective Philip Marlowe and all? So I begin asking questions, and sure enough it's the same story. So that was weirdness number one. Why write a novel based on a movie that's been out more than fifty years?

Tony meanwhile says what does Celia know about real literature since all she reads is the communists. Then he names John Steinbeck, Ellen Glasgow, and Maxim Gorky, two of which I read stories of in high school, and I remember the teacher called them Regionalists, not Commies. So this argument goes further, until Bud jumps in the pool and grabs Tony and pulls him in too. Celia gets terrifically splashed. Their usual horseplay. But she's soaking and pissed, especially as it's a nice skirt she's wearing. She asks me to go in and get a towel, would I? Then Bud and

Tony, who are in the pool, ask for towels too.

So I go into the bath—not the water closet, they're separate—and find a handful and I hear Bud yelling to come out and see something; looks like lightning coming quickly across the hills toward the house. From indoors the sky has turned weirdly dark, rose-colored if that makes any sense, and as I head out to the pool terrace, I yell to them to get the hell out of the pool, and there's this enormous crack of thunder and huge bolt of lightning at the same time, hitting I swear to God right over Ingoldsby, absolutely <u>deafening</u> and <u>blinding</u>. I drop the towels and run outside afraid they're hit and...

Okay I'm going to write, it...and <u>there was no one there</u>. Nothing there. Wait, that's not true. My sweatpants and book were where I'd left them. The chaise lounge too. But only one. No other furniture. None of the flowers or plants Celia fusses with. The pool was there, with water. But they were gone. All three of them. Not a sound. Then, it gets better, when I turned around, the house was closed and locked and indoors completely empty except for what's usually covered with sheets and sealed with Scotch tape. Totally different than I'd left it all not a half minute before!

Even the towels I'd just dropped on the lintel were gone and the bedroom door was closed and, yes, locked. Whatever the storm was, it moved away pretty quickly, as I stood there on the terrace. Believe me, I stood there a while trying to figure out what had happened.

I didn't succeed.

June 19, 2000

One thing's now straightened out. For better or worse.

The guy who hired me, A.J. Torrington? He phoned on his weekly check-up and after we'd talked a while about the place and its upkeep and all, as casually as I could, I asked if any of the Ingals family who owns the place ever came down for a visit.

"They might. But they'd let me know and I'd let you know in advance. Why? Has anyone been bothering you there?"

I told him no, then asked him to clarify: They don't ever come down for a week in the summer, or a weekend?

"Of course not. The elder members go off to Maine and the Riviera. As for the ones your age, they go to the Seychelles and Rarotonga and places like that. No one's used the place in over fifty years! That's why the Trust is thinking of giving it to the state."

"To the state?"

"Yes. As a museum."

I thanked him for clarifying.

Yes, thank you, very much, sir! Oh and by the way, Mr. Torrington, I thought I would let you know that I am <u>totally fucking nuts</u>.

June 20, 2000

Haven't been back to Ingoldsby since Sunday, and you know what happened. It's remained stormy and cool, cloudy, so I've kept all the windows in the gate-house apartment closed. No yard work to do. Have not swum, but I have done some jogging—in the opposite direction.

In town yesterday afternoon having lunch at Joe's lunch counter, got to talking to Doc Stansbury—seems Rodman is his first name. I hinted as I'd not had a physical exam in years. He's semi-retired, but he said I should come over to his office. I did. He had all the equipment, although the office was fairly close and not much used.

Sort of hinted around at what I'd told the librarian, hearing strange noises and stuff. Mentioned what those girls, Ashley and Amanda who always hang around me, said, about Ingoldsby being haunted. He said nothing, then asked if I wanted sleeping pills. Told me I should have more activities to occupy me. He and Joe play gin rummy. They're missing a third for the summer. Would I join them. Said I would.

So Doc didn't exactly brush off the whole thing, and I didn't push it. But as I was leaving, he asked in a low voice, "So these 'events'? Are they just auditory or visual too?"

"Sometimes visual too," I admitted. He recommended lots of beer and movie-going and the sleeping pills he was prescribing.

Why is it I think he knows something he's not letting on? Oh great! Now I'm getting paranoiac too.

Just for historical accuracy, the second movie Bev and me saw was Bertolucci's <u>1900</u>, another sweeping, this time Italian, history movie. Pretty good. Kinda pervy too at times. As involving as the other one.

June 21, 2000

Still haven't been back to Ingoldsby. But I did join Joe and Dr. Stansbury for cards at the pharmacy last night. Joe closed up and pulled down the shades. Lots of fun. Nice guys. Of course, I'm one of those really annoying people who doesn't remember how a card game is played or what's wild or what wins, until I'm told. Then whammo! We were all three neck and neck for an hour or so, then I pulled ahead and beat Joe and Doc.

Won two dollars and seventy cents. Penny a point.

June 22, 2000

Still not gone back to Ingoldsby. But it seems I have a standing date with Bev on Saturday for the movies—read the fuckies, because we skipped the movies, went to dinner at the Chinese place, then I drove her back and we were all over each other. I didn't beat off earlier this time and I came while she was doing me with her mouth, and then another three times. Not since that mulatto chick Gina have I had such hot sex. It's not that we fit so well, or have even once come at the same time. We're sort of like big cats with each other, licking and biting and all. That is, when we're not wrestling or wrestling our way out of the sheets. One of these days that kid of hers is going to walk right in on us. I got away in time. Slept to noon today. Totally fucked out. Didn't even need the pills Doc gave me.

June 23 2000

Okay, so it had been over a week since I'd been there and I was feeling better about my life, so I took my mind in my hands and went for a walk down to, you guessed it, Ingoldsby, Speedo on underneath my shorts and T-shirt. Lovely sunny day. Just going for a swim, right. Like nothing had happened there. Ever.

Okay. I walked down to Ingoldsby and <u>there they were</u>. They were lying around the pool terrace, which of course was fully furnished as before, like nothing had happened. All three seemed to be in various states of prostration. (So If I'm nuts, I'm at least consistent and yet original too, since they're never quite exactly the same as they were before, are they?) Believe me, I resisted the urge to ask: Uh, would any of you care to tell me where you <u>utterly vanished to</u> the other day?

I resisted partly because it seems like they were preoccupied with hangovers. Seems they'd had a quite busy Sunday night at some playboy pal of Bud's party. Bunky Huenecker—seems everyone they know has names like Bunky and Muffy and Fluffy. Rich kids! Or rich whatever they are.

Bud was the least incapacitated. He was actually hitting golf balls off tees. And so up and around. Celia, meanwhile, wearing those funny dark glasses even though it was gray outside, insisted that she was making breakfast for everyone. This would consist of—get this! —three pancakes per person, ham, Canadian bacon, three eggs each and toast with no doubt huge gobs of butter on it. I said I'd pass, I'd eaten. Seems she'd gotten a little tipsy the previous night and, I'm quoting Bud now, "danced the kasaztka with someone who claimed to be Russian royalty." Tony, however, was laid out on a chaise, mostly under a bath towel—yes, one of those towels—moaning now and then. It turns out he also had won a bet by outdrinking some other idiot by downing a magnum of French champagne, i.e., the Good Stuff. Bud meanwhile sported a tiny little shiner, which, when I probed, it turned out was due to a quote political difference unquote he'd had with another party-goer over... (I stop for effect, should any damn fool except me ever read this)...over Mussolini's invasion of Ethiopia. "When I mentioned how repulsive it seemed for Italians with Gatling guns to be casually sipping Chianti and mowing down fellows with spears, he accused me of being a, you know, darkie-lover."

My first thought was—now I've heard everything! Then I asked Bud why he was upset over Mussolini rather than the invasion of Poland or the Anschluss with Austria or the Sudetenland or one of Germany's other atrocities. He looked me in the face with a completely straight face and said, "But Neal, old pal, everyone knows we'll have to go to war with Hitler eventually." Tony asked us to lower our speech to a scream, <u>please</u>.

It was that ever so casually said "eventually" that somehow got to me.

So I watched Bud hit a bunch of balls away from the house, then Celia came out again, with a tray with dishes, silverware, and big glasses of orange juice, saying food would be a few minutes more. And she looked so pretty with her pale yellow short-sleeved little sweater that I said, "Fine. I'll have some of your cholesterol-drenched breakfast!" And she seemed happy about it, although Tony said, "For someone who eats what looks to me like nuts and bolts and plain water, some real food might do you good."

And that was when the idea crossed my mind. "Do you two also think that we'll eventually got to war with Germany?" I asked Celia and Tony when we sat down to eat. They both said they found current events, and European current events especially, far too boring for words. Would I change the subject please.

Afterward, they went indoors for naps and I strolled with Bud to his garage—doors wide open, of course—and we talked about his cars. When I called them antique, he said, "The only antique is that Stanley Steamer my grandfather brought." We then talked about his newest acquisition, an Oldsmobile four-door convertible he told me was ridden in by—get this—"Fiorello when he opened the New York's World's Fair. Look inside on the floor, notice anything different?" Bud asked.

I looked, said I didn't notice anything different.

"You must be <u>blind</u>! This car has <u>no clutch</u>!" Bud exulted.

They came out again and I said I'd bring a "Speedie" for Tony to wear. I also flirted outrageously with Celia. And waited for you know what.

But they never disappeared and I ended up leaving to go do thesis work.

Crazy as all this may be and crazy as I may be, I am developing a "theory" in which I am <u>not completely insane</u>. Which itself is probably a perfect sign of my insanity.

June 25, 2000

Went to town, had lunch in the pharmacy—Bev flew out as I came in, not even looking at me—and afterward I stopped in the library. I was looking up dates in the big Encyclopedia Americana they've got there when Ms. Noonan—""Please, Neal. Call me Tonia! All my friends do!"—asked what I was doing, and when I mentioned the time period I was looking for, she brought over two reference books. One was a <u>Time-Life Book, 1933–1942</u>, the other was a Time Line book, <u>Black Tuesday to Pearl Harbor</u>. So I opened the first and it had photos and there they were, photos of girls with their hair cut like Celia's, wearing those short-sleeved sweaters and long skirts like she does, and guys with those big bathing suits like Bud and Tony's. And there were the photos of the 1939 World's Fair, with Mayor "Fiorello" La Guardia riding in Bud's car, which the caption said was the very first car on sale with automatic transmission. ("You must be <u>blind</u>! This car has <u>no clutch</u>!") And when I looked in the Time Line under "literary best sellers," sure enough I found Chandler's mystery, <u>The Big Sleep</u>, and Steinbeck's <u>The Grapes of Wrath</u>, arguably his most "communistic" book, all of it together under what year?

1940.

1940. Almost two years before the U.S got involved in World War II. Eleven years after the Depression began. About three or four after the country really began to pull out of that depression. A sort of magic twenty-four months of American life—teetering between a bad past and a worse to come future.

Okay, here's <u>My Theory</u>: Bud Ingals, Celia Nash, and Tony Kirby are living in the summer of 1940. And when I'm there with them, so am I.

Comments are not asked for and not required.

So naturally I concentrated on that year and I looked up as much as I could.

I was there all afternoon, taking tons of notes. Finally Tonia stepped out and came back, carrying a Snapple Ginseng Tea— guess she's seen me sipping them—and we talked about the "good old times" together. "I'll bet people were a whole lot nicer then," she mused and really seemed sweet. (If I could only shake off all the powder she wears, like in a shower or something, she might be do-able. She's not that old. And she does seem awfully interested in me and—should I write it—awfully ready.)

By the way, also on that best seller list, a Pocket Book, one of the first paperbacks, costing 25 cents—are you ready?—Thomas Hardy's <u>The Return of the Native</u>.

At any rate, here goes more evidence for my theory: The three occupants of Ingoldsby dress in fashions of 1940 and speak a more formal English, even when trying to be casual. Their slang is, well, let's face it, pretty old hat. If they are, what can one call them? Not apparitions: they're as physically solid and touchable as me—and they're really are living in 1940—though I have no idea how!—still at least that can be tested, proven.

June 27, 2000

So I'm home after dinner last night and I'm about to work on my thesis and playing back some verbal notes on my cassette recorder when I hear this car horn going "Ooga! Ooga!" downstairs. I flip a new tape into it, saying, "Could this be a sound of 1940! Can sounds they make be heard and recorded?" You know, a real Dan Rather. When I hear a shout outside the window and go look, it's Joe Weyerhauser standing up in the passenger seat of this big old red convertible Doc is driving. Seems it's Doc's '55 Buick Roadmaster.

They say they've got two six-packs of beer and three kinds of chips—potato, tortilla, and corn—do I wanna play gin?

What a schmuck I am, thinking it was Bud and the others!

Doc and Joe come up and I clear the table and we begin to play.

Halfway through the game I begin asking questions about Ingoldsby. You know, as casual as possible. How come no one's lived there in over fifty years like Torrington told me. Since I would live there in a second if given the chance, and all. Doc is being close-mouthed but Joe spills that "no one from the Ingals family ever used the place regularly after what happened there."

Now we're getting somewhere. Me, innocent: "Oh? What happened there?"

Seems according to the two of them—mostly agreeing, though not always—back "before the Second World War" there was a freak fire and it killed the heir to the Ingals fortune along with two of his friends. Then Joe says, <u>allegedly</u> killed them, since his grandpa, who was on the volunteer fire force, always insisted that no bodies were ever recovered from the fire.   ·

When I ask more pointed questions, Doc, who's about seventy-two or so and must have been a kid of twelve at the time, tells me lots of rumors he heard, then clams up and tells Joe to do so too. So naturally I ask if the three who died in the fire are the ghosts.

"Why?" Doc asks me, point-blank. "You seeing ghosts at Ingoldsby?"

Very sharp! He already thinks I'm mental. What could I say except of course not, but I'd heard about them in town. Slick escape from that one.

At least I won four dollars off them!

June 28, 2000

The microfiche newspapers at the Fulton's Point Library only go back fifty years. If I want earlier I've got to go to Junction City. I'm driving there today.

June 29, 2000

Saw Bev again last night. We didn't even have dinner. Just sex. No talk, no pretenses anymore, we just got down to the nitty-gritty.

But the real news is what I found at the <u>Junction City Intelligencer</u>, Portage County's newspaper "since 1871!" which for a dollar allowed me to read, select, and photocopy its paper for May 26th, 1940. Went to the J.C. Library too, which carried other Wisconsin and even Chicago newspapers for the time. And sure enough Chester Ingals, Anthony Kirby, and Cecilia Nash were all believed dead or missing after a freak lightning strike and resulting fire that gutted the front half of the Ingals home, outside of Fulton's Point, "around three-thirty in the afternoon."

People driving on Lakeview Drive (now Route 18) saw black smoke, drove to get nearer and were stopped at the gates of

Ingoldsby. They managed to get into the gate-house apartment and call the fire department. By the time the Keystone Kops and Cellar-Savers arrived, the entire living quarters of the house had been gutted, but not the bedrooms. The high winds charred it to nothing and alighted on the multicar garage where Ingals had his collection of expensive and rare automobiles.

The reporter wrote how stormy the past three weeks were: more lightning storms (12) and more tornado touch-downs (6) than in any previous recorded year.

*

Meaning what exactly for me? That they <u>are</u> ghosts.

Except I happen to know they aren't. They're as real as I am. Especially Celia.

Now for something truly sick. While I was screwing Bev the other night, guess who I was fantasizing about? You guessed it, The Long Dead Celia Nash. Nobody but me better read this. Maybe I should stop writing. it. No, all this is so weird, I've got to keep getting it down or I'll really begin to think I've gone over the edge.

Oh, here's the article. I scanned it into the C drive:

FELICE PICANO

The Junction City Intelligencer

Morning Edition 　　*Sunday, May 26th, 1940* 　　*5 Cents*

FIRE RAVAGES INGOLDSBY INGALS HEIR, TWO OTHERS MISSING, BELIEVED DEAD

Unlikely Anyone Escaped Freak Lightning Fire Says Fulton's Point Fire Chief Jackson

★

Celebrated for Its Architecture, Estate Is Partly Fire-Damaged, Rare Autos Unharmed

By Roger Pollets

Fulton's Point, WI—Motor-tourists from Madison, out for a quiet country drive on Lakeview Drive, found instead of blue skies, clouds of black smoke, and drove to its source. They were stopped at the gates of the Ingals fortune heir's recently completed architectural marvel, known as Ingoldsby. Climbing the gates, they could see the main house on fire. Hugh J. Branch got over the gate

and into the unlocked estate gate-house, from which he was able to telephone local operator Minnie Drake, who called together members of the Volunteer Fire Department. When the fire truck arrived, Mr. Branch's wife Estelle let it in and told Chief Jackson that her husband and his brother Samuel had gone to the main house to see if anyone needed help.

By three-thirty in the

afternoon, the entire front portion of Ingoldsby had been wrapped in flames and completely gutted. The fire apparently swept through the living and dining rooms, kitchen and library. Prevailing westerly winds evidently kept it from reaching the bedroom wing, set at an angle to the destroyed section. Small fires were put out around the estate's large garage

INGOLDSBY FIRE, continued on Page 3

FIRE RAVAGES INGOLDSBY

INGOLDSBY FIRE, from Page 1

where they might have destroyed Ingal's prominent collection of expensive and rare automobiles.

Sheriff Edmund Acker and the fire team searched through the ruins for signs of any bodies, as it was understood that Chester Ingals and at least two friends, Mr. Anthony Kirby and Miss Cecilia Nash, both of Milwaukee, had been at the house for the weekend, and seen around in Fulton's Point and environs. No bodies were located, Chief Jackson told this reporter, "We've not found anything but charred ashes. The wind churned the fire up into an inferno. No one could have escaped."

Sheriff Acker spoke of the stormy past three weeks. More lightning storms (12) and more tornado touch-downs (6) have been recorded than in any previous year. He and his deputy were called to six occasions caused by storms this week.

No servants were present on the property at the time of the fire. It was believed that aside from a caretaker who sometimes resided in the gate-house, no help was ordinarily sent down to the estate from one of Ingals city residences. Young Moderns, the three

were either used to fending for themselves and/or preferred impromptu weekend trips to our district.

Twenty-three-year-old Chester Ingals, glamorous heir to the Ingals Iron Works fortune, was a well-known figure in the state, as well as in Portage County. Especially during the past two years when he engaged Charles Sigurd Thurston, protégé of the controversial architect Frank Lloyd Wright and a figure in his own right, to design and build a large new estate on the southernmost sector of the Ingals property. Thurston's much-discussed estate was the height of the modern. One story high, it was a rambling "ranch" style building with the most up-to-date conveniences, including a large kitchen refrigerator, air coolers throughout, built-in wireless sets and record players in many rooms, a sport regulation-sized swimming pool, and of course the separate, heated, ten-car garage for Ingals's conspicuous collection of automobiles, a building larger and more comfortable than most Wisconsin homes. Utilizing rare woods from the East and South America along with gold and aluminum

trim, when completed, the estate at Ingoldsby was thought to cost an amazing $400,000!

An earlier three-story house built in 1907 on the property was destroyed by freak lightning four years ago. Untenanted at the time, two servants sleeping nearby escaped unharmed. Part of the young heir's legacy, when he began building Ingoldsby, Chester Ingals often said that it was his "favorite place growing up."

Although he was rumored by newspapers in Chicago and Milwaukee to be a "playboy" and was even once rumored to have dated socialite Liz Marshall, Chester Ingals was a gentleman with strong ties to our county and town. Junction City Mayor James Wilcomb said, "He was a young man of great probity, charity, and courtesy, who brightened our local life." Mrs. Anthea Huenecker, our social doyenne, said, "Chester and his attractive, well-behaved friends were always welcome at our little soirees. He and they will be sorely missed."

The grieving family has neither commented nor announced funerary plans.

The Junction City Intelligencer

June 30, 2000

It doesn't stop getting interesting, does it? Here's an unexpected turn of events.

I was down at Ingoldsby's pool doing laps late yesterday afternoon, vaguely wondering where the three were, when they drove up in Bud's 1933 Dusenberg. The wheels are made of chromed stainless steel and are huge. The whole thing is gorgeous. At any rate, they had just been to a matinee at the Fulton Theater, and Celia couldn't stop talking about the new movie they just saw which was—ta da! <u>The Philadelphia Story</u>! I.e., that old black-and-white movie I must have seen about a dozen times because Gina played it so many times and wouldn't shut up talking about it all the time.

Celia was completely taken with it, and so was Tony. They were acting out scenes between Jimmy Stewart and Kate Hepburn and getting all the lines wrong but having a good time doing it. Me and Bud were sitting back with lemonades enjoying it all.

They were enthusing about it, really excited, Tony assuring everyone that Hepburn was going to get the Oscar for it that year, and Celia saying, no no, Cary Grant would, when it just pops out of my mouth. "You're both wrong. Stewart gets the Oscar." Moment of silence. They ignored me and chattered on, but a minute later Bud took me out onto the living room terrace and said, "I believe you. But then you know for sure, don't you?"

I tried to get out of it. But he was not about to be diverted. "Just like you already know how to drive a car without a clutch, don't you? You probably drive one every day." Then he lifted up a copy of <u>Popular Mechanics</u> left on the table, with its cover reading "Frequency Modulation: Is it the Wireless of the Future?" And he asked me, "Well, is it?" When I didn't respond, he said that he spoke to the main office of his company in Chicago and they never hired a caretaker named Neal Bartram. Never heard of him. Nor is there such a student currently enrolled at Northwestern University in the History Ph.D. program.

So I told Bud I'd be happy to show him the signed contract I have for my summer work—as well as my student ID, even though both have the current year on them.

The weather started up, thunderheads out of the west, the north, the east, a real mess. A few drops of rain, but distant rumblings so far, reminding me of that newspaper report. Then Celia and Tony's high spirits found us outside, and she waltzed Bud away while Tony foxtrotted me indoors. After a minute or so of awkwardness, he took the girl's part.

After an hour or so of avoiding Bud, I managed to get away. He was so down, however, that when I left I whispered into his ear, "FM radio, yes. And we do eventually fight Hitler." He held my jacket until I said, "Yes. We beat the pants off him."

"But how can you be here?" he asked, following me outside again. I told him I didn't have any idea how. But that we aren't always in sync, somehow. When he asked what I meant, I pointed to the lightning beginning to strike down on the lawns, as close as the garage roof. "Whatever brings us together, this is what separates us!"

"The rain?" he asked. "No, the lightning," I told him. Just then, Kr-rack, loud and blinding, and twice more. I was alone and they were gone and the house was all locked up.

So now I'm sure the lightning has something to do with it. And as the house was burned half up by a freak lightning strike, I just know there is a connection between the two.

July 1, 2000

One of those teenage girls who are always hanging around— Ashley, her name is, the one who actually has some boobies— slipped a note into my hand yesterday as the three of us were talking at my car. I looked at it and it was her phone number. Just what I need. But I called and said, look, this age difference thing and all. But she said no, it was about Ingoldsby. Would I meet her. All cloak and dagger like she's one of the Spy Kids in the movie. So I drive over to behind the town hall section near the police station and she tells me that the estate has a weird reputation and one of the caretakers went missing from there a while ago. Her grandpa was a landscaper and he'll tell me all about it. I humored her. Took down Grandpa's phone number

FELICE PICANO

and all. Won't call him unless I need to.

I had asked the Junction City newspaper's archives to notify me if they found anything else on Ingoldsby in their files. They sent me one from eight months later, about Bud's will providing funds to rebuild the house as it was.

Here it is scanned in:

The Junction City Intelligencer

Weekend Edition   *Friday, January 5th, 1941*   *5 Cents*

FIRE-DAMAGED ESTATE TO BE REBUILT / RESTORED

Ingals Family Reveals Heir's Will Provided For Complete Restoration of Estate Fire-Damaged by Last Summer's Storms

★

Town Receives Gift to "Establish Town Hall"

By Roger Pollets

Fulton's Point, WI— There was relief today with news that the architectural prodigy that brought us fame will not be torn down. Instead, by terms of the Last Will & Testament of Chester Ingals, who perished in the damaging fire, Ingoldsby will be rebuilt to its former glory.

Attorneys for the Ingals Iron Works announced the news in Chicago yesterday. Ingals's will was opened to public record. By its terms, up to $500,000 is allocated for "the complete restoration

ESTATE REBUILDS, continued on Page 3

FIRE-DAMAGED ESTATE TO BE REBUILT

ESTATE REBUILDS, from Page 1
of the estate and replacement of autos in case of an Act of God. With the hope that Ingoldsby will eventually be a public building, open to all." In- gals's estate was reported as "three and a half million dollars." Most goes to the family, but $50,000 goes to "Fulton's Point Town to establish a town hall." Details of the wills of the others who also perished, believed to be smaller than Ingals's if also sizable by Portage County standards, will be made available to the public upon request.

The Junction City Intelligencer

So yesterday that dweeby funny guy Jim Kleinherz phones me and says he found a Follow-Up story from a few days after the fire. And did I want to see it? Did I? I got him to scan it in and then e-mail it to me.

Guess what? <u>They never found the bodies</u>. Let me write that once more. They never found the bodies at all. Meaning what? That they were <u>not</u> killed by the fire.

Then what happened to them? Well, I'm developing a second theory, this one even nuttier than the first. But hey, that one seems to be kind of right, doesn't it?

It means I've got to take one of the three into my confidence and probe. Bud is the "scientific" one and so he might be the one. Not Celia. I don't want to expose her to this. On the other hand, Bud really reacted to what I told him. Or did he? On second thought, he didn't react <u>that</u> much. I thought that was because he'd already thought about it a while, and so had sort of gotten used to the idea. Maybe it's something else. Maybe he knows something that...that what?

Only one thing to do. Ask him.

Here's what Kleinherz sent me:

FELICE PICANO

𝕿𝖍𝖊 𝕵𝖚𝖓𝖈𝖙𝖎𝖔𝖓 𝕮𝖎𝖙𝖞 𝕴𝖓𝖙𝖊𝖑𝖑𝖎𝖌𝖊𝖓𝖈𝖊𝖗

Weekend Edition   *Thursday, May 30th, 1940*   *5 Cents*

HOPE VANISHES OF FINDING HEIR, FRIENDS IN ESTATE FIRE

"We've Searched Every Square Foot and Sifted Every Ash," Sheriff Acker Reports

By Roger Pollets

Fulton's Point, WI— Under pressure from the Ingals family, county and state authorities, Sheriff Edmund Acker yesterday allowed death reports to be written for the Ingals heir and his two friends believed to have perished in the fire that swept Ingoldsby Saturday noon.

"We've searched every square foot of the property now, and we've sifted every square inch of ash, and there's nothing to explain what, besides incineration, could have happened," Acker admitted.

The Ingals family announced a private funeral service in Chicago for its scion and the friends who perished with him.

The Junction City Intelligencer

July 3, 2000

Okay, Tony and me had "the talk." This was his doing entirely and began with Tony asking if I could trust him, really trust him? I said sure, though it sounded so...dramatic!

"Isn't it?" he asked back. Then told me that he was torn between his best friend since school, the fellow who'd treated him best in life of anyone, and the girl he loved...who—get this—loved him back.

• 216 •

I burst into laughter. Seeing this, Tony stared at me and asked what on earth was wrong with me. "Here I am, unveiling my deepest secret to you, and..."

"Your deepest secret?" I asked. Then I said that his deepest secret, if it even <u>was</u> one, which I strongly doubted, was that he was gay and covering it up.

"Of course I'm gay," he said. Then he said they all were. Or tried to be.

I insisted that he <u>had</u> to know what I meant. Gay as in Queer. Homosexual. Like my dormmate Nate in college? Gay Nate the gay roommate? The guy who ended up living with the center from the varsity basketball team?

Amazement. Tony reacted with extreme shock. So I quickly told him that obviously it was totally okay with me. Not that I was personally inclined that way myself, despite my roommate Nate, but that I thought it was great and that he should "Go for it!"

When Tony still didn't respond, I said that with his looks, he should be able to get almost any guy he wanted.

To which Tony drew himself up to his full six-foot, one-inch height. "Mr. Bartram, exactly what universe do you think you're living in, where open...relations between two men is, as you so <u>blithely</u> put it, 'okay'?"

Then he stormed off. Believe me, I got out of his way.

Still, it needed to be said.

July 5, 2000

This is completely nuts. If you've been reading this, you know I'm not the most romantic guy in the world. And yet, and yet, I think I've fallen for Celia Nash.

Jeez. Did I just write that?

Not only have I fallen for her, but yesterday at the little barbecue she and Bud did outside on the living room terrace, he and Tony went off at one point to toss a football on the lawn while the steaks cooked, leaving us alone to talk. She began flirting, I flirted back. Then she said, kind of breathlessly, "I know you've got a woman in town."

How did she know?

Tony told her. "We never hide anything from each other."

Thanks a lot, Tony. I haven't told anyone you're queer, have I?

I told Celia that Bev was a nice woman but that she meant nothing emotionally to me. That I'd stop seeing her if Celia wanted me to. In fact, I would stop seeing her period.

Yes, boys and girls, I actually said those words. And meant them. I was supposed to see Bev tomorrow. But I won't.

Celia said, "Well, the puzzle is that none of us are at all certain of your intentions."

I told her my intentions were "honorable toward her." Can you believe I said that? Yet it's true. It is. Really. Then before she could do more than register that, I said that my intentions were honorable and serious. Gosh, she looked wonderful at that. Did I just write the word "Gosh"? What is happening to me? Then I asked if Bud would allow me to pay court to her, being a lowly caretaker and all.

I knew she'd say that didn't matter a bit to her—hey! she reads Gorky and Steinbeck and they love "the common man" —but that it might to Bud.

Except I added, I was actually appearing under false pretenses, since besides the degree I was close to getting, which would get me a good job teaching in college almost anywhere, I also happened to have some money stashed away myself, with more coming in. I didn't tell her how I got the money (Yet. Do people die in commuter airplane crashes in her time? They don't, do they?), being sixty-five grand per person that's been paid to me from my parents' insurance policies. Or that I've also got about two hundred and seventy-five grand due to me (from the sale of my folks' house).

"Why, Mr. Bartram!" she said, trying to be angry. "You're rich! At least as rich as Tony. And far richer than poor me!"

I'd forgotten, hadn't I, that in a time when most mansions cost twenty grand and a Caddie goes for three or four grand, having four hundred grand in the bank <u>means</u> something. Unlike today when it means bupkus.

I asked her not to hold my being rich against me, and she promised not to, and I think we were both secretly relieved. We kissed for a long time without otherwise touching and I all but swooned and so did she. Wow. I really do think I'm... No, I'm not going to write it.

So I'm paying court to a woman who lives in 1940 and has been dead for more than sixty years.

Nice going, Neal. Really smart.

July 6, 2000

So there I am for once actually working yesterday afternoon, mowing the back lawns and using the trimmer/edger around the garage when Bud comes out wiping his hands and waves. Few minutes later he gestures that I shut off the machine as he wants to talk to me. Here it comes, I think. O. Kay.

He comes up to me, saying whatever is that contraption on your head. I lift it off and put it on his head. He lifts it off immediately and looks down at it. Then puts it on his ears again tentatively. Is once more startled and takes it off again. "What music is this?" Then he gets it. "It's very harsh and strident, isn't it?" he asks. He is talking about the Dave Matthews Band, not the Red Hot Chili Peppers! Then he asks, how in the world did they fit a phonograph in that little thing? He's looking at my CD player and headphones.

I tell him I don't have a clue. I do, of course, but he's never heard of laser technology, so hey!

Change of subject. He's spoken to Celia and he's pleased that I'm so "well-heeled," as he puts it. I'll bet he's somewhat surprised too. Tells me how his father became her protector as his close friend, her father, lost most of his wealth during the Stock Market Crash and dove onto Chicago's Marshall Avenue head-first. Ingals Senior salvaged what he could and put it to work for the girl and she's worth about two hundred grand and change, i.e., not too shabby. When Bud's papa died two years back, Bud got wardship of Celia and has her moola in trust.

I naturally ask if he's got a problem with me and he admits that she's interested in no one. "Of course, there's Tony. They are very close. Girls often choose close pals."

"Except that Tony is gay," I say. Then in case he hasn't gotten it, "homosexual."

Bud admits the truth of that with a shrug, and it's so casually done I believe that maybe the two of them have more than once in their own long close friendship and youth played "Let's Hide the Salami." But hey, I don't care.

"The real problem with you courting her is a bit different, isn't it?" Bud says. "You're not always here, are you?"

"You guys are the ones who keep disappearing," I tell him.

"Whichever," he comments slyly and I have to agree, it is a problem. Right now an insoluble one.

But there's something I want to know. "About Tony... he can't exactly be happy the way he is."

Bud agrees but says Tony's coping as best he can. But no, he's not happy.

"What will happen to him?"

Bud replies that Tony will do what other fellows do, i.e., he'll repress it, hide it, marry respectably and try not to act on it. "It's done like that everywhere daily."

To which I reply that's too bad. And decide to ask Tony what he wants. Why? Well, let's say I've got another theory. Or rather, a theory built upon a previous theory.

July 13, 2000

What did I say? It <u>was</u> the lightning. But not alone. Something else too.

Drove into Junction City to the big Staples there to get a ream of copying paper and a new ink cartridge for my printer. Decided that there might be some use for this journal, so I'm keyboarding it and printing it out. Never know...

While there, I dropped into the library and saw Jim Kleinherz—little heart in German?—and he told me he'd found more about Ingoldsby. Seems that the articles had been listed variably under the place name or under Ingals's name. This one he found under the latter, and as there have been a few Chester Ingalses, he wasn't sure it was applicable.

To make a long story short (too late for that, Neal!), he came up with another piece in the paper, this one from the very end of the year of the fire. Part of the town's fire department yearly report blamed a new electrical generator that Bud evidently bought and had attached to the house at the living room where all the wiring comes together and in and out of the house. Evidently electricity goes out during lightning storms and this goes on. Typical of Bud to find a "new scientific solution." Except this might be precisely what screwed them! Who was it who wrote that character is destiny?

Here's the new article I got:

The Junction City Intelligencer

Afternoon Edition   **Sunday, December 29th, 1940**   *5 Cents*

CAUSE OF ESTATE FIRE— POSSIBLY NEW GENERATOR

Newly Installed Electrical Generator Believed To Have Amplified Freak Lightning Strike

By Roger Pollets

Fulton's Point, WI— In a yearly report to Portage County, town Fire Chief Jackson reported that his team reached the conclusion that a newly installed electrical generator that heir Chester Ingals had installed only days earlier might have been the "conduit" for the freak lightning strike that spread the fire that destroyed more than half of his estate last May.

Purchased by Ingals because of frequent electrical failures due to the especially bad spring weather with its frequent

ESTATE FIRE, continued on Page 5

CAUSE OF ESTATE FIRE: GENERATOR

ESTATE FIRE, from Page 1
lightning storms that took lights out, the generator was supposed to turn over as soon as the electricity failed. A large thunder and lightning storm was said to have dominated the area the time of the unfortunate fire.

"The generator, in effect, strongly amplified any electrical charge hitting the house, in the way a wireless crystal is amplified to make a radio louder," Chief Jackson wrote in the report.

As for Ingals and two others, whose bodies were never found after the fire that destroyed so much, Jackson told this reporter that he stood by his earlier comments. Viz. the savagery of the fire reduced them to ashes.

The Junction City Intelligencer

July 15, 2000

And there it is, happening right now! Yesterday p.m. as I was getting into my Speedo I heard a truck pulling up and going by. Once I realized that it was an old '30s truck, a Chevy I think, I realized they didn't have to ring for me to open the gate—back then it's already open. Two guys inside and on the flatbed, this big weird-looking mechanism.

The generator, sure enough. Two guys from Milwaukee had driven it over and they were already installing it exactly where I guessed they would, back of the living room, not far from the fuse box. Bud was waxing poetic to the others about it.

I asked Celia what she thought about it. "Well, if Bud wants it." Then "I sort of liked it without electricity. Candlelight is so lovely."

Spent the evening with the three of them instead of at my usual Saturday sex-fest. Celia made dinner—tomato consommé, which is a gelatin soup (okay), veal loaf (good), creamed casserole of potatoes (very good), green beans (overcooked), and a dessert made out of rennet (which is what, exactly?) that tasted like regular old vanilla pudding my mom used to make.

Afterward we all took turns foxtrotting with Celia to music coming all the way here to the middle of the country from the Waldorf-Astoria Ballroom in New York City. ("Tony loves the

Waldorf," Celia said. And I thought, "He would!") At any rate the first hour is really kind of nice and old-fashioned, stuff my grannies would love, then guess who comes live on the radio? Carmen Miranda and her band. They're the guest artists. Seems she'd recently made her American debut in a movie—Tony told me—titled <u>Down Argentine Way</u>, and she played what she called the Merengue but sounded to me like Salsa. So I showed them how to do it. Celia got embarrassed trying to copy me. Too much hip involvement.

July 18, 2000

Hot afternoon. Where did today come from!? Tony asleep on his chaise, snoring away, and Celia indoors napping in her room. Bud joins me in the pool. We evidently awaken Tony, who snortles something, then goes inside to nap.

Soon as we get out of the pool, Bud starts in on me. "Maybe you can explain this to me. Yesterday I went to read that <u>Popular Mechanics</u> issue I showed you last week, looking for it on the table out here where I'd left it, and it was gone."

I told him I took it with me to the gate-house.

"Ten minutes later," Bud tells me, "it was right there out on the table again."

I guess it didn't work, I tell him. I tried but I found that I couldn't bring it with me into my own time.

"You mean into the year 1980?" he asks.

"No, the year 2000." I watch his mouth fall open a little. "It's July there. It's what? Mid-May here?"

"So Frequency Modulation <u>is</u> the future of wireless?" Bud asks. "Until those little things with headphones come along. What else? That radio with moving pictures we saw at the New York World's Fair? What was it called? Television? That will be commonplace, won't it? And machines that calculate faster than a million men but that fit into a valise. What else?"

I'm very touched by Bud, for some reason, and almost begin to cry. Then I decide to let him know. "Digitalization and micro-computer chip technology allow computers in most homes. On people's desks. More common than typewriters in your time.

Instant communication with anyone in the world in real time via the Internet."

"Flying automobiles?" Bud asks. I say no. Then he asks, "What is it like? Are we like Stone Age people to you? Is that fun for you?"

And I get really upset and ask why he's saying those things. It's <u>not</u> intentional on my part. I don't have <u>any</u> control. When I least expect it, they vanish and the house is all closed up and empty... I tell him I'm really unhappy when that happens. Really!

After a minute, Bud wants to know why I tried taking the magazine back.

I tell him to prove to myself it's really happening, because what if it stops again for good? What if I never see them again? What then?

Bud says, "You've always got that woman in town and other people." Then he realizes that's lame. He says, "'What then' is right, Neal. We really are a fix, aren't we?"

That's when I ask why he's not so surprised by me and the time thing. Surprised but not <u>that</u> surprised. He's seen someone or something before here at the place, hasn't he?

"Never anything like <u>you</u>! But...as kids...me and Tony."

Then he tells how the first time it happened they couldn't believe it. They were playing behind the older house built here, in the woods, and suddenly, walking past was a family of Indians. He didn't know what tribe. An old and young woman, two dogs pulling a triangular sled filled with gear. Three kids. Two braves. One kid saw them. The dogs sniffed him and Tony as they went by. The Natives all went up to the house, and the old garage, a converted stable, astounded to see it. They looked in the windows, spoke quickly, saw the old Marmon 16, and took off fast!

"It was like a dream. Only, we <u>smelled</u> them," Bus said, crinkling up his nose. "We could have touched them, I'm sure. Totally unfamiliar smells. One dropped this—and he went in and came back with a leather necklace with a polished white stone wrapped in a knot."

I asked if the boys had told anyone.

Bud said they mentioned it to the servants, who said there had been other odd incidents. A laundry woman once saw a Pony Express rider dash by as she hung out wash. He was astonished by her and the house. She said he stopped on the bluff, looked at a map, then at the house, back and forth, map and house. The house wasn't on his map. Other servants, staff members who closed up for the summer, also reported seeing campfires in the wood and hearing chanting and drumming. Bud added, "But you're the first to..."

"To interact? Because I could have been from your time?"

"Yes. And because we've all fallen for you in one way or another."

Such an admission that I said, "I love you guys too. Celia most. But all of you!"

We are, as Bud said, really in a fix. Aren't we?

July 21, 2000

Doc and Joe came over for cards again last night. Caught me coming back from Ingoldsby, where I'd been most of the early evening with Celia. Then she and the others were going to Bud's Grandma's again for dinner. I asked if I could come over later, but Celia said she'd be putting up her hair later and reading movie magazines. She was wearing the yellow sweater thing and I got to second base. I really am crazy, aren't I? But hey, it felt like a big thing.

So they come upstairs and I prepare to take them for a few bucks. Only tonight Doc is kicking butt, so I begin asking him about the property that Ingoldsby is built on. Seems no one in town knows a damn thing about it, I say. Which I'm pretty sure will provoke Doc's inborn know-it-all-ness. He says he knows whatever there is to know. I ask him to tell me about it and why it was that no one lived there before the Ingalses put up a house.

He says, "Plenty people lived there. They just didn't *stay* living there."

Why not, I ask.

Here Joe Weyerhauser says his grandpa told him that the property had a bad reputation from the time of the Indians. "They considered it a sacred place. Or at least a special place, going back fifty years before any whites lived out here."

Naturally I asked what happened back then. And Doc, in his best know-it-all mode, says everyone knows what happened back then. It was the New Madrid earthquake, allegedly the most powerful to hit North America in historic times. 1835. Looking back to letters and records of the few whites living there, and to the Indian stories, scientists figure it was a 9.1 on the Richter scale. That's a thousand times stronger than the San Francisco Quake of 1906. Seems every wooden frame house anywhere in a five-hundred-mile area was shaken to the ground. Horses and domestic animals went berserk, ran off, and some never returned. The Mississippi and Missouri Rivers ran backward for a thousand miles north and south of the earthquake's epicenter. Sounded like a major bitch.

Something happened on the property at Ingoldsby at the same time. Some piece of land either rose or fell hundreds of feet in a few seconds or altogether vanished or came out of the blue, Joe said, his grandpa had heard from some old Indians but couldn't get straight exactly what occurred, and the Natives never again stayed to camp on the land. They abandoned it. Marked it with cairns or something and split for good.

So I'm losing pennies like a fool and asking if anything had happened in modern times to support the Indian superstition and Doc says, "Well, every house built there has been struck by lightning and burnt up."

Then Joe says, and halfway through Doc tries to shut him up but I won't let him, "And of course folks are disappearing all the time." When I ask which folks besides Bud Ingals and his friends, Joe says, "Why, that caretaker fellow, some twenty-odd years ago. That's why we were all so surprised to see you here. We thought that up in Chicago they all understood." Then Doc does manage to shut Joe up.

So <u>someone else</u> vanished here, just like Ashley said. And what they have been describing seems like some kind of unstable rift in time, brought into being by a SuperQuake.

Oh, Mr. Neal, honey. What in the World you got your fool self into?!

Then just as they're leaving Doc turns to me with Joe down ahead of him and asks, "How in hell did you know that they called him Bud?"

"Him who?" I feign innocence.

"Chester damn Ingals Junior!" he replies. Looking at me like an old owl.

Ooops!

July 24, 2000

Fresh with this info from Joe and Doc, I phoned Kleinherz and asked if he could find something else for me a bit more recently, say 1980. He sounded busy, harassed, etc. So I said, I'd find him a date. What was his type? Blonde? Brunette? Did he go for legs, tits or ass?

"I go for males," he replied. "Tall, dark, handsome, slender males," he added.

"And I'm sure that a cool-looking guy like you gets more than your share," Mr. Neal Slick replied. Then I told him I'd keep an eye out for someone for him. I'll admit that I was secretly displeased that he didn't say "short, blonde, with a swimmer's body." But hey, you can't win them all, can you?

But he came through after all. This morning's e-mail contained the following:

Final—   —20 Cents

The Junction City Intelligencer

★ ★ ★ ★ SATURDAY, SEPTEMBER 1, 1979 ★ ★ ★ ★

EMPLOYEE MISSING AT INGOLDSBY ESTATE

By Janet Wagner

Fulton's Point, WI— Police were called to search the interiors and grounds of Ingoldsby, the once-famed and now mostly neglected estate several miles from town, still owned by the Ingals family of Milwaukee and Chicago.

According to Police Chief Frank J. Young, they were looking for Jason Terranova, a U. Wisconsin junior hired as summer caretaker and groundskeeper for the estate who'd been living in the gate-house. He'd disappeared within the past few days according to friends in Madison who tried to reach him by phone, then searched in person. Chief Young confirmed their story that Terranova's apartment looked untouched, and said there was no reason to suspect foul play.

Ingoldsby's main house has not been occupied since it was rebuilt, following a 1940 fire in which the young Ingals heir and two friends died. Chester Ingals's last will ordered the house be prepared as a museum. Designed by Frank Lloyd Wright protégé Sigurd Thurston, it was at one time an architectural wonder, and still has its admirers.

Terranova was not much seen outside the estate, although he was believed to have had many student guests from Madison. Wild parties, sex orgies, and drug use were rumored to be common at the estate by some townspeople. Some believe Terranova's disappearance is the result of a drug deal that went wrong.

The Junction City Intelligencer

July 26, 2000

Ever subtle, I asked the three about Jason Terranova. Celia was actually in the pool—first time I've seen her doing that; cute little pale blue—her color—one-piece bathing suit, and this big rubber bathing cap on top, natch, not that she'd ever get that close to the water. She was sort of dog-paddling about when I got there, threatening to come out. I said nonsense and dived in far away from her so as to not scare her, then swam up to her and we sort of fooled around in the water and I held her so she could try out some swim strokes without fear of drowning in the five feet of water at the shallow end, which let me cop a few feels and, even better, let her brush against my almost constant chubby, before she was tired and climbed out. Very demure and all. But I was more excited than anytime with the postmistress. Imagine! I almost popped right there and scuzzed up the pool.

Meanwhile Bud was trouncing Tony at backgammon. Tony was saying things like "It's only <u>suggested</u> you take my pieces," to which Bud naturally scoffed and wiped Tony out. So after me and Celia dried off, I asked them if she'd ever heard of Terranova. Bud remembered him. "Cheeky sort of fellow, wasn't he? Didn't last here but a few weeks, if I remember." Then Tony remembered, "Wasn't he the one with the (lowered voice) mezz?"

I am not an American History Ph.D. candidate for nothing and well know that "mezz" in Pre–World War II U.S. slang means pot, grass, marijuana. Recalling what reporter Wagner said townsfolk had rumored of Jason T, I said it was more than likely, yes, he had mezz. Tony gets this faraway look in his eyes, but clams up. From which I imply that he personally sampled mezz, and possibly also sampled Jason Terranova.

Then Celia says something absolutely breathtaking which I'm not at all certain how to take. She says, "Didn't Jason quit working here to go marry that pretty young widow whose husband died, leaving her with the diner on Lakeview Drive to run all alone? What was her name, Tony? Janice! Janice Snyder."

Nota Bene that Snyder's Country Inn is, in the year 2000, the largest, poshest, and most elegant restaurant of this part of Portage County, with four dining rooms on two floors, a staff of maybe fifty, and parking for a hundred. I pass it often.

"Ray Snyder didn't die," Bud says. "He vanished. Remember? In fact, some people said he was last seen around my property here. At first Janice said that Ray last mentioned that he was coming to meet up with Terranova and some other people. She changed her story later and said she was mistaken."

That's all they remembered. But for me it was plenty. So another trip to Junction City is needed. Don't want to impose too much on Kleinherz.

July 28, 2000

Well, if Mohammed won't go to the mountain, Bev Freneau will come to the gate-house. At least she did yesterday night. Guess she missed her usual ashes hauling session. She appeared outside, buzzing me through the gate, and when I let her in, she didn't want to talk, not even to hear an explanation why I've not been seeing her (Celia asked me not to; ergo I won't). But once she was inside, what could I say? What could I do? You guessed it, and I feel terrible, going back on my word to Celia. Except I really needed it, and I fantasized she was Celia the entire time! So it's not complete betrayal.

So it's midnight or something and Bev's got to go. I walk her downstairs and see her out the gate. I'm wearing a pair of shorts and not one thing more. Guess who comes around the side of the gate-house but Tony Kirby, dressed in a white silk tuxedo getup. Seems he and the others have just been to a big bash, and he left early, getting a ride with Bunny someone or other. He's seen me see Bev out and he's sniffing the air, literally smelling sex still steaming off my body, I just know it. I really don't want to let him upstairs because who knows what ideas he'll get. On the other hand he does want to chat, and so I take his offer and put on the tux jacket, protesting that it'll smell like me, to which he says with much eyebrows, "You and her too!" nodding in the direction Bev left.

Then he tells me that he and Bud have "naturally, discussed" me and he wants to know if I was fooling him or what about what I said before about it being okay to be gay "where I come from."

Those are the exact words he uses. As though I'm from Pasadena. Or Japan.

So even though I'm dead on my feet, I tell him all about the Stonewall Riots and the G.A.A. and Act Up and the pro-gay laws passed, and all the publicly out actors and musicians and writers, and the neighborhoods filled with gay people, Chelsea in

Manhattan, the Castro in San Francisco, West Hollywood.

"I've always wanted to go to Hollywood. I've always wanted to live in Los Angeles with the palm trees and warm weather all year round as I see in the Moviefone rotogravures!" Tony says.

So I talk more until he lets me go. Then he comes upstairs and gets the jacket from me and I guess puts a blanket over me. I'm dead to the world by then. Nice guy, Tony. Really nice guy. But he's living in the wrong time. Wrong place and wrong time.

And guess what? I've just gotten another idea. And have another theory.

August 9, 2000

I have been to see the estimable Kleinherz, and he let me spend all day in his archive, and that's a good thing, because it pretty much took all afternoon, literally right until closing time at six p.m., to find what I found, virtually invisible and hidden deep within a paper from the other end of the state.

Here goes:

☆ *The Star Journal* ☆

MILWAUKEE'S HOME PAPER

Morning Edition   *Thursday, October 4, 1979*   *20 Cents*

---

32 | *The Star Journal*
   | *Thursday, October 4, 1979*

Bank Robber Cops Insanity Plea

By Don Biggers

Claiming that his client, charged with last Friday's attempted robbery of the Union National Bank on Fond du Lac Avenue, was mentally infirm as a result of a head injury, city-appointed attorney Dale Haslett asked that Raymo Snyder be remanded to De Paul

BANK ROBBER, continued on Page 2

Bank Robber Cops Insanity Plea

BANK ROBBER, from Page 1

Rehabilitation Hospital for a period of no less than six months, saying that jail would be "extremely deleterious." His plea was granted by Judge Andrew Wallgren.

Snyder pleaded no contest to the robbery, in which he was overwhelmed by a security guard and two bank customers. Teller Peggy Gutmanson and guard James Willis backed the attorney, testifying that Snyder appeared "out of his mind" and "completely raving."

Haslett said his client suffered a severe head injury a month ago and has been "rootless, essentially wandering ever since, not knowing where he is or even what year it is." Police doctors said Snyder's head injury was "consistent with severe cranial fracture and contusion." The conditions could have been caused by Snyder being struck by lightning somewhere in the southeast part of the state, as he asserts.

The Star Journal

August 12, 2000

Ray Snyder's still alive!! Of course he would be—if he were in his twenties in 1979, he'd be in his forties today. At any rate I went through some phone books and found a Raymond Snyder living in Elm Grove, an okay suburb of Milwaukee, and left a message with his wife. Said I was a medical history student, specializing in success stories of lightning strike survivors. She said, "Ray never talks about that," but that he might with me. I'm to call back tomorrow.

Meanwhile, driving home from Junction City at what by then was six forty-five, I decided to stop into Snyder's Country Inn, which was having Happy Hour. The bar was packed. Mostly yuppies, a couple of hot women, they and the guys mostly ten years older than me—I'll tell Bev Freneau about it. I went to the john and wandered around the place until I found the photos of the Inn's "founders," Janice and Jason Terranova, aged about sixty-five in the photos (dated 1988) and both looking okay—Jason may have been a druggie but he was a stud too, because he still looked good at retirement age.

Bartender had seen me very obviously checking them out,

so back at the bar I asked if they were named Terranova, how come the place was called Snyder's. He didn't have a clue, said every new employee there asked the same question. He said the founder's grandchildren owned the place now, none of whom are named Snyder, and that Jason was dead a few years and Janice was an Alzheimer's vegetable at a local hospice. Very friendly guy. Half an hour later, he refilled my drink yet again for free and asked me out later in the week. Unfortunately he's not dark, or slender, although he's good-looking, muscled—wore a biceps tight shirt to show himself off—and red-haired. Sorry, Kleinherz!

August 14, 2000

Now <u>this</u> is news! Talked to Ray Snyder yesterday on the phone. He was very circumspect at first. Wanted to know how I knew about him. I told him Dale Haslett, who represented him, had mentioned his name to my father a while ago in my presence.

"Poor Dale, dying like that," Snyder said. I said I didn't know how. Turned out Haslett and his wife he were in a massive car wreck in some tunnel in the Swiss Alps in which a fuel tanker truck caught fire and killed like forty people. "Dale saved my skin. Got me help. I owe my life to him," Snyder said, adding, "So much for the good ending happily."

Took at least five minutes before Ray would talk about his old lightning injury. His memory of it was vague, and always had been, he said. He'd gained consciousness inside the flatbed of a pickup truck on Route 18 outside Fennimore, and the driver who'd stopped on the side of the road to urinate and who'd picked him up had noticed him staggering around the field with a bloody and blackened but already healing gash along his ear and head. He got Ray medical help at Madison, where Ray stayed a few days.

Snyder said he'd lost his memory or it was totally screwed up by the injury. He did know his name, however, and he had some kind of non-photo driver's license from Milwaukee, so he headed there. No one at the address listed knew him or of him. "I was missing big chunks of stuff that ended up making my adjustment really hard." Stuff like? I ask. "Like who was president. Couple of wars. Everyday stuff. All kinds of shit. It was terrible. Stuff five-year-olds knew, I didn't know." Snyder said that Milwaukee had looked familiar, but only parts of it. He had phoned a number for a Snyder and said that the voice that answered seemed familiar, but the old woman said her brother Ray died forty years ago, told him not to bother her again, and then hung up. Snyder grew more confused, couldn't hold a job as he didn't know simple things that everyone else seemed to know. He was fired, lost his rental room, drank, got desperate, ended up on skid row, robbed the bank, and went into the mental ward.

"Best thing that ever happened to me," Snyder said. "I met Janice there. My wife. Janice was a De Paul Rehab volunteer. She ran a mobile library. We met, fell in love, and she got me work and a place to stay. I read books and newspapers and magazines and eventually I caught up with everyone else. We married and the rest is history."

I'd bite my tongue off before I'd dare mention that Ray's first wife was also named Janice.

But I gathered from all this that:

1. Jason Terranova and Ray Snyder had somehow switched times and places at Ingoldsby. Jason was in 1979 and Ray in 1940.
2. Lightning was involved.
3. Jason knew what was he was doing, and may have intentionally made the switch. But not Ray. He had no idea what happened.

Leading to the logical question, what did Jason Terranova discover that I haven't so far?

August 18, 2000

"I'm afraid you can't take it out," Tonia Noonan said, and if it weren't that the book was stamped "For In-Library Use," I might have believed it was her own rule so she could keep me around. However, it was once again hot and nasty outside and cool indoors, so I sat at one of the writing tables of the little, old, admittedly handsome Fulton's Point Library, and perused Portage County: A History by Mabel Normand Freer, published in 1934, by—haven't you already guessed—the Portage County Chamber of Commerce.

However, I hit pay dirt almost immediately, since the book had at one time not been so rare nor so restricted, and among those who <u>had</u> taken it out was—drumroll here, please—on August 12, 1979, one Jason Terranova, who'd signed his name.

I looked for underscored passages, and there were plenty. So I went back to the beginning and concentrated. After an hour and two chapters of bluntly local boosterism, I came upon the following: "The Ingals family purchased this land in 1889 but didn't build on it for several decades. Possibly because it was long thought to be the site of an Indian Holy Place, and had accreted several tall tales. None of them more baffling or colorful than that of 'Injun Ralph.'"

I searched for an index, found none, read on and on, another hour or more. At last my patience was rewarded halfway through the volume. I quote it in full:

Fulton's Point was a bustling trading spot along the route that would later become Lakeview Drive, connecting eastern towns like Milwaukee and Madison with western posts on the Missouri River, when Injun Ralph made his unexplained appearance.

Injun Ralph was the name the townspeople gave him because of his Frontiersman costume of buskins, powder horn, and moccasins. He insisted his name was Ralph Leninger, and when pressed, would offer eyewitness accounts of Chief Pontiac and other long-dead Indian Chieftains he claimed to have met and smoked peace pipes with on his on-foot wanderings through what he called Greater Louisiana Territory, and which he was astonished to see suddenly populated with steamboats, steam locomotives, and "many thousands of settlers."

Like Rip Van Winkle, the by no means aged Injun Ralph—appearing to be less than thirty-five years of age—had gone to sleep, hiding from a ferocious storm of lightning and thunder on what appeared to be the southern edge of what later became the Ingals property, and somehow slept nigh on forty years instead of forty winks, without any apparent worsening for wear. He assured all that Andrew Johnson, not Taft, was U.S. President, and he spoke English with a "lilting, yet distinctly more British than American accent."

Our Modern Rip adjusted soon enough, and he found gainful employment giving speeches about "America The Beautiful: As It Were" for Elks, Chambers of Commerce, and varied women's clubs. After some years of this activity, however, Injun Ralph encountered and then joined up with "Buffalo Bill" Cody and Calamity Jane's "Wild West Show," traveling the Eastern Seaboard and to Europe.

Perhaps the oddest part of Injun Ralph's tall story was that it contained a disturbing instance of provable evidence. In the moment between his sudden awakening from a clap of thunder and his being catapulted into the year 1911, he clamed to have witnessed—not two feet away and very briefly in the blinding re-illumination—another person, male, young, looking astonished, wearing a checkerboard vest and porkpie hat, seated on a "tubular metal contraption" that Injun Ralph later recognized to be a bicycle. He had exactly described Wilfred Dix, a young man whose disappearance on the very day of Injun Ralph's appearance has never been resolved.

August 20, 2000

After a swim and "tea" with not-bad butter cookies Celia made, I got Tony to walk with me back to the gate-house. He'd told me that he'd come in that night after me to retrieve his tux and cover me with a blanket, so I asked him upstairs, wondering what he could see of my time since I can see plenty from his. Turns out a lot, including the "Now What for Gay Rights?" cover story of <u>Newsweek</u> and recent edition of <u>The Advocate</u> and a copy of a book of gay short stories (<u>Men On Men</u>), both of which I'd found in Tonia's library and taken out especially for this purpose.

Having me tell him about gay life today was one thing, but actually seeing it all was another. First Tony was flabbergasted. Then he spent over an hour looking through it, and I assured him he could come read them any time. Now I need something more substantial, not so much historical as sensible. Maybe like a practical guide to being queer. Who'd know that?

Nate the Gay Roommate would know.

From: HistoryKing78@aol.com
Date: Tue, 22 Aug 2000 12:30:18 EDT
To: snakecharming@juno.com
Subject: (no subject)

Greetings Snake Charmeroo. Long time no etcetera. Looking for Nate Smith. Old e-mail address stinks. What's he doing? What are you doing? Is your fiancee still hot for me?

*

From: Bufferzone@msn.com
Date: Wed, 23 Aug 2000 18:10:20 EDT
To: HistoryKing78@aol.com
Subject: (no subject)

Neal, you're just lucky I was cleaning house on that old moniker. Note new address is Bufferzone@msn.com. Dumped the old g.f. Have another rich, pretty one. Nate's new address is SalHepatica@aol.com. He asked Susan E. if you'd died. He lives in West Hollywood, works as talent agent for CAA has big Beemer & his own place. Heard you were in Jerkoffistan for the summer.

*

From: HistoryKing78@aol.com
Date: Wed, 23 Aug 2000 21:01:12 EDT
To: Bufferzone@msn.com, snakecharming@juno.com
Subject: (no subject)

Jerkoffistan is proving muy interesante. Thanks for the tips. Especially re Nate. More helpful than you'll ever know. I owe you a Dominos supersize with sausage and cheese in the crust.

August 22, 2000

In the Junction City Barnes & Noble, I figured out which guy behind the desk of the three there looked the most queer and asked: "What would I get for someone who needs to know like everything about being gay all at once?"

Wild-haired Blondie with noseplugs walked me over to this big sex book, which he showed me inside was like a Dutch uncle and a history and an encyclopedia all in one. The drawings were really wild, some of them, the expected sucking and fucking and kinky stuff, but with blacks, midgets with whips. Woo! Will have to go slowly with Tony.

"I know this isn't for you," Blondie said, ringing it up.

"Oh, why not?" I asked, all innocence.

"Because you've already <u>done</u> it all," he said.

"In your <u>dreams</u>," I replied.

"In <u>my</u> dreams, I've done it all <u>with</u> you!"

I had to laugh.

August 23, 2000

I've decided not to tell Celia anything about my plans and decided not to attempt to explain anything to her should my plans actually work. As for Bud, I'm not sure. He's one of those "scientific" guys and he'll eventually want to figure it out. Luckily I now have the examples of Injun Ralph in Mabel's book about Portage County in addition to his own stories and legends.

I feel bad about depriving them of Tony, however, because really that's what it comes down to, no? I'll make it up with Celia in hundreds of ways. With Bud of course I have the greatest way of all, I know what stocks to invest in, what fields to spread into. But I genuinely like the guy. Did from the beginning, and while I'm still not sure how straight he is, I really don't care. I do know that with Celia and Tony out of his hair, Bud's little forays around Portage County with his own "round-heeled" women will end or get more serious. He might even decide to double-date with Celia and me.

Even so, in the last few weeks as the weather got cooler (for the most part), I've joined him as often as Tony does, playing tennis, a sport I'm coming to enjoy and which Bud excels at, and also in golf, a sport I'm less good at and less interested in. (Mark Twain called it "A good walk in the outdoors—ruined.") Tony doesn't do golf at all, and it's as social as it is athletic. So I'm trying to in advance "be there" for Bud when Tony's gone.

Meanwhile, me and Celia were "petting" so much the other afternoon in the chaise lounge that I came. I think she did too, without knowing what was going on. From being all soft she became suddenly totally rigid, then sort of convulsed, and pushed me away, jumped up, and left me there while she went inside. After a while I took a swim.

But is that amazing or what?

August 25, 2000

Went to an attorney and had my will changed. For this to work, Tony too will have to change his will, signing his estate over to me as I'm signing mine over to him.

And if this doesn't work? If all that about Injun Ralph and Wilfred Dix and Jason Terranova and Ray Snyder is just bull, well then my twin cousins Dean and Daryl, aged seven, will be quite well off when they reach eighteen.

So now all I have to do is convince Tony and wait for a stormy day.

I'm guessing both Tony and me will have to have our hands on that generator when the lightning hits!

Here ends the journal provided by Fulton's Point Police

WISCONSIN STATE POLICE
Cold Case Department
Linklatter Mall, Bldg. E
Eau Claire, WI 54701
Detective-Sergeant Annabella Conklin

TO: Wayne G. King, Asst. D.A.
STATE of WISCONSIN, District Attorney's Office
Government Center, Building C
Madison, WI 53711

November 22, 2001

Re: Missing/Person Cold Case, reopened as Case #324-01.

Dear District Attorney King,

After a six-month investigation by this office as per your request in May 2001, we are able to enclose the following relevant documentation.

A. Newspaper articles.
   1. *Junction City Intelligencer*, May 26, 1940.
   2. *Junction City Intelligencer*, January 5, 1941.
B. Marriage License of Neal Bartram and Cecilia Nash-Ingals, April. 4, 1941.
C. Military Record of Neal Bartram, served U.S. CIVIL DEFENSE, July 9, 1942
D. *Junction City Intelligencer* Obituary of Neal Bartram, December 1, 1989.

ℭhe Junction City Intelligencer

Morning Edition   **Sunday, May 26th, 1940**   *5 Cents*

FIRE AT RENOWNED ESTATE
INGALS & FRIENDS UNHARMED

Celebrated for Architecture,
Estate Receives "Minor Damage"
Residents & Rare Autos Unharmed

By Roger Pollets

Fulton's Point, WI— Tourists from Madison, out for a quiet country drive on Lakeview Drive, found amid blue skies a cloud of black smoke, and drove to its source. They were stopped at the gates of the Ingals fortune heir's recently completed architectural marvel, known as Ingoldsby. Climbing the gates, they could see the main house on fire. Hugh J. Branch got over the gate and into the unlocked estate gate-house, from which he was able to telephone local operator Minnie Drake, who called together members of the Volunteer Fire Depart-ment. When the fire truck arrived, Mr. Branch's wife Estelle let it in and told Chief Jackson that her husband and his brother Samuel had gone to the main house to see if anyone needed help.

By three-thirty in the afternoon, when they arrived, they were greeted by Chester A. Ingals and his house guests, who'd managed to restrain the fire to a section of the living room, saving the remainder of the Thurston masterpiece, one of the state's most famous houses. Also unharmed was the large garage containing Ingals's collection of expensive and rare automobiles.

Sheriff Acker said that Chester Ingals and his friends, Miss Cecilia Nash and Mr. Neal Bartram, both of Milwaukee, had been at the house for the weekend. Mr. Bartram aided Mr. Ingals in containing the fire. No servants were present on the property at the time of the fire. Young Moderns, the three were either used to fending for themselves and/or preferred impromptu weekend trips to our district.

Twenty-three-year-old Chester Ingals, glamorous heir to the Ingals Iron Works fortune, is a

FIRE AT ESTATE, continued on Page 3

FIRE AT RENOWNED ESTATE

FIRE AT ESTATE, continued from Page 1

well-known figure in the state, as well as in Portage County.

Especially during the past two years when he engaged Charles Sigurd Thurston, protégé of the controversial architect Frank Lloyd Wright and a figure in his own right, to design and build a large new estate on the southernmost sector of the Ingals property. Thurston's much-discussed estate was the height of the modern. One story high, it was a rambling "ranch" style building with the most up-to-date conveniences, including a large kitchen refrigerator, air-coolers throughout, built-in wireless sets and record players in many rooms, a sport regulation-sized swimming pool, and of course the separate, heated, ten-car garage for Ingals's conspicuous collection of automobiles, a building larger and more comfortable than most Wisconsin homes. Utilizing rare woods from the East and South America along with gold and aluminum trim, when completed, the estate at Ingoldsby was thought to cost an amazing $400,000!

An earlier three-story house built in 1907 on the property had been destroyed by freak lightning four years ago. Untenanted at the time, two servants sleeping nearby escaped unharmed. Part of the young heir's legacy, when he began building Ingoldsby, Chester Ingals often said that it was his "favorite place growing up."

The Junction City Intelligencer

The Junction City Intelligencer

Weekend Edition   **Friday, January 5th, 1941**   *5 Cents*

FIRE-DAMAGED ESTATE TO BE REBUILT / RESTORED

Complete Restoration of Fire-Damaged Estate to Begin Immediately
Town Receives Gift for "New Town Hall"

By Roger Pollets

Fulton's Point, WI— There was relief today with news that the architectural prodigy that brought us fame will be restored to its former glory.

The restoration of the front room and the addition of new suites by the architect will be completed by Spring 1941, Ingals told *The Intelligencer*.

At the same time the heir announced the engagement of the other two witnesses to the fire, Miss Celia Nash, Ingals's ward, of Milwaukee, graduate of The Eden School, and Mr. Neal P. Bartram, of Chicago, at Northwestern University. The couple will reside at Ingoldsby, abroad, and elsewhere.

As a gesture of re-commitment to our town, Ingals also donated $50,000 to build a new town hall to include administrative offices, a new post office, and a restored public library on the spot of the former William Jeffers Pott Library.

The Junction City Intelligencer

STATE of WISCONSIN
PORTAGE COUNTY
Department of Civil Licenses
Junction City Town Hall
Judge Martin Adams
1209 Old River Road
Fulton's Pt., Wisconsin

Be It Known To All Persons!

That on This Date, April 4, 1941

Mr. Neal P. Bartram
residing at 1340 Lakeview Drive (Ingoldsby)
and **Miss Celia Nash**
of 1340 Lakeview Drive were

Joined in Wedlock

by presiding judge

Martin J. Adams

in a civil ceremony of

Matrimony

after having passed in a satisfactory manner certain
residence and health tests as required by certain
regulations of the State and County, and now reside in
full enjoyment of the civil responsibilities and benefits
of that establishment.

Witnessed by	Date of
Chester A. Ingals	*April 4, 1941*
And by	Date of
Virginia (Bunny) Clarkson	*April 4, 1941*

ATTESTED TO by : *County Clerk, Nicholas G. Strath*

STATE of WISCONSIN
Governor's Office
War Time Civil Defense
Jeffers Federal Building
Madison, Wisconsin
General Thurbert G. Kruger

On this date: July 9, 1942

Mr. Neal P. Bartram
of 3430 Lakeview Drive a. k.a. Ingoldsby

Did Solemnly Swear to Defend to the Best of His Ability

THE UNITED STATES OF AMERICA
and
THE *SOVEREIGN* STATE of WISCONSIN

As a Ranking Member of The United States Civil Defense
With all the Privileges and Obligations of The Position
of
Portage County: Lieutenant Colonel

Note: This Commission Allows Its Bearer to BEAR ARMS in public, to enlist or deputize for a period of no more than two days any other male citizen if deemed necessary, and to make reasonable requests for material and other aid from any citizen of the county and state thereunder.

signed | witnessed
Neal P. Bartram | *Chester A. Ingals*

Evening Edition— **—20 Cents**

The Junction City Intelligencer

★ ★ ★ ★ FRIDAY, DECEMBER 1, 1989 ★ ★ ★ ★

HISTORIAN / AUTHOR NEAL P. BARTRAM DIES

CLOSE INGALS ASSOCIATE AND FRIEND FOLLOWED HIS OWN PREDICTIONS TO AMASS FORTUNE

By Kenneth Gregg

Fulton's Point, WI— Business associates announced the death yesterday of Neal P. Bartram of heart failure. The noted historian and professor, author of several books presciently warning of coming fiscal and ecological trends, was believed to be about 75 years old.

A Ph.D. graduate of Northwestern University and frequent professor of American history and politics at several University of Wisconsin campuses, Bartram is perhaps best known for his 1947 study "Re-Imagining the Future," a text used by many influential think tanks since.

While Bartram's early years are veiled, he was known to have been part of millionaire Chester Ingals's inner circle from early days. Bartram wed Ingals's ward, Celia Nash, in 1941 and became a consultant as well as a friend, steering Ingals out of the iron and steel business into new alloys, then into computer and microchip technology.

Bartram himself profited by following his own predictions. He leaves a personal estate valued in the hundred millions, and helped to endow several universities and libraries.

Prof. Bartram is survived by two children, Bud of Grosse Point and Tony of San Remo, Italy, as well as by several grandchildren. His wife predeceased him earlier this year.

Services to be announced.

The Junction City Intelligencer

That's all of it, Wayne.

Please note that the two newspaper articles differ substantially from those of the same dates enclosed in the journals provided by your office.

This office has spoken in person to various people mentioned by Bartram in his journals, including all those deposed by Sheriff Estes, who encountered Bartram daily in the summer of 2000. In addition we've traced the M/P's contacts with Mr. Kleinherz at the *Intelligencer* and found M/Ps check-out slips at the main library in that city. A copy of his revised last will & testament is also on record. *There is no question* that Neal Bartram was active in Portage County during the summer months of 2000, and he was uniformly described as a slightly shorter than average, very handsome, blonde or light brown haired male with light brown eyes and an excellent physique, aged early to mid twenties.

Unquestionably, according to various documentation we've found, only the most salient of which this office has obtained so far and enclosed for your perusal, Neal Bartram somehow also lived from approximately the fall of 1940 through December 1, 1989, dying around the age of seventy-five [*sic*].

Whatever really happened to the Missing Person Neal Percival Bartram, given all the evidence herein collected, this office cannot assess a finding of Homicide or Death by Foul Play.

I'm afraid it's back to you, Wayne—Happy Turkey Day!

Det. Sgt. Anabella Conklin

About the Author

FELICE PICANO'S novels, short stories, poetry, memoirs, and plays have been entertaining readers and playgoers for decades. He is considered a founder of modern gay literature and a noted post-modernist. He has won the Ferro-Grumley Award for best novel and the PEN Syndicated Fiction award for best short story. He was finalist for the Ernest Hemingway Award and recently received a Lambda Literary Foundation Pioneer Award. A native of New York, Felice Picano now lives in Los Angeles. More information as well as free stories and essays are available @ www.felicepicano.net.

Books Available From Bold Strokes Books

The Moon's Deep Circle by David Holly. Tip Trencher wants to find out what happened to his long-lost brothers, but what he finds is a sizzling circle of gay sex and pagan ritual. (978-1-60282-870-4)

Straight Boy Roommate by Kevin Troughton. Tom isn't expecting much from his first term at University, but a chance encounter with straight boy Dan catapults him into an extraordinary, wild weekend of sex and self-discovery, which turns his life upside down, and leads him into his first love affair. (978-1-60282-782-0)

Raising Hell: Demonic Gay Erotica, edited by Todd Gregory. Hot stories of gay erotica featuring demons. (978-1-60282-768-4)

Pursued by Joel Gomez-Dossi. Openly gay college student Jamie Bradford becomes romantically involved with two men at the same time, and his hell begins when one of his boyfriends becomes intent on killing him. (978-1-60282-769-1)

Timothy by Greg Herren. Timothy is a romantic suspense thriller from award-winning mystery writer Greg Herren set in the fabulous Hamptons. (978-1-60282-760-8)

In Stone by Jeremy Jordan King. A young New Yorker is rescued from a hate crime by a mysterious someone who turns out to be more of a something. (978-1-60282-761-5)

The Jesus Injection by Eric Andrews-Katz. Murderous statues, demented drag queens, political bombings, ex-gay ministries, espionage, and romance are all in a day's work for a top secret agent. But the gloves are off when Agent Buck 98 comes up against the Jesus Injection. (978-1-60282-762-2)

Combustion by Daniel W. Kelly. Bearish detective Deck Waxer comes to the city of Kremfort Cove to investigate why the hottest men in town are bursting into flames in broad daylight. (978-1-60282-763-9)

Night Shadows: Queer Horror edited by Greg Herren and J.M. Redmann. *Night Shadows* features delightfully wicked stories by some of the biggest names in queer publishing. (978-1-60282-751-6)

Wyatt: Doc Holliday's Account of an Intimate Friendship by Dale Chase. Erotica writer Dale Chase takes the remarkable friendship between Wyatt Earp, upright lawman, and Doc Holliday, Southern gentlemen turned gambler and killer, to an entirely new level: hot! (978-1-60282-755-4)

Secret Societies by William Holden. An outcast hustler, his unlikely "mother," his faithless lovers, and his religious persecutors—all in 1726. (978-1-60282-752-3)

The Jetsetters by David-Matthew Barnes. As rock band the Jetsetters skyrocket from obscurity to superstardom, Justin Holt, a lonely barista, and Diego Delgado, the band's guitarist, fight with everything they have to stay together, despite the chaos and fame. (978-1-60282-745-5)

Strange Bedfellows by Rob Byrnes. Partners in life and crime, Grant Lambert and Chase LaMarca are hired to make a politician's compromising photo disappear, but what should be an easy job quickly spins out of control. (978-1-60282-746-2)

Fontana by Joshua Martino. Fame, obsession, and vengeance collide in a novel that asks: What if America's greatest hero was gay? (978-1-60282-675-5)

The Dirty Diner: Gay Erotica on the Menu, edited by Jerry L. Wheeler. Gay erotica set in restaurants, featuring food, sex, and men—could you really ask for anything more? (978-1-60282-677-9)

Sweat: Gay Jock Erotica by Todd Gregory. Sizzling tales of smoking-hot sex with the athletic studs everyone fantasizes about. (978-1-60282-669-4)

The Marrying Kind by Ken O'Neill. Just when successful wedding planner Adam More decides to protest inequality by quitting the business and boycotting marriage entirely, his only sibling announces her engagement. (978-1-60282-670-0)

Calendar Boys by Logan Zachary. A man a month will keep you excited year-round. (978-1-60282-665-6)